Planet of Equus

Rebecca McCullough

Planet of Equus

Rebecca McCullough

Croft
An Imprint of Four Winds

This book is a work of fiction. Any references to historical events, real people, or real places are used fictitiously. Other names, characters, places, and events are products of the author's imagination, and any resemblance to actual events or places or persons, living or dead, is entirely coincidental.

Interior Design by Rebecca McCullough

ISBN: 979-8-9920700-0-2

First Edition

I would like to give special thanks to Miss Bonnie Carlton for being my first reader and telling me Equus had potential and for her editing suggestions.

Additionally, I thank all the horses I have been privileged to be instructed by. Without their patience, nobility, and intelligence this book would never even have been conceptualized, let alone written. I only hope I have depicted them as well as they deserve.

And as always, Jagger, who truly is Thracis in the flesh, uncoordinated clumsiness and all.

And to Myakka, who shared with us all the nobility, courage, and kindness of the horse as a true Hippeus.
You will be missed.

To Sydney, not only for your proofreading and editing suggestions, but also for giving me the courage to move forward with the publication of this book.

I love you,
Mom

<u>*Planet of Equus*</u>

Book One of the Battle for Equus

Coming Soon:
<u>*Skies of Equus*</u>

1

CHAPTER 1

Zephyros Thracis stood on the terrace outside his stall in Thetis Stable and gazed out at the Phthian Sea. The salt-scented wind blew his copper mane back from his muscled neck. From this vantage he could view not only the swirling turquoise water, but also the emerald green of the rich grasses that covered Calabria's rolling hills. The two elements were separated by the white sand of the beaches that made this region a sought-after refuge for those in need of solitude and healing. The trio of colors were a pleasing contrast to the eye and eased the discomforts of the soul. All of which was lost on Thracis in the excitement of this particular morning.

As the province which boasted the richest deposits of achillium, the light-weight but highly durable metal used in Equine weaponry, Calabria was one of three provinces that made up the country of Myrmidonia. Of the other two, only Pendaria could equal Calabria in material wealth. Pendaria was a flat, dry region perfect for growing a variety of grains. The last was Acarnia, a territory of gentle valleys known for its orchards of fruit-bearing trees and full-bodied wines. The three provinces together made Myrmidonia one of the richest countries on all Equus, second only to the alfalfa laden slopes of Baroquia.

Thracis knew he would miss this view of the ocean in the months to come but it couldn't be helped. He would be leaving today to travel to Bucephalus, the capital of Myrmidonia, with his brother on provincial business for their sire, Zephyros. From Bucephalus, they would continue to Lipizza to attempt to pass the grueling trials required to gain access to the Romanium, the most honored military training facility on all Equus.

He turned from the picturesque scenery and trotted down the halls that would take him to his dam's private garden. As he followed the halls to the inner gardens, Thracis glanced at the murals along the walls depicting his herd's history on Equus. The murals began with the story of Bucephalus, Equus' legendary hero and founding stallion of Thetis Stable. The paintings depicted Bucephalus' rise to power from his humble beginnings as the foal of a slave, through his training at the Romanium and on to his most notable battle on the Sands of Troy.

Thracis' sire, Bailus Zephyros, was a direct descendant of the great stallion Bucephalus, who defeated Zaxas on the Sands of Troy in the victory that unified the breeds under the Gaze of Pegasus and brought an end to a hundred years of fighting known as the Age of Strife. In the five centuries from that time to this, Thetis Stable had become the ruling herd of Calabria.

Thracis knew the murals by heart, having looked at them for hours as a colt. He was fascinated by combat and fighting. He yearned to be accepted into the Hippikon, the pinnacle of military power. However, first he had to complete training at the Romanium, the premier facility for any horse wishing to master the higher military maneuvers. Thracis wanted nothing more than to become a Hippeus, a knight, in the Imperial Cavalry. It was the most coveted of military positions.

The Hippeus were the most elite warriors on all Equus, trained in the highest maneuvers of military combat and were living representations of Equine ideals. They followed a code of honor, loyalty, and strength. Becoming a Hippeus was the greatest aspiration a young stallion could claim. Given the strict acceptance codes of the Romanium and the grueling months of training, fewer than a dozen stallions graduated out of every fifty. It had been Thracis' dream to walk among those revered warriors since he was a gangly colt.

As the youngest of two sons, Thracis was required to understand how to command the province, but was unlikely to ever be called upon to do so. That duty was the privilege of his brother, Pyrios. This arrangement suited Thracis perfectly; he was far too blunt to be skillful at the intrigue of politics. Besides, another caveat to being the youngest was that he was his dam's favorite.

Thracis slowed to a walk as he entered his dam's private domain. Calypsa's ears flicked in his direction as he approached. Unlike native Calabrians, whose coats ran the gauntlet from tan to black, Calypsa was true to her Lipizzan heritage. Her coat was glossy white, her mane long and silken. Every morning the Felisian kittens fostering in the stable would spend an hour brushing and braiding the long white mane. This was an easy task for the cats as they were gifted with opposable thumbs. It was Calypsa's unique beauty that first caught the eye of Zephyros on a moonlit night. The meeting of Thracis' parents was legendary in Calabria and a favorite story among the fillies.

When he was a colt his dam told Thracis that she first met his sire as she was walking along the beach of the Phthian Sea one night by the light of the full moon. Zephyros, a flash of copper fire, was struck by the mare's moon-glow beauty. He immediately requested that she become his mate and live with him in Calabria. He was already established and could provide her with all she desired. Calypsa, as attracted to him as he was to her, delighted in the prospect of becoming his mate. However, she was a mare from a high-ranking herd; she could not simply marry some unknown stallion from a foreign land, no matter what his lineage might be, especially since she had been dismissing suitors for months. Calypsa knew she would have to present Zephyros with a challenge in order to legitimize his request.

She told him that she was wandering the beach because she had lost her circlet while swimming the day before. Circlets were a common adornment among the high society mares in the planet's capital of Lipizza. This one had been in her herd for generations. It was crafted of silvery achillium metal and emeralds. Calypsa was heartbroken that she had lost it. She told Zephyros that if he could find the circlet, she would accept his proposal.

This was a daunting task as Equines could not swim underwater and usually gave up anything they dropped in the ocean as being lost forever. Zephyros knew if he could obtain Calypsa's circlet no other stallion could challenge him for the right to have her.

The Felisians, cat refugees from the planet Felisia, had developed a strong relationship with the Equines after their spaceships had crashed on Equus three hundred years previous. Given their dexterities and their advanced technology, Zephyros enlisted the help of the Felisian Adjo to achieve his goal.

Together, and after many months of searching, the two found the circlet. It was one of the defining moments in Zephyros' life. With the circlet packed carefully into a pouch on his harness, Zephyros traveled to Lipizza and presented his prize to Calypsa in the audience of her entire herd. Calypsa's sire was so impressed by Zephyros' achievement that he gave the couple his blessing and they were joined in a formal union within the week.

While Thracis respected the relationship between his dam and sire, he couldn't fathom going through so much trouble to impress a single mare. He often asked his sire why he bothered when Zephyros could have had any mare in Calabria. Or Myrmidonia for that matter.

Zephyros twitched his ears and replied, "There are no other mares save Calypsa. When you meet your true mate, you will gaze on other mares and find them all lacking."

Thracis was wise enough not to mock his sire's sincerity though he doubted he would ever find a mare who would entice him enough to go through such a trial to have her. There were simply too many mares who were easily pleased.

Calypsa turned to her son and tossed her head, the elaborate braids along her neck bouncing in the sunlight. "I would have thought you would be halfway to Bucephalus by this time."

"I am still waiting for Pyrios. Sire keeps him long overdue."

"Zephyros wants to ensure Pyrios remembers every topic he needs to discuss with King Pedasos. Your sire worries about the Baroquian Pact. We all do."

The Baroquian Pact, the reason behind this trip to the capital.

After much debate the Registry of Breeds, the ruling council of Equus, had decided to enter into alfalfa trade agreements with the Caprians. Alfalfa was a plant unique to Equus. It was a miracle plant of sorts, used for everything from healing salves to fuel capsules, depending on what it was mixed with and how concentrated it was. Equine scientists were constantly finding new uses for alfalfa both on Equus and throughout the Anima Galaxy. The Caprians were the most prolific merchants of the galaxy and had been begging for the opportunity to barter alfalfa to the other planets for decades.

Most Equines viewed the trade agreements as a golden opportunity to enter into galactic commerce. The trade agreements were designed to make sure that Equus had nothing to lose and everything to gain. The Registry was thrilled with the Equine reception of the Caprian proposition.

Most Equines were happy. The breeds who controlled Baroquia, and the most fertile alfalfa fields, were not. Baroquia, like all countries on Equus, was divided into three provinces:

Friesia, Lusitania, and Andalusia. Of these three, Friesia was the most powerful. The Friesians controlled their province with iron hooves and were strongly allied with Lusitania. Those two provinces composed seventy percent of all the alfalfa fields on the planet. Those breeds were balked to the point of complete gridlock on the subject of open trade. They refused to even entertain the thought of trade agreements. The Friesians felt that Equus should hoard alfalfa for its own inhabitants and to Pandemonium with the rest of the galaxy.

Representatives from Friesia and Lusitania argued passionately about keeping the alfalfa plants on Equus and sending the Caprians back to their own planet of Capra with empty hooves. They thought of the Caprians as nothing more than foul smelling goats to begin with. The grievance was noted, but the Registry decided to press on with the trade agreements.

To show their anger, the Friesians and the Lusitanians entered into the Baroquian Pact, an agreement promising to keep their alfalfa fields out of the trade discussions. They made it clear that they would be open to any other province who wanted to keep alfalfa on the planet. The Registry, not wanting to incite a war, publicly agreed to allow The Pact to exist while privately drawing up plans to handle the situation. Andalusia, the remaining province in Baroquia, had yet to make a decision as to whose side it was on. And so the planet was in an uneasy peace.

Very quietly, the ruling herds around the planet had begun to enter into discussions as to how The Pact should be dealt with. Rumors were galloping around the larger cities claiming that more provinces were joining The Pact though no one seemed to know which provinces. Whispers claimed that the Friesians were purchasing as much achillium metal as possible. As far as Myrmidonia was concerned, the Friesians might be purchasing achillium, but they weren't getting it from the large deposits.

As a precaution, the ruling herds of the provinces that made up Myrmidonia were sending representatives to Bucephalus to have an audience with the king. It would be a full week of discussion and decision-making. Exactly the kind of thing Pyrios was bred for and Thracis found exceedingly boring.

Thracis stretched his neck to lay an ear against his dam's bulging belly. The filly inside, annoyed at her brother's proximity, kicked against her uterine prison. He pulled away, his eyes smiling. "Our little sister is in rare form today. Not even out and already bossing the stallions around."

Calypsa regarded her roundness with a mother's beam. She had always longed for a filly. After the birth of both their sons, she and Zephyros decided two foals were plenty to contend with. But Equines could live to see a hundred years and Calypsa and Zephyros were still young. Ten years after Thracis first stood, Calypsa convinced her mate that another foal was needed. She had been overjoyed when the seer of Calabria had confirmed the sex of the foal. She was due to birth soon and was becoming anxious, though she hid it well.

"I regret that I will not see my little sister until she's at least six months on the ground."

Calypsa nuzzled her son's chestnut neck. Pyrios was his sire's son in temperament and build, but he wore his dam's coat. Thracis was his dam throughout, but was gloved in his sire's copper. Only the white stripe down his forehead to his nose gave inclination to his dam's lineage. It was a running joke among the herd that Lord Pegasus hung the coats side by side and gave each colt the wrong one before they entered the world. All were curious as to what the newest member of the herd would look like.

"You have never been around a mare after she has foaled. Thank your fortune that the stable will have settled by the time you and your brother return." She shifted her feet. "Besides, it is well past time for you to journey to Lipizza and learn about the other half of your heritage."

Thracis flicked his ears. It had long been his dam's wish to send him to the University of Piber so that he may learn the teachings of the Lipizzans. Interested as he was in history and knowledge, Thracis' true passion lay in combat training. In either case, he and Pyrios planned on going on to Lipizza after their meetings in Bucephalus were concluded.

"Perhaps you should stay longer than a month or two and get to know some of the horses in Lipizza." His dam's tone was light, but Thracis understood her meaning.

"You mean some of the mares."

"Lipizza boasts some of the finest herds of all Equus, not to mention the university is a locale frequented by traveling Equines from all across the planet. Even you might be able to find someone to catch your eye."

Thracis shook his head. His dam didn't put this amount of pressure on Pyrios to find a mate and he was the true heir to Thetis Stable. Of course, Pyrios' problem was that he couldn't choose one mare to hold his eye longer than a season at most.

He would, of course, have to pick a single mare before assuming his role as ruler of Calabria as the practice of polygamy had been outlawed on Equus long ago. Fortunately for Pyrios, with the outlawing of polygamy came the acceptance of divorce.

"Mother, I am happy without the agitation of a mare at the moment. No offense meant," he added as Calypsa pinned her ears.

Calypsa stared at him for a moment, measuring, then turned her head as her belly twitched. "Apparently, your sister is in agreement with you. Very well, I will let the matter drop. For the moment."

"On that acceptance I will take my leave." Thracis reached out and nuzzled his dam's cheek. He dropped his head along her belly. "Take care, little sister. When I first see you, you will already be racing the Calabrian winds." His dam's belly twitched again as the filly kicked from inside.

"Take care, my warrior son," Calypsa called to his retreating hooves.

2

CHAPTER 2

The sun was falling toward the horizon as Thracis and Pyrios trotted along the road to Iliad. They had been on the road for days, having crossed the Acarnanian Mountains and into Acarnia the previous morning. Pyrios was heading for the barter town of Iliad where they could spend the night in a boarding stable. Thracis was just as happy to stay in the wilderness, but Pyrios was craving female company. In Thracis' opinion it was good his brother was meant for politics because he wouldn't last a month in the cavalry without a mare.

The lights of Iliad sparked in the distance. A sprawling township, Iliad catered to travelers of all kinds, be they avarice traders or humble pilgrims. The town was an arrangement of circles that kept the taverns and boarding stables on the outside and the more respectable dwellings on the inside. It was set on an open plain with constant wind to carry scents and few trees to block visibility.

Pyrios came to a stop just inside the entrance posts. He shifted his shoulders, settling his armor harness more comfortably on his back. The harness was made of leather and achillium metal. The leather was made from the tanned hides of deer and was favored by the Equines because of its ability to be strong yet give against the horses' bodies. These harnesses were used to carry grain, water, weapons, and the armor boxes worn just behind the withers and above each of their legs. The harness also had a thick breast collar that held the armor that would encompass the wearer's neck and head.

Equine body armor was designed to compact into a box five inches deep, twelve or sixteen inches long, and eight to twelve inches wide depending on the horse wearing it. Bigger horses carried bigger armor. Leg armor was contained in the smaller boxes above the horse's limbs. To call the containers boxes was a stretch of the imagination. The containers had smooth, rounded edges and a more aerodynamic design than a box could boast. When activated, the armor inside would unfold, encasing the Equine in overlapping layers of metal.

Cavalry stallions preferred armor that covered their whole bodies, while most Equines who felt the need to use armor in their home provinces had variations of design, freeing up their legs or necks by leaving them exposed. This type of traveling armor would only cover the areas that the Equines felt were their weak spots, such as soft bellies and unprotected flanks.

Even Equines who were traveling through hostile areas often did so without armor simply because of the weight. The stallions of the Imperial Cavalry were given pure achillium armor. Achillium was light-weight and virtually indestructible, but it was also very expensive. Few Equines could afford pure achillium and were forced to purchase armor that was a mixture of achillium and some other metal, the best combination of which was achillium and folded steel. Since Thracis and Pyrios came from the planet's richest achillium deposits, their armor, a gift from their sire on departure, was pure and of high quality.

Neither stallion felt the need for this much protection, but it was the first time they were being turned loose without adult supervision and their dam was nervous. So they humored her and agreed to carry not only armor, but an assortment of weaponry that would allow them to take over a small town.

Pyrios turned to Thracis. "I think we can afford separate stalls tonight." This was a warning that Pyrios did not want to be disturbed once he found a mare to spend the evening with.

Thracis tossed his head. "Fine. That will free up me to wander the merchant district and metal smiths." Not to mention keep him far away in case the mare Pyrios chose happened to have a friend also on the prowl for male companionship.

Pyrios snorted. "You should find a mare to bide your time with."

Thracis ignored the bait. "I've plenty of female company back home. Unlike you, I don't feel the need to be with a mare every hour of the day."

Knowing the stubborn look in his brother's eyes, Pyrios let the matter drop. Thracis was only two years younger, but more than age often separated them. They were alike enough to enjoy each other's company, most of the time, but in general they didn't like to spend every waking minute together. Besides, if

Thracis was off venturing into some dusty shop somewhere, Pyrios wouldn't be in competition with his sibling, something that was becoming more common as Thracis honed his combat skills.

Twenty minutes later they had acquired stalls at the Laughing Donkey boarding stable and were dispersing throughout the town; Pyrios off to the taverns for a talented mare of easy virtue and Thracis window shopping the blacksmiths' shops. He was equipped well enough that he couldn't justify buying anything, but it never hurt to look. Most of the proprietors were closing up for the night anyway.

Thracis stopped at an open court café for his evening meal and then began to explore the more eccentric side of the merchant district. As he walked along the narrow streets, he passed stall after stall of fortune tellers, soothsayers, miracle healers, and magical trinket sellers. Equines had been introduced to metaphysics by the Felisians and found the practice was much to their liking.

Not much for having interest in the occult, Thracis passed the shops with little more than a curt nod to the vendors. Halfway down a side alley, he stopped outside a stall door adorned with moons and suns. He flicked his ears. Something about the stall was calling to him, but not in a good way. The hair on the top of his rump was standing on end and he seemed able to hear the minutest sounds. He shifted back on his heels, intending to turn back the way he had come.

Halfway through his turn he was forced to sit back on his haunches and tuck in his front legs to keep from crashing into the mare standing behind him. He came back down to all four hooves and lowered his head in submission.

"I apologize, lady. I did not know you were behind me." This admission was embarrassing as he had been trained as a warrior and yet the mare had walked up right behind him without his knowledge.

She flicked her black ears. Her large dark eyes were amused. She circled him slowly. "Impressive that one who has no formal training could perform such a movement with no trouble." She came to stand before him after her inspection. "I would expect nothing less from Zephyros Thracis."

Thracis blinked. "You know of me?"

The mare walked past him to enter the fortune teller's stall. "I know many things. I have been waiting for you." She paused on the doorstep.

The two half-moons had risen over Equus, outlining the mare in shining silver. She was lithe and toned, like a thoroughbred but with the heavier legs of one of the Baroquian horses. Her mane resembled that of an Andalusian. It was long and full, falling nearly to the front of her shoulder. Her forelock fell straight down her face to curve along the right side of her nose. All these attributes were enough to excite any stallion, but it was her coloring that held Thracis in sway.

The mare's mane and tail were jet black shot through with star trails of silver. Her coat was a patchwork of black and white. Her legs were black from hoof to knee and her ears were black as well.

Her face was her most intriguing feature. The mare's face was a perfect balance of black and white with the division line directly down the center. Thracis had never seen anything like it. All the painted horses he had met either had solid-colored faces or a mixture of two colors, but not split right down the middle the way this mare's was.

"Do you see something that interests you?" Her voice was dry, but her eyes still laughed.

"Yes, no, I-"

She cut him off. "And stallions say mares speak useless babble." She continued into the shop.

Thracis pinned his ears. He still didn't want to go in, but the mare was too enticing to leave. Shaking his head, he walked into the dim interior.

The shop was much larger than it appeared from the outside. It was narrow but long. Feathers, bells, colorful beads, as well as other trinkets hung from pegs on beams or on the walls. The stall smelled of roses and fresh grass, the scents wafting from incense burners.

An ornate box caught his attention. It was about two feet tall with runic designs along its sides. The top was open and inside was a labyrinth of wood and metal. A glass marble sat on a ledge recessed just under the box's rim.

"What is that?" Thracis tossed his head in the box's direction.

"That is a puzzle box. It contains levels of carved wood and worked metal that form a different pattern each time the box is opened. A marble is dropped into the center of the pattern. The player must find a path for the marble to find its way out of the maze."

"Sounds simple enough."

The mare shifted her head, her forelock falling to cover one eye. "Many things look simple though they are not."

Thracis laid back his ears. This mare's riddling was beginning to chafe. He walked around the stall, making a pretense of looking at the knick knacks. He watched the mare from the corner of his eye. She stood within a half-circle of candles and colored stones on velvet cloth. She was hipshot, her casual demeanor making the stallion more frustrated.

He may not be as interested in mares as his brother, but Thracis was not unaccustomed to feminine fawning. He knew he was an attractive stallion and was not above the attention his physique warranted.

But this mare...

She was hardly giving him any notice. Her eyes were half-lidded as if she were dozing. They should be watching him as he was watching her, even if she was not interested in him as anything more than a customer. Any mare should be on alert when sharing the company of a strange stallion. It was common sense. That he should be so easily dismissed caused a protective aggressiveness in him. And an intense frustration.

Giving up his feigned perusing, Thracis came to stand before the mare. Her nostrils flared, the only sign that she was aware of his proximity.

"Do you always act so careless when strange stallions enter your shop at night?"

The mare's eyes opened and narrowed. "I am Hippolyta Psyche, foolish colt. My dam is leader of the Augean Stable and the queen of Diomedea. I have nothing to fear of unknown stallions as my combat training is far more extensive than any but cavalry officers. And even they are lacking by our standards," she added darkly.

Thracis was taken aback. He knew of the Diomedean queen, everyone did. Diomedea was a country far to the south. Its provinces were Athenia, Artemia, and Amazonia. All were shrouded in mystery. It was the only country on Equus that was ruled solely by a mare. Other countries boasted female rulers, but they all had mates. Hippolyta and her following viewed stallions only as breeding stock and therefore did not enter into formal unions. Their combat training was legendary throughout Equus.

Diomedea was the most concentrated area on the planet for Equines with otherworldly talents. The mares, and the few stallions, who called Diomedea home were blessed with the gifts of sight and foretelling. The country was also the location of the biggest Felisian city on Equus. Felisians were well-acquainted with the other planes and spent much of their time communing with spirits and exploring psychic avenues. Thracis half expected to see a Felisian curled on one of the stall's rafters.

He bowed his head to the mare. "I apologize. I should not have spoken to you in such a manner.

"No, but it is in your nature."

"How is that I am so intriguing to you?"

She looked away dismissively. "Interesting, not intriguing, and I dream of you."

Thracis flared his nostrils. He had thought the mare was older than him, given her mature attitude. As her scent filled him, he realized she was closer to his age. Her exterior made him think she was calm in his presence. Her scent told him she was nervous, worried that he would lash out at her for her boldness when addressing him. A fighter she may be, but she was anxious at having to prove her competence.

Psyche turned back to him but kept her eyes downcast. "That is why I am here in this shop. It belongs to another mare. I've...been waiting for you."

"You came a long way. Must have been a good dream." He saw pleasure ripple through her before she could stop herself.

"That is none of your concern. I do not know everything about you, only enough to make me curious."

Thracis raised a back leg, putting the toe of his hoof down to stand hipshot. The mare relaxed. "I thought all the mares of Diomedea were seers. Surely, you've seen my fortune."

Psyche shifted, once more awkward. "All the true seers and oracles are fully black. I only have half a gift." She snorted. "Even a gray has more talent than I. I have learned to interpret a great deal from a hoofprint, however." She looked down. A shallow pan filled with softened clay slid out from under a piece of linen laying on the floor. All Equines, as well as other species in the Anima Galaxy, could move objects with their minds. "I could tell your fortune if you wish."

Thracis twitched his shoulders. "If you came all the way from Diomedea just to meet me, I can at least allow you to decipher my fate."

Psyche took a deep breath to settle herself. "Place your right hoof in the clay. Press down as hard as you like, then pull back."

Thracis did as told, a ripple of power going through his foreleg as his hoof touched the clay. Psyche focused on the imprint, her forelock falling forward to hang in front of her face. Thracis noticed again how long and lean her legs were.

Her nostrils flared as she sniffed the clay. Keeping her head lowered, Psyche rolled her eyes up to look at him. "Your fortune is a language of contradiction."

"That's heartening."

"You have a great destiny, though I see you will not want it. War is coming. In you is the choice of which side will be victorious. Many will ignore the warning you carry. Many will think you unworthy. Look to those the world has forgotten, the tarnished silver, they will be your armor, they your might. In your darkest hour, look to the sky. Your salvation is carried on wings of light."

Thracis waited until he was sure Psyche was finished before shaking his head. "You've gotten me confused with my brother Pyrios. I have no need of laurels and glory."

"Lord Pegasus does not care for your needs, only those of his horses."

"Are you certain you read the clay correctly?"

Psyche's eyes could have frozen rum as she arched her neck to look at him. She was as tall as he was and had no intention of appearing submissive. "I know well enough to see that you will need an ample amount of humility if we are to place our hopes on such a spoiled colt."

Thracis snorted. "Spoiled colt? A moment ago I was the savior of all Equus."

Her ears pinned. "I did not say you were savior. I said you would decide the outcome of the war, whether good or ill."

Psyche tossed her head, her unruly forelock coming to rest behind her left ear. They stood in silence. Outside, a mare called for her filly to come in for the night. Somewhere a few streets away, a band was beginning to play. Psyche's shoulders were set. Thracis could see that this mare was not going to back down anytime soon.

He sighed. "I apologize if I've upset you. Do you see anything else that would be helpful to me?"

Psyche shook her head. "I will read no more this night. I have my own meditations."

"You aren't giving me much enlightenment."

"That is not my concern." Psyche walked around him and toward the back of the stall. "I have a gift for you," she called over her shoulder.

She returned with a stone tied to the end of a colored string. Standing before Thracis, she used her mind to weave the string into his mane, fastening the stone high up on his neck just behind his head. She placed it on the underside of his mane so that it would be concealed.

Satisfied the talisman would not fall, she stepped back and looked at Thracis. "That is a stone of protection. I fear you will have need of it on your journey."

"I thank you, lady. If not for your prophecy than at least for an interesting evening. "

Psyche watched him walk to the doorway without a word. Before he stepped out of the stall he felt a feather-touch on his mind, a request for communication. Equines, like all species of the Anima Galaxy, could speak mind to mind. This telepathic ability was stronger in members of the same herd and could be used to contact Equines traveling throughout the galaxy, though in that instance their abilities had to be amplified by technological means.

He paused in the doorway, looking behind himself at Psyche without turning his head. He could do this because a horse's eyes were set more to the outside of their head than the center, allowing them better peripheral vision than most species.

Take care, Zephyros Thracis. You will meet many individuals who will bear you ill intentions.

I have learned to take of myself, dear lady.

He felt her frustration with him clearly in his mind. *Have it your way then, foolish colt. However, if ever you reach the legendary training rings of the Romanium, seek out Alois Phrenicos. He is accustomed to dealing with one such as you.*

She broke the link between them. Thracis saw her turn and walk to the rear of the shop. She looked over her shoulder once, then stepped behind a dark blue curtain. He shook his mane and walked back down the alley and on to his boarding stable.

Psyche waited until she was sure Thracis had left the vicinity before coming back to the front of the shop. She blew out the lanterns on the doorframe and closed the door. Returning to the clay hoofprint, she settled herself and opened her mind to the will of Pegasus. Despite her modesty, she was far more talented in the sight than she let anyone know.

Images flew to her on zephyr wings. She saw Thracis armored in brilliant achillium. He came to stand on his hind legs. She saw him jump forward at an opposing stallion rising on hind legs to meet him. She did not know the victor as the next image she saw was the Sands of Troy. Armies of thousands, gleaming silver fire, set apart by the colored banners of various stables and herds, the air a cacophony of screams of challenge. She saw crimson rain, heard shrieks of agony, the sun dawning on a painted chorus of death.

Tears streaming down her face, Psyche fought to break the vision, she wanted no more knowledge of what was to come. Not all she saw ever came to be, but she was experienced enough to know that most of what she had seen would come to pass.

But Pegasus, a lord of violence and challenge, was also one of mercy. Before the vision released, Psyche was granted a final image.

A foal, newborn, its coat a puzzle of copper and white. Standing beyond its wobbling frame was a dam with face equal in white and black, her star-shot forelock falling to curve along her sculpted nose.

3

CHAPTER 3

Bucephalus, capital of Myrmidonia, was a mosaic of artistic expression and warrior's steel. It was renowned for the high percentage of its stallions who were accepted for training at the Romanium. The city also boasted some of Equus' finest artists. It was quieter than the planet capital of Lipizza and granted those with artistic talent the peace they craved. The streets and buildings displayed sinuous carvings and arched doorways. Statues and fountains abounded in every square and open café. The training rings themselves were decorated with the likenesses of the many warriors who had forged their foundations in the deep sands.

Pyrios had been to the city on many occasions with Zephyros for some political purpose or other, but Thracis had only been inside the city walls once before. He followed his brother with rounded eyes, trying to look at everything in a single glance. Pyrios noted his brother's astonishment but choose not to comment. Thracis had been on edge and snappish since their night in Iliad.

Pyrios had questioned Thracis about what had transpired in the fortune teller's shop, but Thracis became evasive on the subject. Knowing his brother would never budge once he set his mind, Pyrios gave up his querying. Probably some mare had rejected his advances. He had kept an eye on Thracis nonetheless and noted that his brother was uncharacteristically pensive. This new thoughtfulness made Pyrios more supervisory of his brother than usual, a restriction under which Thracis bridled and complained of loudly. However, it would not do for something to happen to their dam's favorite son.

That Thracis was her favorite had never bothered Pyrios. He was his sire's colt through and through. He and Zephyros mirrored each other in temperament and personality. Pyrios was the one who would carry the honor of continuing his herd's rule in Calabria. It was a responsibility he reveled in.

Where Thracis chafed at any inclination of authority, Pyrios loved his power and prestige. He saw exactly what he needed to do to better the province. Under his sire's watchful eyes, Pyrios was already making his own decisions. He knew how to charm his fellow leaders and manage his subordinates. He wanted only the best for his herd and his horses, which was why the current political climate vexed him so greatly.

Like many Equines and Felisians on the planet, Pyrios knew the benefits the Equines would reap if they agreed to open alfalfa trading with the Caprians. The trade agreements would open many doors between Equus and other planets in the galaxy. It was a winning situation for all involved. But the members of the Baroquian Pact weren't interested in the planet as a whole, they were only concerned with how control of the alfalfa would empower their own provinces.

It was this greed that led to the Age of Strife so many centuries ago. A dark time marked by death and pain, when even traveling between villages and cities became an ordeal if the dwellings happened to be in border provinces. Raids were a daily occurrence in most territories and the majority of Equines lived in fear.

As it was taught in Equine schools, the Age of Strife began because each breed thought they were better than another. They had forgotten that Lord Pegasus created all the breeds in his own image, save for his shimmering wings, and that they were all precious to him. Granted, each breed contained an aspect unique to them that made them stand out, but all had flaws as well. They had been created to work with each other, not against.

The breeds fought among each other for decades. One herd would gain control of a territory for a short while until a stronger herd invaded. This was disastrous for an established herd as the first thing the victors did was kill off all the native offspring and remaining stallions, keeping the mares for breeding stock and slaves. It was rumored that the country of Diomedea was founded by the escaped mare Cassandra and her following. She and her daughters were the first mares to cultivate the talents of the mind.

This turmoil continued until Lord Pegasus sent two great leaders among his horses. In keeping with the balance of the universe, the stallions he sent were polar opposites of each other. The fate of Equus would be decided by them, not by any god or goddess.

First foaled was Zaxas, the red stallion. He came from the western regions that would later become the Baroquian Peninsula. A hard birth, the old ones said, and the mare did not survive. It was thought the foal would perish having been born during the winter with no dam to support him. His sire, an evil creature called Nero, would not hear of his colt dying of starvation. He sent his soldiers to invade the nearest village and bring back a nursing dam. Her own foal would be forfeit so she could see to the needs of Nero's colt. So it was from foalhood that Zaxas learned only his needs mattered.

Zaxas was taught all his sire knew. He was schooled in weaponry and military tactics, accompanying the older stallions on raids when he was only four. His taste for cruelty became common knowledge and all quivered and fled when they saw the black standard with the red bear claw fluttering above a column of stallions. Zaxas' skill in treachery soon became apparent as well after he assassinated his sire and took control of his army. Under Zaxas' rule, the Titans, the name he gave his warriors, began a campaign to enslave as many breeds as possible. The conquered breeds had two choices: fight for Zaxas or be executed.

Unbeknownst to Nero, a mare from his harem escaped to a village along the northern reaches of his empire. She was heavy with foal and beseeched the villages to aid her with the birth. The villagers knew Nero would search for this mare once he discovered her flight and would kill any who helped her and the foal. They turned her away, not for lack of pity, but for pure survival. They told her of an old mare who lived at the base of a sacred mountain that might lend her aid.

The slave's labor was well upon her by the time she found the crone's dwelling. The older mare knew at once that this foal would be special. She cared for the slave and her new colt in the days following the little one's arrival. During that time, the slave, Danae, told the crone of her herd in the north near the Phthian Sea. Danae begged the crone to take the colt to her herd where he could be raised by her kin. The crone would have to find a wet-nurse for the foal as Danae would not be able to make the journey. Nero would destroy every village between he and Danae in order to find the slave. Understanding Danae's meaning, the crone found a willing mare who had lost her foal to sickness, and the two mares took the colt, Bucephalus, to Danae's herd.

Danae returned to Nero, telling him that the foal had died at birth. Not believing her, Nero demanded she take him to the body. Danae led him to the grave of the wet nurse's foal. Enough time had passed that the body had decomposed so much it was difficult to tell the age of the foal. Furious by her escape and refusing to grant mercy even though Danae had returned of her own volition, Nero had the mare executed.

Danae's foal Bucephalus grew strong and healthy on the trek to the northern territories. Danae's herd accepted the foal as one of their own, never judging him by his sire. His foal fuzz shed to reveal a gleaming black coat. He carried the compassion and strength of his dam and soon showed his prowess in combat.

Bucephalus looked to the wet-nurse as if she were a caring aunt, the crone a wise grandmother. The crone taught him how to respect the world around him. She taught him how to communicate with nature and listen to the whispers carried on the winds. The stallions of Danae's herd taught Bucephalus all they knew of fighting and politics. The young stallion was a natural leader and soon rose to become lead stallion.

His belief in the balance of the world became a beacon, drawing all those who feared Zaxas' tyranny and longed for a better life. Bucephalus' army grew daily until it was formidable enough to engage the Titans. Bucephalus knew the breeds must be united in peace, but the path to peace was to be forged in battle.

Years passed before the armies of Bucephalus and Zaxas met on the Sands of Troy, a barren, desolate place where nothing grew and only the wind gave voice as it howled through rock-strewn cliffs. An epic battle ensued. Casualties abounded on both sides. The sand turned red from all the blood. The cries of the wounded and the dying soon drowned out the harsh shrieks of the scavenger birds.

Finally, his army faltering, Zaxas agreed to face Bucephalus in single combat. It would be the red stallion's only hope of keeping his followers from fleeing into the desert sands. The two stallions met in the blood-stained ground between the encampments. The poets claimed the struggle lasted for three days and nights before Bucephalus emerged the victor.

Even before he would allow the healers to see to his wounds, Bucephalus bade the herd leaders come forth and unite all the breeds under the Gaze of Pegasus. One by one he made them touch their heads to his blood-splattered shoulder, so that they would never forget their oath. From that day until just a few months ago, the planet had known peace.

Pyrios pinned his ears every time he thought of the breeds involved with the Baroquian Pact. The Equines had mastered space travel, with the generous aid of the Felisians, and were anxious to form alliances with other planets. If The Pact succeeded in dividing Equus, the other species would be hesitant to allow the Equines access to their own planets. The Caprians were already finding reasons to procrastinate on the final signatures. This was not a trait goats and sheep usually displayed. Once decided on a course of action, goats could hardly be dissuaded. However, Equines not only possessed the alfalfa fields, they also created and used the most advanced weaponry available. Pyrios couldn't blame the other species for being cautious when making commitments.

Pyrios led Thracis up the busy streets to the palace gates. A pair of guards approached and asked Pyrios to state his business.

"I am Zephyros Pyrios, this is my brother Thracis. We are on business from Thetis Stable in Calabria."

The taller of the guards bobbed his head. "We received word that you would be coming." He tossed his head at his comrade. "Take them to the king's audience hall."

As they were led into the main courtyard Pyrios and Thracis paused in front of a life-size statue of Bucephalus. Unlike many of the statues throughout the city which depicted the great stallion in one of the combat maneuvers, this statue showed Bucephalus at ease. He stood relaxed, his ears forward, his mane sculpted to look as though it were being blown back in the wind. His neck was arched as if he were looking at something in the distance, nostrils flaring to catch a scent. His eyes were kind, a tribute to his vision of peace. The statue, like all those sculpted in the likeness of the Equine legend, was crafted out of black marble.

The visiting stallions bowed their heads in respect. Pyrios and Thracis were direct descendants of the great stallion and always looked on his image with wonder that the same blood flowed through their veins. Thetis Stable boasted its own life-sized statue of their founder. In their home stable, Bucephalus was also standing at ease, looking out over the rolling seas. Written along pedestal on which this statue was positioned were the words spoken by Bucephalus centuries before to still the frightened hearts of his stallions at the Sands of Troy.

Think not to outrun your shadow for it is always with you, even in darkness. See it not as an enemy, but as an ally always by your side.

These words held deep meaning for all Equines as almost every foal feared its shadow the first time that darkness was glimpsed from the corner of the eye. Later, after their dams soothed their unease, foals learned to play with their shadows as if they were the best of friends. In times of danger, when every gust of wind or tremble of branch could signal attack, a shadow might cause alarm where no panic should be.

Their respects paid, the young stallions followed the guard into the palace to meet King Pedasos.

4

CHAPTER 4

King Pedasos, or more correctly, Queen Helena, had planned for this week's events with great care. The main audience hall was decorated to perfection. Music played faintly from globes hung in nets around the chamber. Maids, mostly fillies just entering marehood, flitted throughout the room positioning flowers here or moving a table there. These mares would only be under the queen's watchful eye for a year or two before being sent to the schooling rings.

Every horse on Equus, male or female, was required by law to spend two years in the schooling rings learning combat training. After completing this requirement, Equines could either further their fighting ability or move on to other interests. Mares were not allowed to join the military. However, they were encouraged to learn how to defend themselves and their home stables. Mares were taught how to use all weapons and armor and were given the opportunity to attend strategy classes where they were taught how to organize defensive measures and set ambushes. If asked, most stallions would readily admit that they would rather fight outnumbered in open combat than lay siege to a village and have to contend with a bunch of mares in their home territory.

Pyrios and Thracis followed the stone walkway down the length of the hall and stopped in front of the dais designated by a golden inlaid circle where only the king could stand. They bowed all the way down, bringing one foreleg beneath their torso and stretching back on their hind legs until their noses could touch the floor. It was the ultimate show of submission and respect.

King Pedasos, who had favored the sons of Zephyros since the days they first stood, restrained himself as they completed the formalities of court. As soon as they were back on four feet, he trotted down the short ramp from his circle to stand right in front of them.

"I'm so happy you've arrived." The king was all but dancing in place. "Some of the others from the ruling herds are already in residence, but they're all my age and rather stuffy. I'm glad Zephyros chose to send his sons in his stead."

Pyrios tossed his head. "Thank you for the welcome, your majesty. My sire would be pleased to hear we are in your favor."

Pedasos shook his head. "Don't be so formal, young Pyrios. You and your brother are practically family." He tossed his head at a nearby window. His voice lowered. "I did not inform your sire because I did not want your dam to worry so close to her foaling, but we've had reports of Pact activity in the area."

Thracis and Pyrios exchanged a look. Pyrios spoke, keeping his voice low to match the king's. "We did not have any trouble on our journey." He refrained from looking at Thracis. Did Thracis know something about the Pact that he hadn't shared? It would explain his distraction.

King Pedasos sighed with relief. "Thankfully, the Pact associates we have seen haven't done anything to cause trouble. Still, my advisors and I have been in mental contact with all the ruling stallions and mares for the last few weeks. We have also been in contact with the magistrates and mayors of every town throughout the country." He took a deep breath. "I want to know the instant something happens."

"Do you believe the Pact would act out so far from home territory?" Thracis wasn't worried about Thetis, his sire and dam could take care of themselves, but the prospect of being outnumbered on the way to Lipizza was daunting. He had never faced anyone but his instructors in combat.

"I cannot say. The Pact has already shown more defiance than the Registry expected." He twitched his shoulders. "Who is to say what they will do?"

"My lord," Pyrios began, "my brother and I have leave to journey on to Lipizza after your council. Do you believe the Endurance Road to be safe?"

"Your sire told me of your plans. I already have an inclination as to how to make your trip as safe as possible. I have it on good authority that others may want to journey to the capital." The king looked at Pyrios. "Come and speak with me in private, Pyrios. I have things I wish to discuss with you and then we can contact your sire."

Pyrios twitched his shoulders and looked back at Thracis. King Pedasos smiled. "Do not worry about him. My Lady Helena will see that he is well occupied."

Thracis fought the urge to roll his eyes. Entertainment with the queen meant hours of standing around while she gushed about which mare in her court would make an excellent match for each of the young stallions. Such was the lot of the younger son.

King Pedasos nodded to a hall leading off the main chamber. "Her private garden is that way. She is already waiting for you."

Thracis and Pyrios exchanged a look.

King Pedasos flicked his ears. "It is what my lady wanted."

Ignoring the sparkle in the king's eyes, Thracis bowed his head and walked down the indicated hallway. He had to dodge a couple of maids on his way. They were so involved with the placement of a flower arrangement that they didn't even see him. As he stepped out of the way, Thracis caught sight of himself in a mirror. Not usually aware of his appearance, he was now too conscious of the dirt and mud that splattered his copper coat. He and Pyrios should have stopped at a boarding stable to clean up a little before they came to the palace. Thracis twitched his shoulders as he entered the garden, nothing could be done about his appearance now.

Queen Helena and two of her ladies were standing next to a table laden with foodstuffs. Barley oats, carrot cakes, and fragrant mounds of alfalfa grass accompanied clear bowls of honeyed wine. An extravagant meal for a young stallion sent on family business. Thracis took it as a sign that Queen Helena wanted to get on his good side as quickly as possible.

Lady Helena herself was resplendent in the decorative garb common to the ladies of court. Her circlet was golden and inset with an array of colored jewels. Worked metal earrings, something that looked positively annoying to Thracis, dangled from her ears and her back was covered by a light material that resembled shimmering gold. Thracis didn't see the point of all this adornment; Lady Helena was famous for her regal beauty.

The queen nodded as Thracis came to stand before her. "Welcome son of Zephyros. I have prepared a light meal for you as I am sure you have not eaten since arriving in the city."

"You are very insightful, good queen. And this spread looks delicious." *Though hardly a light meal.* He did not add that last. Thracis would be on his best behavior while in the presence of one of his dam's friends. For as long as he could be anyway.

"I'm glad you approve." Lady Helena's eyes danced with amusement.

Thracis sipped the honey wine and nibbled on some oats. In reality, he was starving, Pyrios having told him that they shouldn't eat before going to the palace just in case food were offered. Thracis didn't see the point in this as it would be rude for him to stuff himself and so now he would eat enough just to keep him hungry until the evening meal.

He kept one eye on Lady Helena as he ate. He noted the way her gaze flowed over his physique. He stifled a groan at the conversation he knew was coming. Royalty were all about political alliances and Lady Helena made it well-known to Calypsa that she wished a marriage between one of the Zephyros stallions and a lady of her choosing. Calypsa had forestalled the queen thus far, stating that neither son was old enough to entertain the thought of a mate and foals.

Deciding to make polite conversation, Thracis tossed his head back the way he had come. "I should think King Pedasos will keep my brother well into the evening."

Queen Helena shook her head and took a small bite of carrot cake. She swallowed and looked at Thracis. "My mate is curious about the heir to Thetis Stable. Your herd has ruled Calabria for many years." She inclined her head to the side.

Taking the hint, Thracis left the table and the ladies in waiting and followed the queen to a quieter part of the garden.

"If you wished to speak with me privately, you could have just asked."

Queen Helena laughed softly. "That is why your sire choose Pyrios as his heir. You have many good qualities, Thracis, but subtlety is not one of them." She stretched her neck to sniff a rose. "You have much to learn, foolish colt."

"That seems to be the consensus among the mares I've met recently," Thracis muttered.

The queen looked at him, his comment capturing her curiosity. "Have your parents been introducing you to ladies of note?"

"No, this was a mare I met on the journey here. She comes from Diomedea."

Lady Helena snorted to show her opinion of Equines from that region. "Truly no one of interest, then."

Maybe not to you, Thracis thought. Knowing he could never say such a thing to a queen, he tried to change the subject. "When does the council begin?"

Not to be dissuaded, Lady Helena sighed. "Sometime tomorrow. Has your brother chosen a mate yet?"

Thracis looked away before the queen could see his aggravation. If she wanted to know about Pyrios why didn't she ask him? How was Thracis supposed to know if his brother was serious about this mare or that? Pyrios was always chasing someone new. "As far as I know, Pyrios is still having fun sampling his prospects."

"A shame. He really should settle with someone and produce an heir himself so that your sire will know his line will continue."

"I don't think my sire has any fear about the future of his herd."

"Yes, but Pyrios should begin to establish himself. It is expected."

"Perhaps you should have this conversation with him." Thracis' patience was beginning to fray.

"No, that would not be appropriate." Queen Helena nodded back to the mares standing near the table. "What do you think of that buckskin?"

Thracis twitched his shoulders. "She's fair enough. I'm not really drawn to duns or buckskins, but she has nice legs and a slim neck. She should have no trouble attracting a desirable stallion."

"What do you think your brother would say?" Her tone was mild.

Thracis paused. There could be a trap here. Why was the queen so interested in this mare? She was obviously a favorite of the queen. Thracis couldn't tell Lady Helena that Pyrios would no sooner court that buckskin than he would a deer. He chose he words carefully. "I think he would find her fair as well, but she seems a little smaller than the mares I've seen him with."

"Size means little if the mare has breeding and obedience." The queen nodded as if coming to a decision. "Perhaps at the evening meal I will see what your brother thinks of this mare."

Thankful that the discussion was over, Thracis followed the queen back to the table. Lady Helena nodded to her other attendant, a tall bay mare much more suited to Pyrios' tastes. "This is Desiree. She will take you to your stall so that you can freshen yourself before the evening meal."

Thracis followed the mare through the palace to the wing reserved for guests. He could hear other Equines behind closed doors. The mare said nothing, but her ears kept flicking back to the stallion behind her, revealing that she was keeping an eye on him.

She led him to the stall he would be sharing with Pyrios. "You should find this comfortable for the two of you. The evening meal is in one hour and the morning meal is an hour after sunrise. If you require anything the bell pull is near the door." She bowed her head and left.

Thracis sighed. This visit seemed to be more of a social occasion than a strategy session. Resigned, he explored his surroundings.

The main living area contained two bedding boxes filled to the brim with fluffy straw. The stall also had a floor to ceiling mirror in one corner and a balcony overlooking the public gardens. He walked across the living area to inspect the wash stall. It was large and open with half a dozen faucets in the shower to spray water from every angle. The voiding area was emptied and cleaned with the touch of a button.

Even though Equus was one of the more technologically advanced planets in the galaxy, Equines used very little technology. This was mostly because with the use of their minds and their love of nature, Equines didn't need technology, with the exception of their weapons and spacecraft. Even with the invention of hovering movers that could transverse the planet, most Equines opted to travel on their own four feet. Wash stalls and voiding areas were the exception. Those advances were simply too convenient for city life.

Thracis was in the shower when he heard Pyrios enter from the outer door. He finished, then used a scraper to remove as much excess water from his coat as possible before stepping under an arched metal tube that blew warm air. Thracis only dried himself enough not to drip on the floor of the living area.

"Did the king say anything important?" Thracis asked.

"Nothing more than we already know. He's very concerned about the Pact and is positive they plan on using the trade agreements to incite a war."

"That's becoming common knowledge."

"He is also worried about our home stable. As we control the biggest deposits of achillium, King Pedasos is concerned the Pact may not bother with bartering a deal and just take what they want."

"With the help of the neighboring stables, I'm sure our herd will be fine." Thracis hoped he sounded more confident than he felt.

"To make certain they will be safe, the king has dispatched a contingent of soldiers to keep an eye on things until the Pact associates leave the area."

Thracis shook his head, his copper mane releasing a spray of water droplets. "Mother is going to be overjoyed when all those stallions show up just as she's readying for the arrival of our sister."

Pyrios gave Thracis a sly look. "Thank Lord Pegasus we won't be there to share in her pleasure."

They both snorted laughter.

"I'm sure I'll have to be present at the council tomorrow." Thracis' voice became a growl.

"Yes, and you'll have to play nice with everyone else during the week we'll be spending here. Especially with any of the society ladies you know Queen Helena will invite."

"Fortunately, it's not me she's looking to settle, older brother."

Pyrios snorted. "Good luck to her. I've met every mare she finds suitable already and while I can't say anything bad about their manners or breeding they're all lacking in..." he ruminated, "spirit. I want a mare who's not afraid to stand up and speak her mind."

"Like our dam?" Thracis walked to the balcony to let the wind dry his damp mane.

"I am our sire's son. It's only natural that I would be drawn to the same kind of mare." Pyrios joined his brother. "What happened in Iliad, Thracis? Did you meet an Equine from the Pact?"

Thracis shook his head. "No, nothing like that."

"Then what has you so spooked?"

"It's hard to explain." Thracis took a deep breath. He and Pyrios had always been close, never engaging in any rivalry, but he still found it hard to open up about Psyche.

Pyrios looked out over the gardens. "If it's that hard it must be a mare."

"And if it is?"

"Then you'll have even more trouble fending off Lady Helena's subjects." The two stallions shared another laugh. Thracis felt a lot of his tension drain away, but he could feel his brother's anxiety.

"What is it?"

Pyrios shook his head. "If the Caprians back out of the trade agreements it will be years before we have another opportunity."

"No one knows that. They may just leave for a little while until the Pact is settled."

"King Pedasos says that the Caprians are bringing up the Canans and the overtaking of Felisia."

Thracis twitched a shoulder. "This is not the same as that. The Canans openly spoke of laying siege to Felisia. At least that is what the Felisains tell us."

"The point is not how the Canans did it, but that they succeeded in conquering another planet. That was three centuries ago. Our weaponry and space travel exceeds anything in the galaxy. If the members of the Pact are planning on starting a war and they defeat the Elysian Alliance, what's to stop them from invading foreign planets?"

At the mention of the Alliance, Thracis twitched his ears. After the Friesians and Lusitanos established the Baroquian Pact, a few of the breeds who supported the trade agreements created the Elysian Alliance. The Alliance was not only in favor of the trade agreements, but the breeds involved also believed that Equus should remain united and not be splintered by the Baroquian Pact.

Thracis remained silent for a few heartbeats. Up until now he had thought of the Baroquian Pact as an Equine problem. Now he had to think of things from a different perspective. He looked at Pyrios. "What does King Pedasos think we should do?"

"He believes that is a matter for the Registry to consider." Pyrios shook himself. The sun was sliding toward the horizon. "I'd better shower off before the evening meal, have to look my best for the ladies."

Thracis remained on the balcony listening to the sounds of the city settling down for the evening meals. The wind carried a potpourri of scents from spiced main dishes to sweetened desserts. On a strong gust he could smell the freshness of the Cerulean River, supposedly the clearest river in all Myrmidonia. When he and Pyrios continued on their trip, they would cross the river and enter Levadia.

He thought of what it would be like to stand on this same balcony and look out over ruin, with only the sounds of sorrow to fill his ears and the smell of smoke to burn his lungs. Psyche had said a war was coming.

Thracis shook his head. Despite what Pyrios had said, Thracis still did not think that the issue with the Baroquian Pact was anything like what had happened to the Felisians home planet of Felisia. The Canans had invaded, yes, but it was sibling rivalry and a goddess' stubborn pride that led to the Felisians exile on Equus.

5

CHAPTER 5

Three hundred years previous, two children of Chimera, lord of all the gods, had a dispute. The gods lived in the sacred land of Tranquility where they observed the trials and triumphs of their children on each of their respective planets. As Tranquility was a land of peace, the exact opposite of the netherworld of Pandemonium, the gods often grew bored and argued amongst each other, usually about their children.

The story of the gods, told on every planet, was that Chimera so loved his children that he gave each of them a world where they may create the species of their liking. Only two provisions were placed on this gift: the animals, great and small, must retain their free will and the gods could not incite or resolve a conflict within or between any of the races. If animals wished to battle and obliterate each other, they must do so of their own volition. That was not to say that the gods could not help their followers from time to time, which they did often.

So it was that Pegasus was granted Equus, Pan given Capra, Volga allowed Mustel, and Atla gifted Nekton. Bast and her twin Lupious, the youngest, were allowed Felisia and Canan. As the gods nurtured and guided their children, some species developed faster than others. This was true in the planets Felisia and Canan.

The Felisians, their quizzical minds and dexterous hands enabling them to question and invent, were the first to develop space travel. Their technology was at least a century beyond any other species save the Canans. The Canans, just as intelligent as the Felisians, were less restrained than their cat cousins.

The Felisians believed in balance. They cultivated a deep respect for nature and harmony. They frowned upon overcrowding and congestion. In her lifetime, a female Felisian might have three litters of two kittens each. A Canan might have eight litters of five pups during her fertile years. With overpopulation a serious threat, the Canans wanted to expand their territory to another planet.

Fearing for her Felisians, to whom she had granted not only superior intelligence, but also gifts of the occult, Bast beseeched her brother Lupious to find some way to control the Canans. Lupious, always resentful of his sister's favoritism in the family, ignored Bast's plea for intervention. Bast warned her brother that she would not allow her children to be cast aside by another species.

To save her planet from domination, Bast created a plague to destroy the Canan species. She unleashed it in the water and sowed it in the earth. Within a year, a third of the Canan population was deceased. Infuriated by his sister's destruction, Lupious told their sire, Chimera, of Bast's transgressions. Knowing his children could not be allowed to destroy on a whim, Chimera dispelled the plague and told Bast that because she had thought to annihilate her brother's planet, hers would be forfeit. She was forbidden to engage with any Felisian for a hundred years. Bast was devastated and withdrew from all her family to wait out the century in seclusion.

Feeling her daughter's heartache and well-aware of her son's jealousy, Chimera's consort and mother of his children, Hippocampia, spoke to her mate on her daughter's behalf. Hippocampia knew well that Lupious would turn Bast's punishment to his advantage and endeavor his Canans to besiege planet Felisia. And so Chimera relented. He granted that Bast could contact her Felisians, but only through dreams and visions. It was their faith in her, Chimera said, that would secure the survival of their species.

The Canans, believing the plague was sent by the Felisians and fearful of another attempt to destroy their planet, forged an alliance with planet Mustel to overtake Felisia. The Canans promised to share all their technology with the Mustelidaens in return for their help. The Mustelidaens, eager to harness the power of space travel, agreed to the proposition. It didn't matter to them who they were fighting as long as they obtained the technology they craved. Lupious, delighted that his Canans were seeking vengeance against his sister, secretly aided his children in their endeavor, while fueling their hate for the Felisians.

It was Volga, vigilant to the change on her planet of Mustel, who told Bast of their brother's intentions. Knowing she could not directly intercede and incur her sire's wrath again, Bast visited the young queen Nefertiti in a vision and told her of the Canan's planned attack.

"With their weapons and superior numbers, and with the aid of the Mustelidaens, the Canans will destroy your people and my children." Bast walked through the queen's mind as a tiger of gold and silver. "Save what you can. Convince as many of the breeds as possible to leave the planet with you."

"Many will balk at this exodus."

Bast's voice held all her conviction. "You must make them see that this is the only way."

Nefertiti's mind spun as she thought of all her species she would have to save. All their history, all their culture. She bowed her gray and black head. "My Lady, where will we go?"

Bast's tail ticked back and forth. "My older brother Pegasus has agreed to see that the Equines grant you sanctuary on their planet. Share with them your knowledge and culture. They will be your strongest allies in the dark days ahead."

"Lord Pegasus is most kind." Nefertiti raised her head and squared her shoulders. "How long do we have?"

Bast blinked ruby eyes. A golden clock appeared in front of Nefertiti. The clock was simple in design and could easily be overlooked as nothing more than an ordinary timepiece, with one exception. This clock did not tell time in minutes or hours, but in years. It only used one hand. The top numeral, a fifteen, was sculpted out of red metal.

Bast nodded at the clock. "When you awake from this vision, the clock will stand in your chamber. You will have fifteen years to save all that you can. On the day the hand points to the fifteen, the Canans will attack and your planet will be lost."

Nefertiti bowed her head again. "I will do all I can, my Lady."

Bast walked away into mist. As the tiger body faded, a final comment flowed to Nefertiti's pointed ears. "See that you do. And see that you leave a parting gift for those who would take what is not willingly given."

In the fifteen years afforded them, the Felisians built great arks that would carry their history and their people to safe harbor. Nefertiti had no intention of leaving anyone behind. They built the ships to appear identical and launched them a few at a time. In this fashion the Canans believed the arks to be used for scientific exploration and gave them little thought. The arks landed on Equus where the first Felisians built the colony of Sanctuary in Diomedea and from that humble beginning migrated across the planet, integrating themselves in Equine culture.

When the Canans launched their attack on planet Felisian all they found were empty cities and broken pottery. In queen Nefertiti's chambers they found the golden clock, the single hand pointed at the fifteen. The Mustelidaens, sensing a trap and wanting to distance themselves from the Canans, withdrew their forces at once to their own planet. They took with them all the ships and technology they had been granted by the Canans.

Queen Nefertiti, all too happy to acquiesce to her goddess' request, made sure that even though she had to leave her beloved planet, the Canans never would. The Felisians, always more advanced, had many machines the Canans coveted. Nefertiti knew this. She bade her most talented technical cats build a virus into the technology they left behind that would corrupt and destroy all the Canan technology as soon as the systems were linked.

Lord Chimera, having discovered Lupious' deception, banished Lupious to Pandemonium and vented his fury on the Canans left on their home planet. The planet Canan left a barren rock, Chimera turned his attention to the surviving Canans on planet Felisia. Wanting to end the destruction, Bast beseeched her sire to allow the Canans on Felisia to live out their lives and learn from their mistake.

Over the years the Canans who had ventured to Felisia built their own humble civilization. They were slowly regaining their technological advances, but they now lived in fear of retaliation from the other planets in the galaxy. Wanting some peace of mind, the Canan leaders had signed a truce with the Felisians and for the past fifty years the two species had shared a tenebrous civility. Even though they had signed the treaty, the Felisians feared that the Canans still harbored a deep resentment.

The galaxy had been in upheaval after the discovery of the seizure of planet Felisia. The other planets, learning about the act years later through interplanetary traders, were horrified by the prospect of a hostile race descending from the sky and starting a war. In an attempt to mollify the planetary leaders, the Equines proposed an assembly known as the Anima Federation. This association was given the task of monitoring the planets in the solar system.

Even with the best design, every system has its flaws and corruption. Because of these issues, the Federation was becoming little more than a figurehead. Many of the planets kept to themselves, secretive of their intentions and advancements. That was why the trade agreements between Capra and Equus were looked at with mixed feelings of excitement and trepidation.

6

CHAPTER 6

Thracis stood hipshot just inside an alcove off the ballroom. He wasn't hiding, exactly, but he needed a breather from all the mares Queen Helena was introducing him to. At last count, he had met thirteen eligible ladies.

Thracis sighed. He had hoped Pyrios would face the same torture, but his older brother had slinked his way out of Queen Helena's matchmaking by being uncharacteristically gregarious to the lead stallions of the ruling herds. Pyrios wanted to obtain as much information about the Pact as he could. The council had begun four days prior, but new Equines were arriving daily from the outer territories. It was the newcomers that held Pyrios' interest.

Thracis watched the shift and flow of Equines and Felisians. All the Equines wore the traditional braids and pendants identifying their herds and home stables. The Felisians also wore pendants about their necks or between their ears in elaborate headpieces depicting their home city and house. As an integral part of the Equine courts, Felisians were invited to all the social events. Several Felisian families were longtime friends of the Thetis herd, but Thracis didn't see anyone he knew among the cats in the room.

Since more representatives had arrived, Thracis and Pyrios weren't the only young stallions at the council. Lady Ithia and her entourage had arrived yesterday and she had brought two of her sons, Phlegon and Aethon, with her. Ithia's sons were close in age to Pyrios and Thracis and the four stallions had spent the better part of the day together. Phlegon and Aethon, not coming from a ruling herd and with their paternity in doubt, were well below Lady Helena's manipulations. Thracis envied their freedom.

He sighed again, flicking his ears and shifting to lift his other back foot for a while. Thracis was bored to cribbing. He understood enough about politics to know parties like this were important to his province and his herd. Pyrios would make many of his own connections here now that their sire wasn't present. It was Pyrios' first chance to stand on his own four legs and show the ruling stallions his caliber and Thracis wouldn't rob him of it. But waiting chafed.

"The queen is requesting your presence, Lord Thracis."

Thracis flicked an ear in Desiree's direction. He had heard the mare approaching and had known why she was seeking him out. He hadn't seen Lady Helena in thirty minutes or so, more than enough time for the queen to have located another suitable mare.

"Why don't you tell her I stepped out for a minute?"

Desiree tossed her brown head, her forelock bouncing to reveal a white star. She was wearing an ornate headpiece and her ears had been pierced in the way that was fashionable these days. As was also custom, she was wearing a wrap that swirled about her shoulders and flowed over her back and rump to hang a foot above the floor. The wrap was made out of a light blue gauzy material and was embroidered with flowers in dark blue thread. Thracis didn't see the point in wearing anything as she had a beautiful coat and shouldn't hide it, but female fashion was a mystery to him.

"You aren't outside now."

"I will be if you would be kind enough to show me how to get out of this corral."

Her ears flicked making the dangling earrings dance. "Follow me."

She led him farther into the alcove and back against the wall so that they would be hidden in the shadows cast by the pillars. The harsh electric lights on the ceiling had been turned off for the party and the room was lit by softly glowing energy globes suspended in delicate nets made by Felisian ladies of court. The globes varied in color from light pink to deep violet and gave the revelry its festive edge. Even against the wall and behind the conversing Equines taking a break from the formal dances, Thracis felt exposed. He kept waiting to hear Queen Helena's voice ordering him to halt and come meet this wonderful mare from somewhere.

Thracis exhaled a pent-up breath of relief when Desiree led him through an archway and out onto a wide terrace. Thracis walked to the terrace wall and breathed deep of the night air.

He wondered if he would be missed if he jumped the wall and disappeared into the warren of streets that made up Bucephalus. Deciding Queen Helena would send out a search party, he sated himself with just being able to stand outside in the quiet for a few minutes.

He turned, expecting to have the terrace to himself, but Desiree was still standing by the doorway. "Are you making sure I don't bolt?"

The mare snorted. "You wouldn't get far with all the guards patrolling the walls."

"Since you plan on foalsitting, you may as well join me over here so we may talk without shouting."

Twitching her shoulders, Desiree walked over to stand across from him. She sniffed the wind and relaxed. Seeing her so at ease, Thracis unwound as well. He hadn't realized how much tension he had been under.

"How long have you been with the queen?"

Desiree shifted to stand hipshot. "A couple of years. I am only required to serve one more before I can choose another profession."

"Are you from Bucephalus?"

She shook her head. "I come from Emor. It's in Acarnia. It is a small town and my herd is not prominent, but my dam knew Lady Helena when they were foals and Lady Helena felt obligated to teach me the ways of court life. She doesn't introduce me to any eligible stallions, however." This last was followed by a dry laugh, but Thracis saw a hint of something in her eyes before she looked away. Had it been hurt?

"Who is that buckskin that follows the queen? I think she's the only lady I haven't been introduced to."

Desiree's voice was amused. "That is the princess Salia." She stretched her neck to speak almost in his ear. "The queen is most anxious to introduce Salia to your brother."

Thracis snorted. "I don't think she's his type."

Desiree pulled her head back. "And what is his type?"

Thracis flicked his ears at the feigned disinterest in her voice. "Tall, dark, and opinionated, though he won't admit the last."

"Is that supposed to be amusing?"

Thracis blinked at her hostile tone. "I apologize, lady. I meant no disrespect. If I offended you, I am sorry. I seem to be stepping on a lot of hooves lately."

"What does a foolish colt know of a mare's feelings?"

"Not much, apparently."

She sighed and looked off across the darkened gardens. Thracis let the silence stretch for a few minutes, then dipped his head to get her attention. "My brother is many things, but not loyal. He has a lady in every town from here to Thetis and would have more if he were able. He is my blood, but you will find better."

"In one such as you?" Her unblinking eyes unnerved him.

He looked away. "No. I'm not interested in any one mare as yet."

"None here at least." Desiree stepped closer to him.

Thracis' nostrils flared as he inhaled a light scent of flowers, some perfume she was wearing. As he was not stepping away, Desiree reached out and lipped the underside of his jaw, along his neck. The sensation was not unpleasant. Thracis felt his skin tingle as the mare's lips moved farther along his neck and she moved closer. It occurred to him that Pyrios would be busy talking for hours and his stall would be the last place Lady Helena would think to look for Thracis.

He curved his neck to nuzzle the soft hair along Desiree's cheek when an image of Psyche appeared in his mind. It wasn't mind to mind contact with the mare; it was a memory of Psyche standing amid her stones and candles. Thracis' ears went back. He had no loyalty to Psyche, she was just a mare he had met on his journey. Still, the image wouldn't dislodge itself. Sighing, he stepped back from Desiree.

The mare looked at him, equally confused and embarrassed. She glanced around, making sure they were still alone. "I'm sorry, Lord Thracis. I-I should not have been so brazen."

Thracis, his emotions again under control, reached out and nuzzled her shoulder. It was the same show of affection he would have given a family friend. "It's fine. I'm quite flattered."

She didn't look as though she believed that last, but she tossed her head, regaining her composure. "We should go back inside."

Thracis wanted to say more, to make her feel more at ease, but he was at a loss.

Desiree looked out over the garden. "I never should have tried to tempt you, I knew you would not want me." Her voice was musing, not bitter.

"What makes you think that?"

"I've been watching you. You are making a comparison every time the queen introduces you to a new mare. Making a comparison and finding that mare lacking. She must be something."

"Who?"

"Whoever it is that holds your heart."

With that Desiree strode passed him and back into the building. Thracis stood watching her go with his mouth unhinged. In his mind he heard his sire's voice from so long ago. *When you meet your true mate, you will gaze on other mares and find them all lacking.*

7

CHAPTER 7

Thracis stood in his customary position on Pyrios' left in King Pedasos' audience chamber. It was the fifth day of discussion and most of the representatives were thoroughly acquainted with the problems of the Baroquian Pact. It was no secret that the Pact wanted Myrmidon achillium. None of the ruling mares or stallions had any intention of aiding their old enemies. Today they would decide whether or not they would continue to treat Pact representatives with curt politeness or open hostility.

"The Baroquian Pact is beginning to make inquiries about purchasing large amounts of achillium from the Acarnian mines."

The disquieting news fell on silence. Lord Quintus stepped back out of the circle formed by the representatives of the ruling herds. Quintus was the ruling stallion of Acadia Stable in Acarnia. He was accompanied by his son Aeos, a dun who said little but watched the proceedings with vigilant eyes. They had only arrived that morning, having had the farthest to travel.

King Pedasos sighed. "This tale is commonplace all over Myrmidonia."

"It was only a visiting party. Three stallions and one mare. All were very charming." Lord Quintus tried to keep the disgust out of his voice. Acarnia had suffered more than either Pendaria or Calabria during the Age of Strife.

"I'm sure they were." This came from Lady Ithia. She was from Calpernia Stable on the far side of Pendaria. Her stable was small, but held much influence in the surrounding towns. She had come with an escort, but was currently not attached to any one stallion. A fact she made clear at the ball last night when she retired for the evening with a member of King Pedasos' court.

King Pedasos turned to Pyrios. "Has Thetis Stable received any requests for an audience with anyone representing the Baroquian Pact?" Pyrios had already spoken about this to the king but had yet to discuss the subject at the council.

Pyrios shook his head. "No, they haven't approached my sire as yet."

"Good. Calabria has the richest achillium deposits on the planet. They must be protected."

Pyrios pinned his ears. "If the Pact wants Calabrian achillium they'll have to go through my sire to get it. He bears no love for those opposing the Registry of Breeds and we are descendants of Lord Bucephalus himself. We will never aid the Baroquians in an act of war."

The other Equines in the meeting bobbed their heads in approval.

King Pedasos settled himself squarely on all four feet. "The reason you have all been summoned here is that I wish to discuss what part Myrmidonia will play should the Baroquian Pact and the Elysian Alliance go to war. From what I have heard over the last five days, all of us wish to be true to our heritage and keep the breeds unified."

The council members uttered agreement.

Lord Minas stepped forward. He was old and had long since passed control of his herd over to his daughter Lydia. Still, he held the respect of all the Equines in the meeting and had been offered a place on the king's council many times. Each time, Lord Minas had declined, professing he did not enjoy palace life. This statement only deepened the respect of his peers.

The old stallion cleared his throat before beginning. "I believe I speak for all of us assembled when I say that should a war come to pass, we will fully support the cause of the Alliance. We all know the breeds cannot thrive if the world is divided. Such is the lesson of Lord Bucephalus."

All the horses bowed their heads at the mention of the legendary stallion. Minas waited a moment before continuing. "I feel it would be in our best interest to send a group of horses to the capital at Lipizza and inform the Registry of our intentions."

Lady Ithia spoke. "Wouldn't it be more convenient to make contact with someone in the Registry via our minds and tell them of our intentions?"

"That is a wise suggestion, Lady Ithia. However, it has come to our attention that one of the Baroquian representatives who approached us was a practitioner of the occult and capable of eavesdropping." Lord Minas looked at King Pedasos. "We should be careful of what we say mind to mind unless we have the protection of a psychic to secure the connection."

Eavesdroppers were Equines or Felisians who had honed their psychic talents to be able to pick up on private mental conversations between individuals. They were often used in courts to keep alert for any treachery. It seemed that they were finding new employment as Baroquian spies. If the Pact learned of Myrmidonia's firm stand to join the Alliance, they might decide to send a raiding parting to Myrmidonia to take the achillium they wanted.

"As this is the case, we will be forced to send actual representatives to the capital." King Pedasos looked around the room at the members of the council.

Thracis' ears pricked, but he kept silent. He and Pyrios would be heading to Lipizza in any case, a fact of which King Pedasos was well-aware. Thracis knew the king would have no objections to he and Pyrios accompanying whoever the council sent to inform the Registry about Myrmidonia's affiliations.

Lord Quintus cleared his throat. "It may be wise to send some of the younger horses as we must return to our home stables to keep order."

Lord Minas nodded. Lady Ithia stepped forward. "The Zephyros stallions have told my sons that they are journeying to Lipizza. My sons have also expressed a desire to see our capital. That would make four."

The dun stallion from Acarnia stepped forward. "I am Aeos, only son of Mykas Quintus. I would also go if my sire will give me leave."

Aeos stepped back. Lord Quintus all but beamed at his son. "I give it and wish you luck. The Registry will be most interested in speaking with someone who dealt with the Pact firsthoof."

King Pedasos nodded at the remaining council members. "I believe five is an adequate number. No one has reported more than four Baroquians in a group. These stallions are young and strong and trained in combat. They should be able travel to Lipizza with little trouble."

Lord Minas drew the council's attention again. "These stallions should contact their home stables at least every other night during their journey. This communication will not arouse interest as young stallions on their first adventure often contact their parents."

The parents in the council nodded. Those who were not sending their children were grateful that King Pedasos had stopped the nominations at five. Safe as Myrmidonia and Lipizzania were presumed to be, they were living in uncertain times.

"I will keep in touch will all your stables as well," King Pedasos said to the five young stallions, "If I or your parents do not hear from you for more than two days, I will inform the Hippikon and request military assistance."

The young stallions nodded. If the king was planning on contacting the Hippikon, the most illustrious military complex on all Equus, in the event that he lost contact with Pyrios and the others, he was more concerned than he was letting on. This knowledge would ensure that each of the nominees would be contacting someone, probably every night.

King Pedasos bobbed his head. "You will be leaving tomorrow. Spend the day talking with my military council who will tell you how to avoid a confrontation to the best of your ability and get a good night's rest tonight. I fear you will not sleep well again until you are safely in Lipizza."

8

CHAPTER 8

The five young stallions trotted along the Endurance Road. The Endurance Road was the main highway that crisscrossed the countries of Myrmidonia and Lipizzania. Even though Equines had the ability for space travel, their technology was used strictly to benefit them as a whole. In times of need, movers were used to move horses rapidly from one area to the another. The general opinion shared by both Equines and Felisians was that technology was disruptive to the natural world. That was why spaceships and movers were never used in conflicts on planet Equus. The destruction would be disastrous.

The sun was inching toward the horizon when Pyrios, who had become the unofficial leader of this little herd, began to look for a place to bed down for the night. He knew he should have made them stop in Criticos, a village several miles back, but the evening was so cool after the heat of the day and they were making such good time, he hated to stop early. Now, surveying both sides of the road for a suitable camp, Pyrios regretted his earlier decision. They had passed few travelers in the last hour and were now entering a desolate, open plain. It was the exactly the type of situation King Pedasos' military strategists had warned the stallions to avoid.

In general, Equines preferred open spaces. They didn't like forests or hills because of the blocked view. An Equine's first instinct was to run from threats, not attack, and so they depended heavily on knowing where danger may be hiding. This was true in most cases, which should have made the open plain an excellent location, but the hair on top of Pyrios' rump had been standing on end for the last twenty minutes and the panoramic view was making it worse.

Up ahead, he saw a rock outcropping that would offer some cover. The outcropping was big enough that all of them could easily bed down and get below the constant Levadian wind. During the day the breeze was a welcome reprieve from the spring warmth, but the nights were still cool. Pyrios headed in that direction.

The field running perpendicular to the outcropping and parallel to the Endurance Road was a mixture of timothy and clover grass. This was common sight along the major thoroughfares. Equines, in recognition that grain and water were heavy enough, planted fields of rich grasses so that travelers could have plenty of sustenance on their journeys. It made things easier for everyone. The fields weren't a bother to anyone as they were left to the will of nature in the hopes that they would be fertile. Roads were also built along waterways whenever possible. At this point on the road, Pyrios' herd was only a quarter mile or so from the Cerulean River, but they had all drunk heavily at midafternoon and wouldn't need any more water until tomorrow at midmorning. Each stallion was also carrying his own waterskin in case of emergency.

"Should we build a fire?" Aeos was fidgeting in the dirt, preparing to dig a pit to contain the coals.

Pyrios, still gazing over the open plain, shook his head. "Not tonight. The rocks should be enough of a windbreak."

Twitching his shoulders, Aeos walked away to graze with Aethon and Phlegon. Thracis, more in tune with his brother, came to stand beside Pyrios. "Something wrong?"

"I'm not sure. The wind smells fine and the only sounds are birds and rustling grasses, but something feels off to me."

Thracis flared his nostrils and took a deep breath. He couldn't smell anything out of the ordinary. His ears flicked back and forth finding nothing unusual. He looked at Pyrios. "Perhaps you're spooky because you are under king's orders." He meant the comment to loosen his brother's tension, but Pyrios continued to stare.

"I think we should keep our ears up tonight. News of our departure was widespread in the city and the Pact won't be happy with the decision the herd leaders have reached."

Thracis tossed his head. "They would be foolish to try something so deep in Lipizzania. Maybe they only want to talk."

"I doubt it. Talking has gotten them nowhere." Pyrios looked at his brother. "Get something to eat and let the others know we may have company."

Thracis bobbed his head and stepped away to join the other stallions. He relayed the message to the others. Aethon and

Phlegon smirked at the idea of a fight so close to their home province. They had been sheltered by their dam most of their lives and had not seen the dangers of Equus.

Besides other horses, Equines had to be aware of the predators of Equus. In addition to native threats, such as heinas, pack forming canine-type animals with ferocious jaws and razor claws, and bears. The Felisians, in an attempt to save all that they could of their home planet, had brought tigers and lions to Equus. The bigger cats had never evolved to the same intellectual level as the smaller Felisians. They had a crude form of intelligence and were adept hunters. Their four to five-hundred-pound bodies and razor claws and teeth made them a serious threat to any Equine.

Aeos, heir to the Acadian Stable, had traveled far and wide with his sire and was well-aware of the dangers of the road. He was a seasoned fighter and had trained with his sire's best warriors. Of all the stallions in the group, Aeos had the most experience in the lands outside Myrmidonia. He took Pyrios' warning to heart and suggested they set a watch for the night.

"That's an excellent idea," Pyrios said around a mouthful of timothy.

"I think the two of you are overreacting to being out on the road alone." Aethon's voice carried the bored arrogance of a spoiled brat. He was the younger of the two and thus far had shown that he was his dam's favorite.

"I'd rather overreact than regret not being prepared." Pyrios was trying to be patient.

Aethon and Phlegon snorted their disapproval, but kept silent.

"I'll take first watch," Pyrios offered, "I feel awake enough and it would allow you all to get settled."

Thracis bobbed his head. "I'll go next, then Aeos if he doesn't mind." Aeos shook his head and Thracis continued, "then Aethon. Phlegon can go last."

Pyrios flicked an ear at his brother's shrewdness. By setting the watches so that Phlegon and Aethon would stand last, those two would get the most sleep during the night. And would be more cordial on the road tomorrow, presumably.

The decision made, the Equines settled down to pass the night. Some slept lying down while others remained standing. Pyrios stationed himself on the edge of the outcropping so that he would have some cover, but still be able to see the rest of the plain. He noticed, and not with a little unease, that both Aethon and Phlegon had removed their armor harnesses to be more comfortable as they slept. Not wanting to start an argument, Pyrios kept quiet on the subject.

The night passed sedately enough, growing almost silent three hours after sundown. Thracis and Aeos stood their watches without complaint, vigilant to the minutest sounds or shifts of light as clouds drifted across the double moons. The wind had died in the night and the lack of scent carriage had the stallions on edge.

When Aeos awakened Aethon the other horse groaned to his feet and spent several minutes stretching before taking his post. Younger than Phlegon and not an early riser to begin with, Aethon stood watch for ten minutes before cocking a back leg, hanging his head, and falling back to sleep. Five minutes later, the night exploded.

Thracis was shocked awake as the silence filled with a cacophony of screamed battlecries. He had been lying down, the most vulnerable position for an Equine. Letting instinct guide him, he rolled completely over and activated his armor even as he gathered himself and sprang to his feet. Encased in gleaming achillium, Thracis spun back to the camp.

Pyrios, his armor covering him from ears to hooves, was on his hind legs and grappling with a similarly shielded opponent. Both Equines were using hooves and muscle to inflict deep tissue damage as neither could break through the other's achillium coating.

Cavalry armor was equipped with sharpened spikes of various lengths and size as well as customizations such as electrical charges or poisoned ridges. The armor worn by the stallions in this little group was designed for defense rather than offense. Pyrios' and Thracis' armor were both equipped with three-foot-long retracting spikes set in the middle of their foreheads that was accessible after the armor was engaged. However, for this weapon to be useful Pyrios would first have to distance himself from his opponent.

Even as he saw his brother in combat Thracis knew Pyrios could take care of himself. He surveyed the other stallions in the herd and realized that Aethon was in the most danger. Aethon had taken off his armor earlier in the evening and now fought with no protection at all. Although Thracis could see no wounds in the star-studded darkness his nostrils were assaulted by the copper tang of blood.

Still free from attack, Thracis extended the sharpened horn on his forehead and charged Aethon's opponent. He angled his head so that the horn would slide between two of the over-lapping metal plates on the other horse's armor. Thracis took the shock of impact all the way through his body. The other horse screamed and reared, striking Aethon in the chest and wrenching Thracis' head to one side as it tried to pull free of the wicked horn. Thracis' aim was true; he impaled the other horse at the juncture of neck and shoulder blade. That blow would incapacitate the Equine's entire right front leg, effectively hobbling it.

The horse pulled free of Thracis and took several stumbling steps backward on its hind legs. It knew it wouldn't be able to use the front leg and was trying to get as much distance between itself and Thracis before Thracis could strike again.

Seeing his advantage, Thracis lowered his head for another strike. Before he could charge forward, movement to the left caught his attention. Rearing back into a levade, Thracis tucked his front legs to his chest just as a raptor, a disc that opened into a razor-winged shuriken with five talons when fired, whirred right in front of him. It flew past to embed itself in the side of the rock outcropping.

Thracis dropped to all fours and turned to face this new enemy. The horse in front of him was clad in achillium armor fashioned with curved ridges around the faceplate and neck regions. The ridges curved backward into vicious hooks. If another horse tried attacking from the front, it would be effectively secured on the barbs of the armor.

With a rearing assault out of the question, Thracis spun and started kicking as hard as he could to keep his attacker at bay. The other horse, more experienced, sidestepped the first barrage of kicks and came up beside Thracis. The horse slammed its flank into Thracis' side, pushing the stallion off balance.

Thracis stumbled and spread his legs to keep from going down. He tried to pull away from the other horse and was alarmed to find that the two of them were fused side by side. The other horse, its head only coming to just behind Thracis' own, began to batter Thracis' neck and withers with its upper body. The barbs on its armor caught onto Thracis' own. Thracis, fearing that his enemy would have some electrical component modified into its armor, struggled to get away. The more he struggled the deeper the barbs worked into his flesh. He continued his efforts until his neck was slick with blood.

In desperation, Thracis did the exact opposite of what most horses would. Where other Equines would jerk and pull away, Thracis crashed up against the other horse and pulled straight back. The ploy had the intended effect and Thracis was free. He backed rapidly, keeping his eyes on the other horse.

The other horse, disgusted by the ability of this country bumpkin to get away, came forward. Thracis watched the enemy approach, mind calculating. He couldn't kick this horse and couldn't attack head on. That only left one option.

The other horse lowered its head and charged. Thracis held his ground until the very last instant. Then he threw himself to the ground and rolled into the other horse. The horse's legs tangled in Thracis' armor and the two of them ended up in a heap. Knowing it was his only chance, Thracis scrambled to his knees and brought his head around, piercing the underside of his opponent's armor. The horn slipped between two ridges and sank deep into the horse's gut.

Screaming, legs kicking in all directions, the horse wiggled free and dragged itself to its feet. It stood, shuddering, watching as Thracis got up a few feet away. Thracis readied himself for another onslaught, but his opponent had had enough. It backed slowly, feet stumbling and head bobbing in pain with every step. Thracis ears flicked back as he heard hoof beats.

Not wanting to let them all get away, Thracis swung his head low and to the right. His horn caught one of the retreating party across the knees. Thracis was jarred to his knees even as the other horse somersaulted to land sprawling several yards farther on. Thracis stood and walked to the fallen Equine.

The Equine, blood spilling from the armor's nostril holes in two streams, was panting. It looked up at Thracis with pleading eyes.

"Please...please help me." The voice was gargled as if the Equine's throat was filling with blood.

With that much blood pouring out of its nostrils and now from the corner of its mouth, there was only one way to help this Equine. The final way.

"I will speed you along if you tell me why."

The other Equine gave a gurgled laugh. "Because you are not allies and so are enemies."

"Myrmidonia has made no stand as to whose side of this conflict they are on." That wasn't exactly true, but Thracis thought it was true enough.

The stranger snorted. Blood sprayed across the grass. By the time the sun rose, that patch of scarlet would have rusted. "We've all chosen sides." The horse retracted his armor to grant Thracis a clear strike.

Shaking his head, Thracis plunged his horn behind the horse's shoulder, piercing its heart. Getting down on his knees, Thracis wiped the horn clean as well as he could before retracting both it and his armor. His neck felt hot and swollen. Blood ran from dozens of cuts to drip on the grass.

Thracis turned to see how his companions had faired. Pyrios stood with his left foreleg raised. In the starlight, Thracis couldn't see how bad his brother was wounded, but when Pyrios stepped forward he looked as though he were trying to put weight on the leg. Thracis took that to be a good sign. Aeos was standing a few yards away, sniffing his back and shoulders, inspecting his wounds. Aethon and Phlegon were nowhere to be seen.

Aeos and Thracis went to Pyrios so that he wouldn't have to stress his leg. Thracis was about to ask where Aethon and Phlegon had gone when a baleful wail filled the night. The three stallions made their way as quickly as possible to the wail's source. The heat in Thracis' neck was turning into a low burning.

They found the brothers on the other side of the outcropping. It looked as though they had tried to run once they realized they were outmatched. They hadn't gotten far.

Phlegon was on his knees, keening. Stretched out on his side, Aethon lay motionless. A pile of something lay tangled and glistening in the starlight. As they approached, Thracis saw that the tangled mass were the intestines that had fallen out of Aethon after an opponent eviscerated him. In the chancey light, Thracis saw that Aethon's body was a mosaic of punctures and slashes. Phlegon had also sustained numerous injuries, but physical pain was overshadowed by loss.

Pyrios stepped forward, searching for the right words. Before he could open his mouth, Phlegon told them what had happened. The words poured out, tumbling and crashing into each other like white water rapids.

"He was always lazy when it came to fighting. Always trying to get out of practice." Phlegon's breath hitched. "I-I tried to get to him, but they kept me away. I couldn't fight them without any armor. I tried, Pyrios, I really did."

Pyrios set his nose on Phlegon's withers for comfort. Phlegon took a deep breath and continued. "They separated us. Driving him farther away. Do you know they didn't even kill him in honest combat? Three of them ganged up; he didn't have a chance. And then they couldn't even make it quick." At this last his voice broke and he began to keen again.

Pyrios waited until Phlegon fell silent before speaking. "Come now, we have to assess the damage. After we've seen to each other you can grieve all you want. We must clean your wounds. Aethon would want you to heal and help catch the Equines who did this to him."

Phlegon rose slowly and waited as Pyrios inspected him. In the starlight, the gray coat showed little blood. Most of the wounds were scratches and bruises. Deciding there was nothing life-threateningly wrong with Phlegon, Pyrios turned to Thracis.

"Thracis, do you have that salve our dam sent with us? Thracis?"

Thracis wondered why Pyrios was swaying from side to side. He opened his mouth to tell Pyrios he didn't know where the salve was, but his throat felt so dry. Why was Aeos looking at him like that?

Tossing his head, Thracis stepped forward and found himself on the ground. The whole world seemed to be rocking back and forth as if they had left land and were somehow out at sea. He was so tired. Thracis laid his head on the ground, straining to fill his lungs. His neck was on fire. Faintly, he could hear Pyrios and Aeos calling his name. He tried to tell them all he wanted to do was close his eyes for a minute or two. Before he could form the words, he was engulfed in darkened silence.

9

CHAPTER 9

Thracis was surrounded in fog. His ears flicked back and forth rapidly. He could see nothing but gray, smell only damp heaviness in the air. But the sounds. Concealed by overlaid veils of gossamer, the sounds in the fog were dangers without shape. Thracis could hear hoofbeats, but they were odd. The hoofbeats made a dragging, scraping noise as if whatever was making them had been injured and could not take normal steps any longer. He heard the click of talons. He heard tearing and chewing. His armor harness was gone, leaving him without protection.

His heart began to pump faster, his breath coming in rapid and shallow. Thracis pivoted on his hind legs, trying to seek out any solidity in the mist. All he saw were shadows that flitted close then danced away. The ground under his feet felt spongy and unsteady, scaring him even more. He was afraid to walk anywhere and risk losing the fragile footing on which he stood. How had he gotten here? Where were the others?

He lowered his head and tried to remember. Fragments of fighting came to him. He saw the horse with the barbed armor coming at him. Thracis shuddered at the recollection of the barbs digging into the flesh of his neck. He turned his head to inspect the wounds on his lower neck and shoulder and noticed a darker shadow standing behind and to one side of him.

Thracis tried to whirl, but he was overcome with dizziness and collapsed to his knees. The shadow advanced, parting the swirling mists. Thracis tried to lift his head, but the dizziness returned and he knelt, shaking, waiting for a crippling blow. He closed his eyes.

He felt the brush of hair against his cheek. His nostrils flared at a familiar scent. Thracis opened his eyes and saw the dark side of a balanced face.

Foolish colt to get locked with a barbed warrior. Psyche's eyes held amusement and concern. Then he realized she was speaking inside his head.

Following her lead, he kept the connection open. He was careful to shield his feelings from the contact, just as she was. *Where am I?*

We call this place the Deceptive Mists. It is the borderland between waking and dreaming, life and death. It is a gateway to the other planes of existence.

Thracis, still unable to stand, trembled. He had never been comfortable with the powers of the mind that went beyond telepathy and telekinesis. *Why can't I lift my head?*

It is the poison from the barbs. It is very strong to affect you even here. Let me help. She nuzzled the soft spot just behind his front shoulder where the girth of the harness would lay. Thracis felt a soothing cool spill down his legs and follow the upward curve of his neck. His head cleared and he rose cautiously to his feet.

Psyche stepped back from him. Her sides heaved slightly and a light sweat coated her neck.

Thracis grew alarmed. *What's wrong?*

Psyche lowered her head and took a deep breath. *I am too far away from you to use this much psychic and healing energy. I've done as much as I can for now.*

She came toward him and lipped the protective stone she had secured to his mane in Iliad. *This has kept you alive so far, but its power dwindles. I have given you as much of my energy as I dare. I have sent help for you.*

She looked into the mist, then back at him, catching and holding his eye. *You must stay in this place, no matter what you hear or see in the mists. My friend will know how to call you home.*

Her body was fading, loosing substance. Thracis reached out to her and felt nothing but mist. *Will you be alright?*

Psyche tossed her opaque head. *I will be fine, foolish colt. It is you who needs help.*

Thracis watched until even her outline was gone. He had never felt so lonely or tired. Shutting out the noises around him as best he could, Thracis folded up his legs and lie down on the patch of spongy ground, waiting for someone to show him the way home.

"What are we going to do?" Pyrios' voice was reaching its highest pitch. He paced back and forth next to Thracis' prone form, his limp deepening with every step.

On his knees, his ear pressed to Thracis' side, Aeos blocked out Pyrios' question and concentrated on Thracis' breathing. What he heard left little encouragement.

Thracis' breath was shallow and rapid and every inhalation was accompanied by a liquid rasping sound deep in his chest. Aeos stood and sniffed the ragged gashes on Thracis' neck. They had a sweet, spoiled smell that made him gag. The wounds were already swollen and beginning to ooze a viscous fluid and they gave off a feverish heat. Aeos did have some experience with poisons but he had never seen anything like this.

He raised his head and looked a Pyrios. "This is bad. This poison is faster than any other I've encountered. It's a wonder he isn't dead already."

Pyrios pinned his ears. "Don't speak of such things. We have to help him."
Aeos and Phlegon looked at each other. The sun was rising, a silver light signaling its arrival. As the day brightened, the gashes on Thracis' neck looked more and more infected. The poison seemed to be rotting the stallion's flesh away.

Pyrios lowered his head to sniff his brother's face and ears. When his breath blew against Thracis' neck the other stallion's mane fluttered, disclosing a stone with strange markings. The markings were glowing white in the dawn light.

"What is that?" Pyrios asked Aeos.

Aeos shook his head. "I have no idea, but I bet it's the reason he's still breathing."

Pyrios looked passed Aeos and down the Endurance Road. "What is the closest town?"

Aeos didn't hesitate. "Weyrother." He paused. "But it's at least a day's gallop from here. Pyrios, even if we all used our minds to carry him, we couldn't make it in less than two days."

"We have to try."

Phlegon, silent until now, stepped forward. "Pyrios, I know the pain you are suffering. My brother lies dead beside you. But Aeos speaks true. We can do nothing save ease his passing."

Pyrios snorted and turned from them. He walked to the edge of the road and breathed deep of the morning wind. A strange scent had him pivoting on his hindquarters and cantering back to the herd. Aeos and Phlegon, their nerves on edge, spun to face outward, their back legs almost touching Thracis on the ground.

"What is it?" Phlegon's voice held restrained panic. He had replaced his harness and now engaged his armor. Phlegon had no intention of being caught off guard again.

"Don't know. A strange scent on the wind." Pyrios flared his nostrils. He wasn't going to engage his armor unless an enemy showed itself.

"What kind of scent?" Aeos was sniffing the air.

Pyrios shook his head. "A kind of spicy, musky sort of smell."

Aeos opened his mouth, intending to make Pyrios explain better, when a tinkling sound caught all their attentions. Coming around the rock outcropping where the stallions had been attacked was the small figure of a Felisian. The cat was wearing a harness securing several pouches to its body. Behind it came a dwarf, or miniature horse as was the more polite term. The miniature wore a similar harness adorned with hanging pouches as well as several tiny bells. The two were moving fast, the Felisian stretched in full run as it came around the rocky corner.

"By Bast's Mercy we come to help. It was the *ammoni* mare who sent us." The Felisian's voice rose and fell in time with his gait.

"What's he talking about?" Phlegon's voice was a whisper.

Aeos bobbed his head. "I don't know, but an *ammoni* is the Felisian word for seer or witch. If she sent him that means she knew something like this would happen."

"Can we trust him?" Pyrios' ears were pinned.

Aeos twitched a shoulder. "What difference does it make? Thracis is dying anyway."

Pyrios dropped his head in agreement as the Felisian skidded to a stop in front of the three stallions. The miniature halted behind him. Balancing on his hind legs, the cat extended an orange paw. "Time is short. I have the necessary antidote and medicines. Please allow us to help."

"I don't know who sent you, but I believe you are the only hope he has, but I swear by Lord Pegasus if you make his suffering any greater I will pike your head on the road for all to see." Pyrios' voice was a growl.

The Felisian bowed. "I would rather you kill me than return to milady and tell her that I have failed."

Not waiting for a response, the Felisian darted between Pyrios' feet and hopped over Thracis' neck. The miniature trotted around the three stallions and began to dig a fire pit. At the same time, the tiny Equine used his mind to unpack a pot, a flask, and half a dozen labeled leather pouches. Minutes later the smell of an herbal brew of some kind filled the air.

As Pyrios, Aeos, and Phlegon watched, the Felisian and miniature began to bleed the wounds and apply steaming pumices to draw as much of the poison as possible. Every hour or so, the Felisian forced a pungent liquid down Thracis' throat. As the day wore on the Felisian sent Aeos to the Cerulean River to get fresh water time and again. As he worked the Felisian sang a soothing song under his breath. Occasionally he would pause in his singing and call Thracis' name. Pyrios looked at Aeos for an explanation, but the dun stallion only twitched his shoulders.

Two hours into the exhaustive healing, Phlegon left Pyrios and began to dig a hole under the one sprawling tree in the vicinity. He used both his legs and his mind to do this. The work was slow, Phlegon was worn out physically and mentally, but he was making progress. After ascertaining that he was more in the way than any actual help, Pyrios went to aid Phlegon. Aeos continued to help the Felisian and miniature throughout the day.

The sun was resting on the horizon, painting the sky with streaks of orange and pink when the Felisian came to sit next to Phlegon and Pyrios. The stallions had finished burying Aethon an hour before and Phlegon was dozing next to the fresh grave.

Pyrios was keeping watch as best he could, but felt as if he would collapse at any moment.

The Felisian was wiping his paws on a scrap of towel. "I believe he will live. He must stay here for at least a day, then you can move him to Weyrother if you are careful. He is very weak and his wounds must be kept clean else they will become infected. In his weakness a fever could kill him."

Pyrios bobbed his head and sighed. His relief was a crushing weight that threatened to take his feet out from under him. "I thank you. We didn't know what to do for him. I have no experience with poisons."

"I've a fair amount with the poisons used all over Equus and can tell you that the one used on your brother is not common in this region. I don't know how the *ammoni* knew which poison it was, but it was her knowledge in herb lore that saved this stallion."

Pyrios flicked his ears. "I am sorry, I do not know of who you speak."

The Felisian smiled and stretched out on the grass. He gripped the earth with his claws, leaving dark furrows. "I didn't think so. She's a funny one. Knows that stallion well enough. That talisman in his mane is one of the strongest I've seen." The Felisian gave Pyrios a sly look. "He must have made an impression at some point."

Pyrios was too tired to give his brother's conquests much thought. Still, Thracis hadn't told Pyrios of any one mare in particular that he held in special regard. It must have been the mare Thracis met in Iliad, she was the only one Pyrios had not seen. He would have to ask his brother when Thracis was co-herent again.

He lowered his head to look the Felisian in the eye. "Forgive me. I am Zephyros Pyrios, son of Bailus Zephyros. That is my brother, Thracis, but you already knew that."

The Felisian smiled and nodded.

"The one who aided you is Quintus Aeos and this is..." Pyrios paused. When Phlegon had been introduced to Pyrios, his dam had neglected to mention a sire.

In Equine society it was customary for a foal to take their sire's name in front of their own. This was true except for those of Diomedea where stallions were considered breeding stock and nothing more. In that country, a foal took their dam's name in front of their own. This practice was becoming more popular among mares who did not have a formal union with any one stallion. It was also popular among the aristocracy where certain mares held more authority than their male coun-terparts.

In Lipizzania, it was traditional for a foal to take their sire's bloodline and keep it in front of their own name, such as Pyrios' and Thracis' dam, Maestoso Calypsa had. The Lipizzans were very proud of their foundation bloodlines and wanted to see their ancestors remembered with every new generation.

Pyrios looked at Phlegon, hoping the other stallion would make his own introduction.

"Ithia Phlegon," Phlegon said. He sniffed the grave. "This is my brother, Aethon."

The Felisian rested a paw on the fresh earth. "May he find comfort in the herds of Lord Pegasus."

Phlegon nodded in reception of the condolence.

The Felisian turned back to Pyrios. "I am Kamuzu, a son of Anat." Felisians always followed the matriarchal line, in deference to their deity Bast. He nodded to the miniature, standing watch over Thracis and speaking with Aeos. "That is Alcander. I do not know his lineage and have never asked. He is a good companion and well-versed in the healing arts."

"I thank you both and will gladly compensate you in any way you see fitting." Pyrios was sincere, but knew there were limits to what he could grant the Felisian and the miniature.

Kamuzu shook his orange and white head. "Nothing but thanks are necessary." He looked back at Alcander. "For me that is enough, but perhaps you could accept Alcander into your herd for the night."

"Why wouldn't we-"

The Felisian cut off Pyrios' inquiry. "He is a gelding."

At that, Phlegon raised his head. His ears set back, but he did not pin them, a sign of his indecision. Pyrios knew what he was feeling. His own ears were vacillating between lying flat and standing up.

Gelding a stallion was the worst punishment on all Equus, more feared than even death. It was reserved only for the most heinous crime in Equine society, rape. For a stallion to force himself on an unwilling mare was unforgivable. A gelding was an outcast of society, a useless thing unwanted and shunned. Stallions challenged all geldings who came too close to any mare, often killing the intruder. During the Age of Strife, Zaxas ordered the captured stallions who led others against him to be gelded so that their lines would never continue and they would not even have an honorable death. It was the ultimate price for standing against him and his army. After being gelded, many Equines took their own lives, refusing to live with only the memory of what they once were. Some moved on with their lives but existed as hermits, far removed from society.

"He was wrongly accused and punished." Kamuzu was sitting up, his tailing tick tocking in the grass.

Pyrios snorted. "Is that what he told you?"

Kamuzu shook his head. "He has told me nothing of how he came to be in his current state. The *ammoni* mare who sent us trusts him and that is all I need to know."

Pyrios and Phlegon exchanged a look. If a mare was willing to put her trust in the gelding then perhaps Alcander had been unjustly punished. No matter what his tale, the miniature had worked alongside Kamuzu to save Thracis' life and that was all Pyrios was interested in.

Pyrios raised his head and hailed Alcander over. The miniature came slowly, keeping his head down. As he approached, Pyrios could see the scars that marred the white coat. The stallion would bet that Alcander had been tortured long before he was finally gelded. Pyrios wondered what the miniature could have done that would have incurred such wrath.

Alcander stopped in front of Pyrios. Even with his head held high, the miniature's ears would only reach the center of Pyrios' chest. Pyrios lowered his head to look in Alcander's face. "I do not know why you have been punished and have no right to ask, but you have saved my brother and for that I give you my deepest thanks. You are welcome in my herd whenever you wish."

Alcander bowed his head and took a deep breath. "You honor me, stallion of Thetis Stable. It has been many years since I was welcome in a herd outside Diomedean borders."

Diomedea again. Pyrios raised his head to hide his surprise. The miniature must have been wrongly punished indeed to be able to walk among those herds. Diomedea was a female dominated country. If the miniature had done anything to any mare, they would have skinned him alive. What kind of mare had Thracis become involved with?

Phlegon bobbed his head at the miniature. "Welcome, little friend. It was fortuitous that you were sent to help."

"The mare who sent us is a very talented lady."

Kamuzu nodded. He stood, stretched, and went to dig through the pouches on Alcander's harness. A few minutes later the Felisian came back and settled on the grass to eat a dinner of dried meat. Alcander moved off to graze. After a few minutes, Phlegon joined the miniature. Pyrios walked over to where Thracis lay.

"How is he?"

Aeos, lightly dozing, jumped at the sound of Pyrios' voice. The dun stallion yawned and stretched before answering. "He's sleeping sound right now. I've been massaging his legs every thirty minutes or so to make sure the blood flows to his feet. Kamuzu said something about getting him up in a bit. We'll have to sleep in shifts again to stand watch and keep up with the massages."

Pyrios flicked his ears to show he had heard, but the bulk of his attention was on the deep breaths Thracis was taking. Pyrios lowered his head and sniffed the bandaging on Thracis' neck. The good odor of strong medicine filled his nostrils.

Thracis flicked an ear at Pyrios' sniffing. "Stop hovering like a new dam." The words were a whisper without force, but they made Pyrios' heart break.

He gently nipped Thracis' shoulder. "Given the last twelve hours, I'm allowed to hover."

Thracis groaned and tried to shift to a more comfortable position.

"You should keep still for now. Kamuzu, he's the one who saved you by the way, wants to get you on your feet in a little while."

"I want to get up now."

Pyrios called to Kamuzu. The Felisian trotted over to Thracis and inspected the wounds. He looked up at Pyrios. "Problem?"

"He wants to get up now."

"Alright." The cat looked at Pyrios and Aeos. "The two of you will have to steady him. Use your minds as that way you won't disturb the dressings."

Pyrios and Aeos nodded. Thracis gathered his legs underneath himself. He waited until he felt the mental bands grip him, ready to catch him in case he buckled. Kamuzu stepped back out of the way. Phlegon and Alcander stopped grazing and came to stand behind the Felisian.

Thracis took a deep breath and pushed himself up. His back legs tried to buckle, but the mental bands tightened, holding his legs straight. He stood, legs shaking, head swimming. His legs were splayed as far apart as he could get them and still remain upright. To all around Thracis looked like a newborn foal trying his legs for the first time. It felt so good to stand. Standing up, even with the help of Pyrios and Aeos, did more to lift Thracis' spirit than any medicine could. After only five minutes, Thracis folded his legs and lay back down. He was exhausted, but content. He would sleep better knowing that he would recover.

Pyrios and Aeos were sweating lightly from the mental strain of holding Thracis up. They stepped back a little and hung their heads while Kamuzu took the opportunity to redress Thracis' wounds and then pour more of the healing tea down the stallion's throat.

When he was finished, Kamuzu looked at the other members of the herd. "We will let him sleep now for a few hours before getting him up again. Those of you who have not eaten should and then get some sleep. I will take the first watch and see to Thracis' legs. I have placed a containment field around your dead opponent."

Pyrios and the others exchanged looks. In all that had happened they had forgotten about the horse Thracis had killed.

Noticing the look, Kamuzu continued, "Tomorrow you should inspect the body with fresh eyes and see what clues you can find about the fighter's identity."

Pyrios nodded and walked off toward the timothy field. He felt too tired to eat, but forced himself to graze for several minutes before coming back to collapse close to Thracis. He and Phlegon had gone to the Cerulean River for water earlier in the day and now Pyrios silently thanked the other stallion for coaxing him to get a drink then. The thought of making the trip to the river now made Pyrios want to groan. After a final check to make sure Thracis was sleeping soundly and that the others had settled for the night, Pyrios closed his eyes and went to sleep.

CHAPTER 10

The next morning, Pyrios woke to see Thracis standing next to Alcander and speaking quietly with the miniature. Thracis looked much better, he did not sway as he stood in the clear morning. Pyrios got to his feet and shook to remove the dust and debris from his coat. Despite his assurance that he would wake the stallions to stand watch, Kamuzu had let them all sleep through the night. Pyrios was more grateful to the Felisian than he wanted to admit. Seeing that Aeos and Phlegon were still sleeping, Pyrios tried to be as quiet as possible as he joined Thracis and Alcander.

"It's wonderful to see you standing on your own this morning."

Thracis sighed. "I won't be up much longer, but Alcander has helped me take a few steps."

The miniature tossed his head at Pyrios. "He was up several times last night and has taken half a dozen steps this morning.

Kamuzu said that he should sleep as much as possible today so that you can continue on your journey in the morning."

"Where is Kamuzu this morning?"

Thracis looked toward the rocks. "He's there, inspecting the attacker." Thracis took a couple of steps before settling down in the high grass of the timothy field. He looked up at Pyrios. "Kamuzu said I don't have to drink any more of that vile liquid today and so I plan on taking advice and resting."

Knowing better than to tease Thracis this morning, Pyrios addressed Alcander. "I would like to get a drink and soak my leg for a few minutes before joining Kamuzu. Would you care to join me?"

Alcander looked at Thracis, already beginning to snore. "I don't think he'll need me anytime soon and I could use a drink."

Pyrios and Alcander walked the well-worn path that the Equines had been using to reach the Cerulean River. Pyrios moved slowly, working the stiffness out of his leg. The leg had become entangled with that of his attacker and some of the muscles in his shoulder were pulled. The injury was more of an annoyance to the young stallion than an actual hardship, but he did like to soak the leg when he went to the Cerulean to drink.

Alcander was silent on the trip, trotting along at a good pace next to Pyrios. His little legs made walking along a normal-sized horse impossible. The miniature had removed his harness before leaving the camp and the scars on his white coat became more prominent. Pyrios wanted to ask about the gelding's ordeal but did not want to be rude. He also didn't want to bring up bad memories on such a fine morning.

The Cerulean, as blue as its name, flowed at a brisk pace. The spring melts of the Acarnanian Mountains far to the northeast were running and the river was swollen to half-again its usual size. The river teemed with fish and supported several Felisian settlements along its length. The water was crisp and cool and felt soothing on Pyrios' injured leg. Alcander stood on the shore taking little sips of the clear water.

"This mare that sent you." Pyrios tried to sound casual. "Is she from Diomedea as well?"

Alcander looked across the river at a flock of birds feeding in the shallows. "She is."

So much for conversation, Pyrios thought. He decided to press on. "I do not know her. Thracis must have met her in Iliad as I've been introduced to all the ladies he entertained in Bucephalus."

Alcander flicked his ears. "You and I both know Thracis entertained no one in Bucephalus. Spoke to yes, but nothing went further."

"How would you know that?"

Alcander snorted. "Because if it had, milady would not have sent Kamuzu and I to help him."

Deciding to use the same blunt tack Thracis often employed, Pyrios said, "Who is this mare and why is she so interested in my brother? Did they have a tryst in Iliad and now she feels he is obligated to her?" His voice had risen as he spoke. He hadn't realized how much this mare had been on his mind over the past few days.

Alcander pinned his ears, the first show of emotion since beginning the conversation. "You would do well not to speak of this lady in such a manner. I know not what happened in Iliad. What I do know is that she contacted Kamuzu and me not long after you and your brother reached Bucephalus and instructed us to follow you. We would have been with you as soon as the attack happened but we are healers, not warriors, we had to wait for safety."

Pyrios took a moment to collect himself. If he wanted to know about this mare, insulting her was not the way to go about it. "I'm sorry, I've been worried about Thracis. I really do wish to know about this mare, will you not tell me something?"

Perhaps taking pity on the younger stallion, perhaps grateful that Pyrios was not asking about the gelding's own troubles, Alcander sighed. "Her name is Hippolyta Psyche. She is a daughter of Queen Hippolyta of Diomedea. She is strong in the psychic arts and feels Thracis is important."

"In general, or to her personally?"

The gelding offered Pyrios a sly look. "I think both, although she won't admit the latter."

"Why not? Diomedean mares are not known for their timidity when seeking a suitable stallion."

"Psyche is young and not as…aggressive as her herdmates. She is still trying to find her place among her sisters."

"And admitting she might be smitten with a warrior stallion from Calabria would cause issue for her?"

Alcander nodded. "It may."

Pyrios snorted and walked out of the water. "Well if you speak with the lady, tell her I am in her debt and also that she has been much on Thracis' mind since we left Iliad."

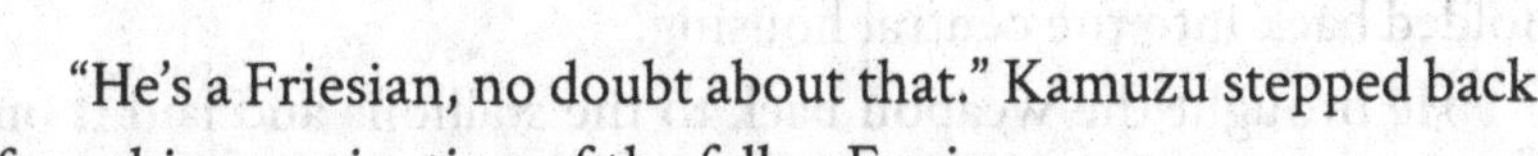

"He's a Friesian, no doubt about that." Kamuzu stepped back from his examination of the fallen Equine.

Pyrios, Aeos, and Phlegon stood in a semi-circle around the Felisian and Friesian. Alcander was back at the campsite with Thracis. The containment shield, a triangle of electricity created by placing three small metal projection units on the ground around the prohibited area, had kept earthbound scavengers away, but the birds had been making a meal of the dead combatant. Once Kamuzu was done with the body, Pyrios and the others would bury the remains. Enemy he may be, but the Friesian deserved a burial, for Pyrios conscious if no other reason.

"Why would he and his group attack us? If we are stopped, King Pedasos will send a message to the Registry one way or the other and attacking us would only strain the relationship between Baroquia and Myrmidonia more." Aeos' statement made sense.

Kamuzu wrinkled his nose and spoke to Pyrios. "Have any of you been in contact with the king since the attack?"

Pyrios nodded. "I gave him and my sire a full account while you were healing Thracis. Phlegon and Aeos have also been in contact with their dam and sire."

Kamuzu nodded. "That is good. This skirmish should not be the cause of a war between the two countries, they've hostility enough already." He hopped over the body and walked to the raptor sticking out of the rock wall. After a couple of attempts to pry it free using his paws, Kamuzu resorted to mind power. The raptor's blades squealed as the Felisian pulled it free. He pressed a button on the weapon's underside and the five blades folded back into the central housing.

He brought the weapon back to the stallions and laid it on the ground in front of them. "That warrior is Friesian, but this weapon bears a symbol more common to these regions."

Pyrios used his mind to lift the raptor up to eye level. Branded on the center of the weapon was an ornate C overlaid with two diagonally crossing unicorn horns. Pyrios and Aeos exchanged a look.

Phlegon, who knew nothing of Lipizzan history, cocked his head. "Isn't that pretty foolish if you don't want to get caught? Why would you brand your weapon?"

"Because those fighters were meant to kill all of you. They must not have been expecting such opposition. I did not see a projectile unit on the Friesian's armor. That raptor must have come from another attacker." Kamuzu had returned to the dead horse and was searching the pouches on the Friesian's harness.

"You know what the crest stands for?" Aeos was watching Pyrios.

"The Conversano bloodline, one of the oldest lines in all Lipizzania."

Phlegon looked from Pyrios to Aeos and back again. "What is that supposed to mean? Members of the Alliance are aiding the Pact?"

"A breed's decision has nothing to do with individual desire." Kamuzu was making a pile of useful equipment taken from the Friesian's pouches. "History has taught us that betrayal and intrigue are as common to war as death and bloodshed."

"He's right," Aeos said.

Pyrios weighed the significance of the raptor. "We'll take this with us but not show it to anyone until we are certain they can be trusted. I think somehow we've gotten involved in much more than a simple message delivery."

"That shows much wisdom. You have stumbled on information the Pact would prefer to have kept hidden. The four of you will have to be on guard from now on. This ambush is proof that not all are what they appear. No one in Myrmidonia has reported a herd of Baroquians this large." The Felisian took his pilfered items and began to walk back toward camp.

Pyrios and Aeos watched the cat retreat then began to dig a hole for the Friesian. Phlegon looked on, watching them. "How can you bury him after what his herdmates did to my brother?"

Aeos paused in his digging. "We cannot leave him here to be scavenged by animals, that would make us no better than the ones who killed your brother."

"I've always thought that those who take the high road are just in denial of their baser instincts."

Aeos tossed his head. "Don't misjudge me. This is a task I wish I could avoid, but it is the right thing to do. It won't make any difference to anyone but me and Pyrios, but at least we can sleep better at night."

Twitching his shoulders at the dun stallion's logic, Phlegon said, "I understand your meaning Aeos, but I cannot join the two of you."

"That is fine. It is a personal decision. Go and wait with the others if you like. We'll be along in a few hours."

Four days later the herd stood next to a sign reading: Weyrother two miles. This was as far as Kamuzu and Alcander were willing to go. Even with the acceptance of Pyrios and his group, Alcander would not be permitted inside the village.

The miniature and the Felisian had traveled with the stallions to make sure that Thracis' healing continued to progress. Kamuzu also wanted to keep an eye on the other stallions' various injuries. It never failed that a healer would spend all his or her time on the most wounded member only to have another in the group develop an infection. The Felisian forced the stallions to travel slowly, with frequent stops for both Thracis' and Pyrios. As a result, Thracis was over the worst of the poison's effects. He had lost weight and was taxed almost to exhaustion every time he stood up on that first day, but he was getting stronger as every hour passed.

"I cannot thank you enough for what the two of you have done." Pyrios was surprised by how much he would miss the two healers.

Kamuzu bowed his head. "It was as the lady wished. I am only happy that everyone recovered from the ordeal."

"Where will you go?" This came from Thracis. He would miss the Felisian in the coming weeks. It was, after all, Kamuzu who had called Thracis out of the Deceptive Mists. The orange and white Felisian had appeared in Thracis' mind, reciting the conversation Thracis had shared with Psyche in Iliad verbatim so that Thracis would know the cat was an ally. The Felisian had left a trail of glittering stones in the Deceptive Mists that Thracis had followed to the more familiar areas of his mind. From those known surroundings, Thracis had risen to consciousness.

Over the past few days, the stallion had tried again and again to glean information about Psyche from the Felisian with a marvelous lack of success. Kamuzu wouldn't talk about Psyche to Thracis but offered that the stallion should contact the lady if he was so interested in her well-being. Thracis had declined as of yet.

"We will go where we are needed." The Felisian never gave anyone a straight answer about his intentions, not even Alcander.

Aeos inclined his head at the small pouches Alcander and Kamuzu had attached to his harness. "Thank you for the salves and poultice herbs. I'm sure they will be put to good use."

"As am I." Kamuzu smiled at Aeos, revealing pointed teeth. "Remember my offer, Acadian stallion. It would do you good to learn more about the healing arts and anything else you question."

The other stallions exchanged puzzled looks. Of all of them, Aeos had spent the most time with the Felisian, the two of them talking long into the night. They always kept their conversations private however, and Thracis felt that Aeos and Kamuzu had also spoken at length using only their minds. It didn't matter either way to Thracis; Aeos' priorities were none of his business.

"We must be going if we want to cover miles before sunset." Alcander was looking across the open meadow to their left.

"True, enough. Good journey, young stallions." Kamuzu waved a paw and bounded away, disappearing into the high grass. Alcander nodded to the other Equines who bowed their heads in return. Then he turned and followed his feline companion, the bells on his harness tinkling with every step.

The four stallions waited until they saw the top of Alcander's head at the far edge of the meadow before continuing on to Weyrother. It wasn't long before they reached the outer posts marking the village limits. Pyrios led them to just inside the outer wall before nudging them into a small alley out of the main thoroughfare. Now that they were back in civilization Pyrios planned to allow all of them a few days to recover, but they had to discuss a few things first.

"I have to go on to the magistrate's office before it gets too late and tell him what happened." Pyrios nodded to Aeos. "Find the closest boarding stable and get us two stalls. I don't want anyone alone until we make sure we're safe."

Phlegon tossed his head. "With that in mind, I'll go with you to the magistrate. His questions will keep you until after dark and you shouldn't be wandering the streets with that leg."

"Good idea. The most important thing is to keep our suspicions about who attacked us to ourselves. We don't know anyone around here and the ones who ambushed us couldn't have gone far with the wounds we inflicted. They may be holed up here somewhere."

Aeos and Thracis nodded and moved off to find a boarding stable. They would contact Pyrios or Phlegon with the location later. Pyrios and Phlegon headed toward the center of the village. As they walked Thracis and Aeos noticed the local Equines giving them curious looks and talking quietly amongst themselves. This secretive attitude did little to settle Thracis' nerves. Knowing there was nothing he could do about what other Equines thought, Thracis lowered his head and concentrated on following Aeos to a boarding stable.

11

CHAPTER 11

"The Equines around here are a little too skittish for my liking." Thracis was standing in the center of the stall he was sharing with Aeos. He had taken a long, hot shower earlier and was now trying not to fidget while Aeos replaced his bandages. Aeos had announced that the wounds were healing well and Thracis should have normal use of his neck in the next week or so.

"We don't know what things the Pact has been saying, the kind of threats they've been making." Aeos focused on the bandaging, refusing to get into a pointless conversation with Thracis about the local horses.

Aeos understood Thracis' frustration. This was the fifth boarding stable they had approached and they would still be looking for a place if Aeos hadn't offered to pay twice what the stalls were worth. Even with the hearty bribe, the stablekeeper had asked them to stay in their stalls for the evening and not cause any trouble with the other patrons.

"They treat us as if we're the ones who caused an ambush." Thracis stomped a foot.

"Stop moving around, I'm almost done." Aeos secured the final bandage and stepped back. "Lines are being drawn whether the Registry wants to admit it or not. It doesn't strike me as odd that little villages like this don't want to be involved in a conflict."

"They're involved whether they want to be or not."

"True. But-"

A knock at the door cut off Aeos' response. He went to see who was calling and then opened the door to allow a maid pushing a hovering tray into the stall. The tray was loaded with the evening meal: grain, water, wine, and even molasses cakes for dessert. Aeos thanked the mare and let her back out. Thracis noticed that unlike Pyrios, who would have charmed the mare to a giggling fit, Aeos kept his conversation with her polite but short.

Thracis sniffed the wine. "I don't know if I should have any of this. My mind is still a little swimmy."

"Then I would stick to the water."

They ate in silence for several minutes. Thracis was finding that he liked Aeos a great deal, maybe because the dun stallion was so much calmer than Pyrios. Because of his injuries, Thracis was spending more time with Aeos and Pyrios was spending much of his time with Phlegon. Understanding that Phlegon needed a strong shoulder to lean on following the death of Aethon, Thracis had stepped back to allow Pyrios and the Pendarian stallion room to build a friendship. This would have been more difficult if Thracis was alone, but he had found that he and Aeos shared many of the same ambitions.

Wanting to know more about the dun stallion, Thracis said, "You handled yourself better than the rest of us in the fight, you were barely scratched. Why haven't you continued with any formal training?"

"My sire needed me at home stable. He has no other heir."

"All the more reason for you to be fully trained."

Aeos stepped back from the table and turned away, a clear sign he wanted nothing more of the conversation.

Thracis, feeling revitalized with this new mystery, was not to be avoided. "If Lord Quintus is worried about someone carrying on his line, he is still young enough to sire a dozen more heirs. Though they might not all be legitimate."

Aeos spun back and pinned his ears. "You know nothing of my herd."

Thracis ignored Aeos' threatening posture. "Then tell me. You're a good fighter and have obvious knowledge of the healing arts. You should have trained in Bucephalus and then moved on to the schooling rings of the Romanium."

Aeos tossed his head, but his ears came up a little. "I was not at liberty to go. My sire did need me and I could not travel to the schooling rings. Now I can and I will."

Thracis bobbed his head. "Then we can train together."

"We can if you pass the entry tests."

Thracis sniffed his bandages and turned back to Aeos. "Even with this I don't think I'll have much trouble." His voice carried doubt and Aeos raised his ears the rest of the way.

"The way you took on the stallions who attacked us should carry some weight. From what I saw you have a lot of natural talent, but you will have to learn how to measure your opponent better and not rush into a trap."

Thracis wanted to defend himself, then decided that he would have to learn to take criticism if he was going to make it at the Romanium. And he respected Aeos' opinion. "I think I have a lot more to learn than simply not running into a trap."

"Apparently injury brings with it a certain amount of humility." Aeos' eyes sparkled as he returned to the table and took a long drink of wine.

Thracis glared at him. "I think you're enjoying my predicament."

"Not as much the mare who holds you in such high regard would." Aeos flicked his ears as Thracis looked away. "Not so brazen now, are you?" He ate a couple mouthfuls of grain before continuing. "So, who is this *ammoni* mare? Not a member of Lady Helena's following."

"No," Thracis mumbled, "she's not from Bucephalus."

"Where then?"

Thracis took a long drink of water before answering. "I met her in Iliad."

"And?"

"And what? I met her Iliad, she gave me a talisman, and then I went on my way."

Aeos suspected there was much more to the story, but knew Thracis wouldn't tell him willingly. He decided to tease the other stallion a little. "She must have thought you were very handsome."

Thracis thought of Psyche's disinterested demeanor. "Not really."

"Well for her to have gone through all the trouble of locating Kamuzu and Alcander and then convincing them to foalsit, you must have made an impression."

Thracis snorted. Finished with his meal, he went to one of the bedding boxes. The soft straw was a welcome luxury after the nights on the road. "Pyrios and Phlegon said they were eating with the magistrate. Do you think they'll insist on discussing their meeting with us tonight or wait until morning?"

Aeos smiled at the tiredness in Thracis' voice and the other stallion's efficient change of topic. "I think even your brother knows you won't be much use until you're fully healed. He will wait until morning."

Thracis nodded and snuggled deeper into the straw. He was asleep in five minutes.

Aeos drank some more of the wine, then went to look out the stall's only window. He knew eventually he would have to tell the others the real reason why he had not continued with his formal training. If this mare from Diomedea, the *ammoni*, continued to be involved, Aeos would have to tell the truth soon. If she even brushed against his mind, she would know him for what he was. Kamuzu and Alcander had known but Kamuzu had kept the knowledge between himself and Aeos. Aeos owed the healers as much of a debt as Pyrios did and felt strongly that he would see them again. Contemplating his options, Aeos settled against the wall and waited for Pyrios and Phlegon to return.

The next morning the four stallions had breakfast in Pyrios and Phlegon's stall. They were still avoiding the common areas out of respect for the stablekeeper, but Pyrios soon informed them that the stablekeeper was doing them a favor, not the other way around.

"The Equines in this village were approached by the Pact several weeks ago." Pyrios spoke as he ate. "As a province of Lipizzania and therefore in the middle of the tensions between the Baroquian Pact and the Elysian Alliance, Levadia is having its own internal turmoil. The Pact has many supporters here as Lipizzania was built on tradition. The breeds here are not as enthusiastic about the trades agreements as those in..." He paused.

"Less privileged regions," Phlegon finished for him.

"Exactly."

Thracis flattened his ears. "So, basically what you're saying is that these breeds have already made their money and have established themselves so they don't care about the trade agreements either way."

Pyrios nodded.

Aeos flicked his ears. "Even if they think their way of life is comfortable, the breeds in these provinces must realize that the trade agreements will only make them wealthier."

Pyrios sighed. "They do and they don't. They worry that their way of life will change. Some think it will change for the better and so support the Alliance. Others think their lives will get worse or at the very least, less comfortable. Those Equines support the Pact."

"Is it like this all over Lipizzania?" Aeos asked.

Pyrios shook his head. "I don't think so. My sire said a lot of Zaxas' followers settled in Levadia after the Battle of Troy. I think old loyalties are rising."

Thracis took a drink of water before asking, "What does that mean to us?"

"It means we're on our own." Phlegon's voice bristled with anger.

"It means," Pyrios said evenly, "That the magistrate of Weyrother will not help or hinder us in our journey. This is the same response he gave the horses who ambushed us."

"Did you get any information about them?" Aeos was starting to clean up the breakfast table.

"Very little. The magistrate told us that a group of badly beaten Equines came to Weyrother a couple of days ago. They stayed two nights and left on the morning of the day we arrived. He wouldn't tell us who they were or where they were going, but I gathered that they were in bad enough shape that they won't bother us again." Pyrios looked at Thracis. "Do you feel up to getting back on the road? I was planning on giving us a few days to rest up but I don't think we're welcome here." Thracis twitched a shoulder. "I think I can make it to Lipizza without much trouble. As long as we go slow."

"We can leave after I see to the bandages." Aeos was already walking toward Thracis.

"Good." Pyrios stepped to the door. "Phlegon, you and I will go and resupply. I think the merchants will be more than happy to help us when they find out we're leaving."

Phlegon tossed his gray head and followed Pyrios out of the stall. Aeos and Thracis used an adjoining door to return to their own stall. Aeos told Thracis to take another shower and wash the wounds as diligently as possible since it would be the last time the injuries would get a good cleansing before they reached Lipizza.

On his way to the wash stall, Thracis paused and looked back over his shoulder. "Does this mean Levadia is already preparing to go to war?"

Aeos twitched his shoulders. "After the ambush I think it's clear that these trade agreements cannot be resolved without violence."

12

CHAPTER 12

The planet's capital of Lipizza made Bucephalus appear a sleepy hamlet. Thracis was stunned by the sheer number of Equines that thronged up and down the city streets. Everywhere, Equines, and a fair number of Felisians, bartered with merchants, window-shopped, or hurried along on some urgent business. Thracis' battered body was jostled and bumped by passersby, reawakening his half-healed injuries. Seeing his discomfort and worried the wounds would reopen, Aeos walked along one side of Thracis and instructed Phlegon to walk on the other. Pyrios led the way, trying to decipher the labyrinthine streets and find the location of the University of Piber.

The University of Piber was the educational mecca of Equus. It was one of the oldest buildings in Lipizza. Many Equines held that without the University, Lipizza would have never grown into the planet's capital. The University had been founded by the Maestoso bloodline five centuries ago, following the truces forged under the Gaze of Pegasus. The Maestoso herd had believed that an edifice should be constructed that would hold all the history and knowledge of the Equine race. After their colonization, the Felisian's were also invited to share their history with the university professors.

From its humble beginnings, the University of Piber, named after the stallion who funded the project, Maestoso Piber, grew to more than six hundred acres of unlimited knowledge. The University was celebrated as being the one place on all Equus where every breed was represented equally. The curriculum held everything from ancient histories to psychic development. The library was filled from floor to ceiling with the history and culture of every breed to ever walk the planet. It was here that the Registry of Breeds held office. The university had ever been a location of neutrality and was a place of protection where anyone could speak their mind and not fear persecution.

The influence of The University could be seen all over Lipizza. The streets flaunted dozens of open cafes and ornately decorated fountains. The shops sold everything and anything imaginable. Art dealers were side by side with technological gurus, jewelers operated stalls next to rug merchants. The abundance of choices was overwhelming. Thracis was dizzy with all the options by the time Pyrios led them down a tree-lined street leading to what looked like a city park.

As they approached the park, Thracis could make out two statues on either side of the wrought iron main gate. The statues were made of white marble and depicted full-size Equines performing the movements of the piaffe, a preliminary movement to many combat maneuvers. The piaffe, like the passage, was considered one of the High Dances and aided in conditioning and warming up the muscles required for extended combat.

The gate itself was worked wrought iron inlaid with all the crests of the founding six bloodlines of the Lipizzans: the Favory F emblazoned on an Equine faceplate and overlaid with a pair of wings, the Maestoso M depicted on a scroll next to a quill and inkwell, the Pluto P facing a horse performing a levade, the Neapolitano N overlaid by a horseshoe with the Cerulean River in the background, the Siglavy S on a heavily decorated breastplate. And of course, the ornate C of the Conversanos.

The four stallions stopped at the gatehouse and waited as a sentry came out to speak with them.

"What can I help you with today?" The sentry was a white mare with black spots and a black mane and tail. Her mane was braided along her neck and secured with a discreet piece of green ribbon. In place of an armor harness, she wore a simple leather surcingle, a band with rings that encircled her just behind her withers and front legs. A couple of the rings on the surcingle held cloth bags that looked as though they contained books or writing blocks.

Pyrios arched his neck and used his most charming voice. "I believe you can. We have just traveled from Myrmidonia and are trying to find the Registry of Breeds."

The sentry, young and not used to this type of male attention, beamed. "The Registry is easy enough to find. Come to the gatehouse and I will show you a map."

Tossing his head at the other stallions, Pyrios followed the mare to a map fastened to the wall next to the gatehouse door.

Aeos looked sidelong at Thracis. "Is he always like this?" "To be truthful, we're lucky he made it to the university. He's been noting every single mare he's seen since coming through the city gate this morning."

"Good thing he's going into politics."

"That's what I always tell him."

Pyrios was coming back to the group. The sentry was leaning against the side of the guardhouse, watching as Pyrios walked away. She wore a dreamy, pining expression. That one wouldn't get much studying done today. Thracis fought hard not to roll his eyes. He would bet that Pyrios would be back pursuing this mare as soon as he was able. Unless he saw someone better between now and then.

Pyrios tossed his head. "Come this way. It's only a few blocks."

"You'd better be careful. I'm sure that mare has connections around here." Aeos looked over his shoulder as he walked, keeping an eye on the spotted mare. She was still leaning against the wall.

"Trust me, Aeos, I know how to keep a mare satisfied. All my ladies are well-aware they are not the only mare I hold dear."

Aeos and Phlegon looked at Thracis for confirmation. Thracis twitched his shoulders. "He speaks the truth. I know of half a dozen mares in our village of Peleus that vie for my brother's affections."

"That is a talent I wish I possessed," Phlegon said with a wistful look at the spotted mare.

"Spend a few weeks with me, Phlegon, and I'll show you how to be pined after by every mare on this campus."

Thracis tossed his head. "Your boasting will get you into trouble one of these days."

"Perhaps, but not today." Pyrios trotted the last few steps to the massive building that contained the Registry.

"It's going to be a long stay." Aeos rolled his eyes at Thracis as the two of them followed Pyrios and Phlegon into the building.

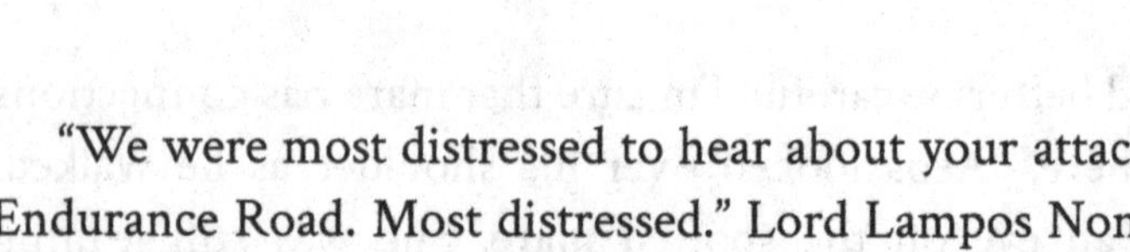

"We were most distressed to hear about your attack on the Endurance Road. Most distressed." Lord Lampos Nonios busied himself with a stack of papers. Nonios was the Head Sentinel in the Registry. He was the one who deemed whether or not an Equine's business was important enough to be brought to the attention of the Registry. He was a prissy little sorrel from Trakania and Thracis didn't care for him in the least.

Pyrios and the others had waited in the Registry's lobby for over an hour before Nonios deigned to meet with them and the Sentinel had spent the last few minutes trying to get the young stallions out of his office. He seemed ill at ease at their proximity to his pristine surroundings. In the Sentinel's defense,

Pyrios' little herd was covered in road dust and smelled like a compost pile.

"But, you see, I can't let every Equine who has a bad day on the road simply walk in to the council chamber."

Pyrios laced his voice with as much honey as he could muster. "We understand, Lord Nonios, but we didn't have a dispute, we were ambushed by hostile Equines."

"That is what you say. Without them here to argue the point leaves your 'attackers' at a severe disadvantage."

Thracis kept one thought in mind as the little runt spoke: keep your ears up. Thracis didn't want to show any signs of frustration while standing in this plush office. The Sentinel was just one more obstacle in the road. All Thracis had to do was keep his ears perked and his mouth shut and let Pyrios do the talking.

"Of course." Pyrios inclined his head toward the door leading to the council chamber. "Our report does not need to be a public affair. Perhaps one or two of the representatives will listen to us in private and then we can be on our way."

Nonios set back on his heels and regarded Pyrios. The Sentinel had been more than happy to listen to their account of how Myrmidonia would stand behind the Elysian Alliance, but now he was showing all the signs that the four stallions were wasting his time.

"I don't think the four of you appreciate how important a representative's time is." He ruffled a few more papers. "I will mention something at tomorrow's meeting, but I do not promise any action on the council's part. For the time being I suggest you find a comfortable boarding stable and settle in for a few days. Perhaps take a bath."

And they were dismissed. Thracis continued his mantra until they were safely in the outer hallway before pinning his ears at the closed door to the Sentinel's office. "Self-important little runt. Who is he to judge what is important to the Registry?"

"He must be capable if he holds the office of Head Sentinel." Aeos was already walking down the hall, leading them away from prying ears. "You should keep your voice low. You don't know who is listening in these corridors."

Thracis flushed and ducked his head.

"I'm sure the Registry had good reason to give Lord Nonios his position," Pyrios suggested.

"Or he's well connected." Phlegon's voice held his distaste for the Sentinel.

"His family is very influential in the city."

The four stallions jumped at the sound of the unfamiliar voice. They turned to see an older stallion walking a few strides behind them. "You should be careful what you say within these walls."

The stallion was a dun with a black mane and tail. His coat was a tawny red color and his dorsal stripe was black. He was shorter than the younger stallions but walked with an air of influence. His voice was stern but his eyes held a glimmer of amusement.

Pyrios looked at his three companions before speaking to the newcomer. "I apologize for my comrades. They spoke out of turn. We have had a long and arduous journey."

The other stallion tossed his head. "They spoke truthfully. I am Representative Xanthos Kantaka. I am from Mongolea, a province of Arabea."

Pyrios and the others bowed their heads. "I am Zephyros Pyrios. This is my brother Thracis. This is Quintus Aeos and Ithia Phlegon"

Kantaka bowed his head, his ears flicking. "I have been waiting to meet the sons of Zephyros. You have been the subject of discussion among my comrades and I. "

Pyrios and Thracis exchanged a look. Pyrios thought he saw something flicker in Thracis' eyes before his brother turned his head. Pyrios wondered who else the mare from Iliad had spoken to. Surely, she didn't know a horse in every city across Equus. He cleared his throat, meaning to tell Lord Kantaka that they would be leaving the Registry in search of a boarding stable when the older stallion spoke.

"It might not be prudent to converse in this building." The Mongolean's eyes shifted back toward the Head Sentinel's door. "If you wish, you may come with me to my stable here in the city where we may talk more openly."

What do you think? The thought, sent by Thracis, flitted through Pyrios' mind.

I think we need to talk with someone.

Another voice filled Pyrios' head. It took him a moment to recognize Aeos' arid demeanor. *We can trust this stallion. He truly wants to aid us.*

Not taking the time to question how Aeos could be so certain about Lord Kantaka's intentions, Pyrios bowed his head at the representative. "We would be happy to accept your invitation, Lord Kantaka."

13

CHAPTER 13

"Well, then, this is much more comfortable. Don't you agree?" Lord Kantaka was standing hipshot next to a polished table filled with an assortment of refreshments.

The five stallions were in Lord Kantaka's study. The representative's stable was modest compared to the ones around it, but it was a far cry from staying in a boarding stable. The furnishings, bookshelves and tables mostly, were simple but elegant. The floors were the hard rubber material used in most Equine stables. The material was easy on joints and easy to clean. It could be obtained in every color imaginable and was often laid in ornate patterns. The flooring in this room was a dark mahogany that complimented the deep brown bookshelves. The walls were painted a dusky sand color to give the room a larger feeling.

"We can't thank you enough for your hospitality." Pyrios nodded to his colleagues. "We haven't been very welcome anywhere since the attack."

"Not surprising given the current mood in Lipizzania. I"m surprised you made it this far without an armed escort." Kantaka tossed his head to lighten his sarcasm. "Do you know who attacked you?"

Aeos flicked his ears. "We have a good idea."

"Until you are certain, I would keep your suspicions to yourself. Even I am not sure as to who are friends and who are enemies in this city. Felisians are not the only beings capable of keeping secrets."

"That doesn't sound encouraging," Thracis sighed.

"I do know of one who is trustworthy and will be very interested in your ambush. I have already contacted him to come here, but he has been delayed."

Thracis lifted his head. "Can he help us with the Registry?"

"No, his influence lies elsewhere. But he can help you in other ways."

Deciding to change the conversation, Pyrios shifted his weight to stand hipshot. "Lord Kantaka, do you have any influence in the Hippikon? My brother, not to mention Aeos, have high ambitions to begin training at the Romanium. As it was told me by my sire, they first have to spend several weeks in basic training before they can move on to the more advanced maneuvers."

Kantaka shifted his feet to a more comfortable position. "I believe my friend can help the two of you with that. As for you, young Pyrios, it is often custom that young stallions join the Registry as aides to established representatives. As it happens, I have an opening in my office for just such an aide. Or two," he added with a nod to Phlegon.

Pyrios was silent for a moment. "That is a very generous offer, Lord Kantaka."

"Generous and shrewd. You see, as my aides, even Lord Nonios will have no right to keep you out of the council chamber. You will not be able to speak before the representatives, but I can speak for you and you will learn a great deal about the politics of our planet. As you come from the province with the highest yield of achillium, you should learn how the planet is run."

"Is there not already a representative from Calabria?"

Kantaka paused before speaking, gathering his thoughts. "There is, his name is Claudius Adonis. He is a capable enough representative but his ambitions lie elsewhere. He longs for more power than a representative can wield."

Pyrios bowed his head. "My stable would be in your debt if you would grant me this boon."

"No more than any other stable who has sent their stallions or mares for instruction in the Registry."

Pyrios inclined his head at the obvious statement. He looked at Phlegon. The other stallion looked overwhelmed at the prospect of navigating the political arena. To be allowed entrance into the council chambers, even as an aide, was the first step to a political career. It was a station a horse from his dam's small stable could hardly dream of. Lady Ithia would be overjoyed with her son's fortune and of her own rise in Equine society.

"I will contact my sire as soon as possible and tell him the good news." Pyrios ducked his head. "It may be a few days or even weeks before he can send funds for food and board."

Phlegon nodded. "It would be the same for my dam. Though my stable will be hard-pressed to come up with the necessary funds."

"There is no need for either of your stables to become taxed. I am doing this mostly out of spite for the practices that are becoming commonplace in the Registry. Only promoting those Equines who come from money or privilege." Kantaka shook his head. "That is not what the Registry was founded on. The Registry was built to ensure that all the nations of Equus had an equal representation, whether their country was rich or poor."

He was silent for a moment before continuing. "The two of you will stay here with me. As you can see, I have plenty of room for even the four of you, but I suspect Thracis and Aeos should have no trouble gaining acceptance into the academies. Until then, they may stay here as well. It would be nice to have some company."

"You are very gracious," Phlegon said.

Kantaka twitched shoulder. A knock at the door halter further conversation. Kantaka excused himself and went to answer the caller. He had a butler and a cook, but both had left earlier in the in evening. A few moments later Kantaka returned with another stallion. The new horse was a broad bay with chiseled muscles. The stallion walked with an air of authority and surveyed the four younger stallions as he would a group of new recruits.

"This is Commander Talos Dias. He is the Asapatish of the Hippikon and my good friend." The Asapatish was the head commander of the Imperial Cavalry. He handled every major military decision. His office was stationed at the Hippikon.

The four young stallions bowed their heads and waited for Kantaka to go through the necessary introductions. As the Mongolean stallion spoke, Commander Dias looked the other stallions up and down, measuring each of them as he would his soldiers. Pyrios and Phlegon shifted under the Commander's gaze but Thracis and Aeos held their ground. This seemed to please Commander Dias.

"I am happy to finally meet someone who has had firsthoof experience with the Baroquian Pact's military tactics." He looked at Thracis. "And you are of particular interest, Zephyros Thracis."

Thracis flicked an ear. The statement didn't really surprise him. It seemed as though everyone he met had a hidden agenda where Thracis was concerned. "Why am I interesting?"

Dias looked at Kantaka. "I haven't told them anything yet. I thought it would be better to wait until we were all together so that I would not have to repeat myself," the representative explained.

Dias cleared his throat and turned to look back at Thracis. "We, meaning Kantaka and I and a few select others, are concerned that you may be more to the Baroquian Pact than a young stallion with ambitions to join the military." The commander settled himself. "Like the Pact, we employ our own eavesdroppers. From the moment you set hoof in Bucephalus, the members of the Pact throughout Myrmidonia have been discussing your whereabouts and actions. Intrigued, we set our best Felisians to find out why you are so important."

"Did you ever find out?" Thracis thought of Psyche's prediction. Maybe these horses could shed some light on his future.

Kantaka shook his head. "No, but the Pact was ecstatic when they learned that the younger brother of the traveling stallions had been killed." He looked at Dias. "We feared the worst until your parents contacted us and told us the stallion who perished was Aethon of Calpernia Stable."

"The Pact is still unaware of their mistake. That will change now that you've announced yourselves to the Registry. I'm certain the Pact has been told of the error and will send others to complete the task." Commander Dias looked at Pyrios.

Pyrios hung his head. "I guess I should have felt the footing first before galloping on ahead."

"Don't take it too hard. You didn't know the state of the politics in the Registry. And you and your brother are young stallions from a distant province. You had no reason to believe you were of specific importance." Kantaka's voice was compassionate.

Thracis thought it best to keep Psyche's vision to himself. He felt guilty enough for not warning his comrades, but in his defense, he had not really taken the mare's warning seriously. He looked at Commander Dias. "What do you want us to do?"

"The easiest way for me to keep an eye on you is for you to attend the academy at the Hippikon. As we are filled to capacity right now because recruits are clamoring at our gates day and night that is not an option. The next best thing is to send the two of you," he nodded to Thracis and Aeos, "to the Romanium."

Thracis' breath caught. "I thought a stallion needed military experience before they would even be considered for training at the Romanium."

"They do, but as Asapatish, I have a certain amount of pull. Plenty of instructors in the Romanium owe me a favor and we'll craft a story so that your fellow cadets think you've already spent time in the military. It will make assimilation easier for you." The commander did not add that even if the story they came up with was perfectly plausible, those stallions with military experience would soon realize Thracis and Aeos had never spent time in the cavalry.

"I don't know what to say." Thracis glanced at the floor.

"Don't say anything yet. Without a strong foundation, you are starting your training well behind your comrades. They have spent months or years extending their stamina and endurance. You will have to work hard to keep up with them."

"I will do my best." Thracis looked over at Aeos.

Aeos bobbed his head. "I am familiar with military foundation training. My instructors thought it important that I train as though I was entering the cavalry. I can help Thracis with his exercises."

Commander Dias addressed all four stallions. "These are dangerous times. You don't know who you can trust and have each other to count on. Until we discover why Thracis is so important to the Pact, all of you could be targets. Lord Kantaka's stable is protected and watched by guards of my choosing. Spend tonight in ease. Tomorrow I will come and personally escort Thracis and Aeos to the town of Sparta and the Romanium. It is the only way to be sure they will reach their destination."

Dias turned to Kantaka. "I will take my leave. I have much to do before tomorrow in preparation for their acceptance into the Romanium. I will arrive early in the morning."

Kantaka saw Commander Dias to the door then returned to the study. He regarded the nervous expressions on the faces of his guests. "Don't look so worried. We have no intention of leaving the four of you to your own devices. Pyrios and Phlegon will be under my watchful eye and Commander Dias will make sure to keep informed of Thracis' and Aeos' progress."

"We've made so many missteps already," Pyrios said.

"All necessary to the journey." Kantaka tossed his head at the stallions. "Tomorrow is a big day for all of you. Go to your stalls and rest easy. In my stable you are in good hooves."

The four trooped up the ramp that led to the stable's second floor. This two- or three-story design was common in cities where space was limited. The ramps were something the visiting stallions had to get used to as they came from single story stables.

They could have each had their own stall but they were still on edge from their recent experiences. Pyrios was staying with Thracis and Aeos was with Phlegon. Thracis wondered if Pyrios would move in with Phlegon after he and Aeos left in the morning or if Pyrios and Phlegon would keep their privacy. He thought the latter. He had noticed that Pyrios was relaxing more and more as the evening progressed.

Shaking his head, Thracis settled in his bedding box and tried to get comfortable. His healing had slowed after they had left Weyrother because Aeos had been unable to tend the wounds as well as he liked while they were on the road. The salves Kamuzu had given them were working wonders, but Thracis' tired immune system could only do so much. He would have to bear the pain, however, as he doubted he would get much time for convalescence once they reached Sparta tomorrow.

"You think you'll get much sleep tonight?"

Thracis flicked his ears in Pyrios' direction. "It will probably be the last good night's sleep I'll have in a while."

"Are you excited?"

Thracis thought about it. He should be excited, should be ecstatic. But he wasn't. He was tired and sore. He couldn't tell Pyrios that, though, because his brother would worry that Thracis wasn't up to the rigors of combat training. "I don't think it has settled in yet. I have mixed feelings."

"I know what you mean. It will be the first time we have gone on separate paths."

They were silent, each lost in his own thoughts. Pyrios spoke first. "I guess it's time for each of us to find our place in the world."

14

CHAPTER 14

The streets were shrouded in ethereal silver the next morning when Commander Dias came to collect Aeos and Thracis. The commander was accompanied by five other stallions. All were wearing achillium armor harnesses. They waited on the street while Thracis and Aeos said their good-byes at Kantaka's doorstep.

"It isn't as if you are traveling to the other side of the world." Pyrios was trying to sound jovial, but Thracis could feel his brother's sadness in the mental link between them. *Be careful, little brother. The Pact will have sent their own stallions to Sparta and despite Lord Kantaka and Commander Dias' confidence that you will be fine, I feel you will have to take care of yourself.*

Thracis tossed his head, keeping with his brother's charade. "Yes, but with your political career beginning, I doubt I'll hear from you often." *Aeos and I are aware that we may have opponents at the Romanium. We will keep our ears up.* He nipped Pyrios' neck in an affectionate gesture.

"Take care, the two of you," Lord Kantaka called from the doorstep as Thracis and Aeos joined Commander Dias on the street. The two tossed their heads in farewell. Pyrios and Phlegon watched until their companions vanished in swirling vapor. Pyrios had the sinking feeling that he would not see his brother for many months.

The stallions didn't speak as they walked along the early morning streets. Few other Equines were out this time of day and those that were gave the passing group little notice. Most were merchants getting their stores ready for the day ahead. A few Felisians trotted along the city streets. Thracis noted with surprise that several of the Felisians were wearing harnesses from which the fat corpses of rats hung. Well, the city had to be kept free of vermin somehow. An hour later the group was out of the city and trotting down the country road that led from Lipizza to Sparta.

Thracis, feeling secure at being surrounded by six experienced warriors, took the opportunity to survey his surroundings with interest rather than suspicion. From the corner of his eye he saw that Aeos was doing the same.

The road led through a manicured pine grove and then the view burst open around them. Tended fields, the green of new sprouts peeking through the dark earth, abounded on both sides giving an unobscured view for miles. The breeze carried the good smells of pristine growth and fertile soil. It blew through Thracis' mane and filled him with strength. The fog was burning away and the day sparkled with miniature water droplets. Thracis' ears twitched as a couple of birds argued over a berry bush. This was the peace of Equus, what every Equine strove for: to live in harmony with their world. It hurt his soul to think that the Baroquians would destroy all this just to rule ashes.

No one would say it out loud but it was obvious to Thracis that the Baroquians were using the trade agreements to complete the conquest started by their founding stallion, Zaxas. The Registry could agree with the Pact and send the Caprians away and within months Thracis was sure the Pact would find another grievance. The trade agreements had allowed the Baroquians to test the waters and see which breeds would be receptive to a change of government. Thracis was not alone in his surprise as to how many breeds were supportive of the Pact's stance.

Aeos took a cleansing breath, drawing Thracis' attention. "I was not aware the countryside around here was so agricultural. I expected it to be more rural, with the farmers on the opposite side of Lipizza, not between the capital and Sparta."

Commander Dias laughed. "This area used to be forest for miles. We performed countless training exercises in those trees when I was a cadet. But times have changed and with the invention of the movers and our ability to move entire platoons to different regions, the city council decided to open this land to the farmers."

"What happened to the trees?"

"They were harvested and milled for building materials and Equine bedding. In addition to the harvesting, the city council decreed that other forests must be planted in the surrounding areas not suitable for crops." Dias looked over his shoulder at Aeos. "The project has worked well for all those involved."

"The fields look as though they will produce good crops this season." Thracis had never been particularly interested in farming, but he wanted to be part of the conversation so that he could hopefully turn it in a more appealing direction.

"The rains have been kind this spring."

Aeos swished his tail at a fly. "I come from Acarnia. We are not as rich in achillium as Calabria and so my sire leases much of our land to local farmers for cash crops. The arrangement is profitable for both parties. I would guess the city council has created a similar bargain."

The stallions around Thracis and Aeos chuckled. Commander Dias flicked an ear back. "You are very observant for a young stallion. And closed-mouthed. A dangerous combination. I always have openings for Equines such as you."

Thracis felt a moment's irritation that Aeos would be considered a favorite. It was as if Aeos was stepping right into Pyrios' shoes, finding his place in society. And Thracis was being left behind. Even Phlegon was on his chosen path. Psyche had told Thracis what his destiny would be, but she had neglected to give him a map. He felt lost and unsteady as he walked along with the other stallions.

Noting Thracis' uncharacteristic silence, Aeos said, "I would have thought you would be full of questions now that we are finally on the road to Sparta. You've only been talking about it since we met in Bucephalus."

"I've got a lot on my mind this morning."

"If you want my advice, you'd best clear it." Commander Dias was slowing his stride to fall back with Thracis. Aeos and the others sped up to give the two some privacy.

"This should be an exciting day for someone who's been longing to get to Sparta."

Thracis looked sidelong at the commander. "My dam wouldn't think so. In fact she wouldn't think much of me going to Sparta at all."

"She thinks you should be more like your brother?"

"No, but she thinks little of fighting. She wants me to become a scholar or something, find a society mare, and sire half a dozen foals."

Commander Dias laughed. "Something she shares with my dam. I feel the only mares who embrace combat as we do are those behind Diomedean borders."

Thracis pricked his ears. "Do you know many Diomedean mares?"

"Only the few my daughter has introduced me to. I rather enjoy their company. They're very direct."

"Not the one I met," Thracis mumbled.

He meant to keep his voice low but Commander Dias heard the comment. He flicked his ears at the younger stallion. "Perhaps she was being coy."

Thracis shook his head. "I don't think that's in her nature."

"Mares are prone to act differently depending on their feelings toward a stallion."

Thracis sighed. He thought of Desiree, all but throwing herself at him, and Psyche so careful to keep her actions that of a concerned friend. He wanted to go back to dealing with the mares of Calabria. They, at least, he understood.

Commander Dais said, "What your dam thinks, what the other mares you've met think...none of that matters now. In the weeks ahead you will need all your focus and concentration and cannot afford to let yourself become distracted with what other horses want."

"I think the longer my dam doesn't know about what I'm doing the happier she'll be. She doesn't want me to become a soldier."

"My dam wished for me to be a farmer like my sire."

Thracis looked at Commander Dias. "Is your dam happy with your decision?"

Commander Dias twitched a shoulder. "She is happy that I am happy."

Thracis walked next to the commander in silence for a few paces before saying, as casually as he could, "What is your daughter's name if you don't mind the inquiry?"

Commander Dias snorted. "Think she might be the mare you met?"

"At this point, anything is possible."

"Well, she may be friends with the Diomedeans, but she would have introduced herself using my name as her mother passed on long ago. My daughter's name is Dias Eno. Does that sound familiar?"

Thracis shook his head. He did not give Commander Dias Psyche's name. If the commander thought this was odd, he gave no sign. In any case, Commander Dias was looking ahead and ignoring Thracis. He tossed his head to the rise above them where the other stallions had stopped. "Go and see your future home."

Thracis trotted up the small rise and stood next to Aeos. A valley spread out before them. Sprawling in the center of the valley next to a narrow river, the Romanium. It was more beautiful than Thracis could have imagined.

From their vantage point Thracis and Aeos could see dozens of schooling rings. Large, open-walled buildings abounded, allowing the Equines to train no matter what the weather. Huge barns were built in along one side of the main training areas. Other buildings, lecture halls, feeding rooms, and wash stalls, were sprinkled throughout the complex. Far from being open to the heat of the sun, the Romanium was covered with sprawling trees that shaded every walkway and street. Tended lawns stretched between buildings and schooling rings. Even from this distance, the stallions could see the sparkle and flash of the water filling the many fountains and ponds located within the complex.

The town of Sparta itself, the shops, the boarding stables, and the more discreet districts found near any military compound, sprawled beyond the Romanium farther up the valley. In this way, the town would be protected by the Romanium in the event of an invasion. The valley narrowed as it rose into the mountains and in the distance Thracis could see a massive structure blocking the far end. The structure was a gate that could be closed to halt the advance of an opposing army.

Thracis felt a weight lift off his shoulders. This was the place where he would see his dreams of becoming a Hippeus fulfilled. To be a knight in the Imperial Cavalry was the highest honor a stallion could hold in the military. It was a position even more respected than that of the Asapatish. This respect was a direct result of the grueling training a cadet had to complete to become a full Hippeus. Of all the Equines who were accepted into the Romanium only thirty percent would graduate. This statistic further established how elite the Hippeus were.

Commander Dias strode up the rise behind Thracis and the rest of the small group. "Come along. The schooling rings are waiting."

15

CHAPTER 15

Thracis staggered across the paddock, fighting hard to remain on all four feet. The stallion he had been facing, a juggernaut of a Calabrian, waited for him to catch his breath. Thracis stood straight, shook himself, and walked back to begin the exercise again. The Calabrian, a patient, good-natured fellow, began to circle Thracis at once. Thracis tried to focus on the other stallion, always keeping him in sight as they moved around each other, but his mind kept wandering.

He was tired for one thing. Over the past month, Aeos had been drilling him without mercy, forcing him to catch up on years of training in a fraction of the time. He was hardly asleep in his bed box before the morning bell rang outside the barns he shared with the other recruits of the Romanium. As a consequence, Thracis was falling farther and farther behind the rest of his group.

The Calabrian, sensing Thracis' distraction, darted forward. He rammed Thracis with his chest, throwing the other stallion off balance and giving himself time to spin and kick. Thracis grunted as the stallion's back hooves hit him solidly in the side. Instead of stepping away as would have been prudent, Thracis threw himself forward. He slammed the other stallion's flank with his shoulder. The Calabrian was caught by surprise and struggled to keep his balance. Thracis reared, settling himself on his hind legs while striking with his forelegs. His aim was a little off and he struck the Calabrian in the face rather than the neck as they had been instructed.

Thracis immediately fell to all fours, an apology on his lips. He wasn't able to utter a syllable before he felt a pair of iron jaws clamp on the topline of his neck. Thracis dropped his head, trying to relieve the pressure of the teeth. The ilarches, a schooling ring instructor, followed Thracis down, holding the other stallion in a submissive position. The ilarches held on until Thracis dropped to his knees.

Releasing him, the ilarches stepped back. "Cadet Thracis, have you forgotten the basic rules of sparring?"

Knowing that admitting he had would result in a more lenient punishment, Thracis nodded. His knees hurt but he didn't dare stand until the ilarches gave him leave.

The instructor examined the Calabrian's face. The damage wasn't severe and he gave the other stallion leave to see the asklepiade, the Romanium veterinarian. He turned back to Thracis. "This is only the most recent in a string of mistakes, Cadet Thracis." The ilarches didn't try to disguise the irritation in his voice.

"I am sorry, Ilarches Platon. I will try harder."

"I don't believe that's possible." The ilarches' voice was dry. "Stand up."

Thracis did as told, swaying on his feet as a wave of dizziness filled his head. The ilarches walked around him, noting his dull coat and protruding ribs. The heaving of the young stallion's sides.

"Cadet Thracis, though your heart is in this instruction, your body cannot keep up with the rigors of training." The ilarches stood in front of Thracis. "I will speak with Commander Dias."

Thracis bowed his head as low as he dared, he was still a little shaky. "Thank you, Ilarches Platon."

The ilarches tossed his head. "Go back to the barns, take a cool shower, and try to sleep the rest of the day. Tomorrow I expect you to be able to keep up with the pace I set in my ring."

Thracis bobbed his head. He walked out of the schooling ring, head and tail low. He could feel the eyes of the other cadets on him as he left. They didn't believe he was the same caliber as they were. They felt he was holding them back. He agreed with them.

The voices of the ilarches filled the air as Thracis made his way back to the barn he shared with forty-nine other stallions. The barn was sectioned by bedding boxes, the communal wash stall attached to one end. His hoofbeats echoed on the walls of the deserted building. Thracis paused as he passed Aeos' bedding box. Aeos was doing very well in the schooling rings, moving to the top of the herd. Of course, Aeos already had combat experience and was getting a good rest every night.

Thracis entered the wash stall and walked back to the twenty separate shower stalls. He stepped into the closest one and turned the water on, using only the cold. The cool water sluiced away the dirt and sweat of the schooling rings. Thracis sighed, pushing away the guilt of having a day to recover. His body ached, his head swam. He tried to focus on the drills Aeos had set the night before and realized he couldn't even remember the first steps.

Turning off the water, Thracis used the scraper to slowly shed as much as the surface water off his coat as he could. He dropped the scraper several times, his mind too muddled and exhausted to hold the small object. His feet stumbled as he reached his bedding box and he didn't so much lay down as collapse into the aromatic wood shavings. With summer only a week away, the bedding boxes had been stripped of straw and filled with the cooler shavings. Thracis was so tired he would have slept on the ground if that was all that had been available.

He closed his eyes and tried to sleep. Worn out as he was, his mind refused to quiet long enough for him to fall into unconsciousness. Myriads of conversations melded together to produce a tangled mass of unanswered questions. His head began to ache.

Over the past month, Lord Kantaka and Commander Dias had asked Thracis about everything from his foalhood to the ambush in Levadia. They were looking for any clue as to why he was so important to the Baroquian Pact. So far they had found nothing.

Thracis' herd, while descended from legend, was not significant in any way. Thetis Stable did control the wealthiest deposits of achillium, which was highly coveted by the Baroquian Pact, but if the Pact wanted to obtain that achillium, killing Thracis was not a smart way to go about doing it. Lord Kantaka was beginning to think the message was wrong. He was convinced that it was Pyrios who should be more important to the Pact.

Thracis had not told anyone about Psyche's vision. He couldn't explain why, but it seemed prudent to keep Psyche's prediction to himself. He couldn't remember all she had said, but he felt he held a pivotal role in the coming war. This lack of clarity was keeping him off balance. He wished he were on as sure a footing as his brother.

Since coming to Lipizza, Pyrios had flourished in the political arena. He and Phlegon accompanied Lord Kantaka to all his political and social engagements. Pyrios was making acquaintances with all the important herds. His schedule was almost as busy as Thracis' and so far the brothers had spent little time in communication.

Thracis shifted, trying to get comfortable. He didn't want to worry Pyrios with his inadequacies. What he wanted was rest. He wished Aeos would give him at least one night off. He felt so lost in the schooling rings, stumbling around and barely able to keep his footing. He knew if he could concentrate on one instructor at a time he would at least be able to keep up with the rest of his class.

Training had always come easy to Thracis and his frustration was beginning to show to the ilarches and other cadets. He understood the maneuvers and light exercises, but his body simply refused to obey his commands. The asklepiade examined him frequently and was convinced that Thracis' overall weakness was a result of his poisoning. The asklepiade had suggested that Thracis take a month off and resume training when the summer recruits began their rotation. Thracis stubbornly refused, stating that he could keep up with his comrades. The asklepiade hadn't offered any other suggestions since.

Thracis closed his eyes, hunting for sleep.

Foolish colt, you should heed the advice of others.

Thracis jumped. He folded his legs under himself, preparing to stand. The barn was empty. A bell rang outside, signaling the midday meal. Shaking his head, Thracis settled back into the shavings.

A little skittish, aren't you?

Thracis' lips curved into a smile. His heartbeat quickened. *I've missed you.*

Psyche's pleasure warmed the mental link between them. *You hardly know me.*

I know you well enough. You saved me with that talisman and sent help to heal me.

The talisman sustained you, but it would not have saved you. That deed was accomplished by Kamuzu and Alcander.

You did send them, though.

After what I've seen I knew you would need assistance.

Thank you for saving my life, even in an abstract way.

Psyche's delight at the compliment flowed through the link. *You are welcome, stallion of Thetis.*

An idea occurred to Thracis. *Can I see you?*

A pause in the link, then Thracis' mind filled with mist. He felt a moment's fear before Psyche stepped out of the swirling fog. She tossed her head, her forelock falling over one eye. *I apologize for the mist, but this is the easiest vision I can present from this distance.*

It's fine. Thracis longed to have the energy to envision himself in the mist alongside the mare, but the mental link was already draining his limited reserves.

Psyche stood with her head high. Her black and white patchwork coat shone and her mane and tail were black and silver silk. Thracis yearned for her. He wanted nothing more than to brush his nose along her delicate cheek. An action for which he would most assuredly get a fierce nip. It was custom in Equine society for the mare to make the first move and as yet Psyche hadn't given him a clear signal.

You seem to be feeling better. Psyche's voice held her customary amusement.

I feel strengthened now that you're here. Thracis felt himself sliding toward sleep, comforted by her presence.

Psyche settled herself, standing hipshot, and looked around. *I will stay until you find sleep.*

Just before he drifted away, a thought floated through his mind. *Do you know why the Pact tried to kill me?*

Psyche tossed her head. *Such a foolish colt. I told you of your future, did you not listen?*

Of course, Thracis snapped. Psyche pinned her ears at him and he spoke more softly. *I apologize. I did listen to what you said but... well since I was poisoned I can't seem to remember everything that you told me.*

Psyche sighed, her body relaxing again. *I told you that you would decide the fate of the coming war.*

She had told him more. Something about warnings and tarnished silver, forgotten ones and lighted wings. Thracis was too tired to puzzle it out. His was sliding back to sleep. Another thought occurred to him, his mind refusing to rest.

Do you know who it was that attacked us? We know our ambushers are associated with the Conversano bloodlines.

Psyche's voice held a note of caution in Thracis' mind. *Step with care, stallion of Thetis. You are a stranger here. The herds are loyal.*

Yes, but if rogues blatantly admit their heritage, someone at the university or in the capital must know who they are.

Psyche continued to be cautious. *They may. But I warn you not to accuse anyone of intrigue. The bloodlines are old. They will not listen to an outsider's warnings.*

They should know of hunters among the herds.

Do not force your way into their associations like a simpleminded ox. This is a matter for which your brother is more suited.

At the mention of Pyrios, Thracis' ears flattened. *You don't even know my brother.*

I know him well enough.

Knowing the relationship between Pyrios and most mares, Thracis twitched in his bed box.

Psyche ducked her head and looked at him from beneath her lashes. It excited her that he would be so jealous on her behalf. *I thought you didn't envy your brother.*

He has no business with a mare that I-, the thought broke off. He wasn't about to let her get him into a frenzy and admit feelings he hadn't examined yet.

Psyche laughed. *I will not goad you any further. I know of your brother because I have seen him in visions as well. And his reputation for politics is not unknown.*

Thracis stopped fidgeting. He could feel his exhaustion even here in this semi-dreaming state.

Psyche smiled in his mind. *Enough. I will go now and leave you to sleep. You will remember the words we've spoken.* She was beginning to fade. *I give you permission to contact me if you wish. Please wait until you are stronger,* she added when she felt excitement flow through the link.

Thank you for the invitation. This was a bit more formal than what he wanted to say, but Thracis was still unsure as to how this mare viewed him.

Psyche bobbed her head. She looked at him for a few more heartbeats, then turned and faded into the mist as she had before. The mist was growing darker as Thracis slid deep into unconsciousness. His thoughts of guilt evaporated as he fell into a sleep that even dreams could not penetrate.

16

CHAPTER 16

"The Romanium asklepiade, as well as several of your ilarches, have told me you are struggling through your courses." Commander Dias stalked in a wide circle around a swaying Thracis. "I see there is much they left out."

It had been two weeks since Thracis had struck the Calabrian and been dismissed from the schooling ring. In the interim, Thracis had thrown himself into training, refusing to fall behind. His practice of the many maneuvers, all basic, became manic. He spent every free moment training until exhaustion caused him to collapse in his bed box. His body was showing the signs of his demands. His coat was dull and beginning to show bare spots from lack of proper grooming. His ribs and spine protruded. His hooves were splintered around the edges. Thracis was in far worse shape than he had been during the asklepiade's examination.

Psyche, somehow sensing his condition, came to him almost every night. She berated him for being such a fool; how was he supposed to complete training if he died from exhaustion? She kept her time with him brief, afraid the mental strain from keeping the connection would drain him even more.

Aeos had told Pyrios of his brother's determination and Pyrios had contacted Thracis and said pretty much the same things as Psyche. He promised Thracis that he and Lord Kantaka were looking into the Conversano bloodline, but the herd was aloof to any outsiders. It was hard going but Lord Kantaka refused to be discouraged. Pyrios told Thracis not to worry about politics and concentrate instead on getting enough food and rest. Thracis heeded Pyrios' advice as much as Aeos or Psyche's.

Which was why he was now standing in front of Commander Dias for an impromptu inspection.

"You will not complete training if you continue on in this manner." The commander's voice was thick with disapproval. "You should have taken the asklepiade's suggestion and waited for the summer rotation. Your body has not yet healed from the ambusher's poison."

Putting as much humility in his voice as he could muster, Thracis asked, "Do you think the poison is affecting my ability to retain the sequence of maneuvers?"

Commander Dias flicked an ear. "In what way?"

Thracis sighed and spoke rapidly, letting the commander hear all his uncertainty and frustration over the past weeks. "I cannot do them. Any of them. I follow the instructor's drills, watch the other cadets, even practice on my own and still I cannot flow and spin like my fellow students. I have never encountered this problem before. It's as if my body refuses to listen to the words of my brain." He stopped, catching his breath.

Commander Dias stood silent for a moment. "I do not think the poison is affecting your cognition. If it were you would not be able to use telekinesis or telepathy. I think it more likely that your inability to master basic maneuvering is simple fatigue. You push yourself too hard."

"I must keep up."

"No, you must *learn*." Commander Dias used the stern voice he reserved for his daughter, Eno, when she became irritable and stubborn because one of her precious inventions wasn't working as it was supposed to. In Eno's case, the stern voice usually worked and the mare took a moment to reassess her agitation.

Thracis, familiar with a parent's anger and discipline, hunched his shoulders and dropped his head.

Taking a deep breath, reminding himself that Thracis and Eno were not much different, Commander Dias spoke with the voice of a sire, not a superior. "You must be patient, Cadet Thracis. Advanced combat maneuvers take time. They take discipline and guidance. You are clever, you will learn them."

"It just appears to me that a step is missing somewhere."

Commander Dias cocked his head.

Knowing he could not say such a flippant remark without reasoning, Thracis continued, "I'm having difficulty proceeding from a simple walk or halt to a pesade or levade. It seems as though I should be doing something else to prepare for the movement."

"You have done the movements before with no preparation."

Thracis tossed his head. "Those actions I did by instinct, not instruction."

Commander Dias twitched a shoulder. "Long ago, when I was a cadet, we were first instructed to learn the movements of the High Dances before continuing with the advanced maneuvers. However, from that time to this, command of the Romanium has gone to another Headmaster. He does not feel it is necessary for young stallions to learn the passage and piaffe before the more advanced maneuvers as long as they have a firm understanding of proper collection and balance."

Thracis' ears pricked at the mention of the Romanium's Headmaster. "May I ask a question, Commander?"

"You may."

"Before coming here I spoke with someone who knew a little of the Romanium. They told me I should look for Alois Phrenicos. I have been asking the ilarches, but none will tell me this instructor's whereabouts."

"He has been exiled."

Thracis stared, stunned. Psyche had neglected to tell him that. Had she even known?

Thracis ducked his head lower. "May I ask why?"

"Because he and the current Headmaster had a difference of opinion."

Thracis knew there had to be more to the incident than that. He also knew he was in no position to ask. Perhaps he would tell Pyrios to query Lord Kantaka on the subject. The

Mongolean was generally more apt to share information than Commander Dias.

"Let the matter drop, Cadet Thracis. We are here to discuss your troubles, not those that happened before you were foaled."

Bobbing his head, Thracis waited to hear the commander's judgment.

"I am ordering you to take a weeks' rest. You are to eat properly, rest often, and groom yourself to the standards of the Romanium. I do not want to hear any rumors that you are working yourself to bare bones. I will be having the ilarches and the asklepiade keep an eye on you. That is all."

Thracis bowed his head and walked to the stall door, stumbling as little as possible. As he stood on the threshold, he heard Commander Dias' voice behind him. "This is your last chance, stallion of Thetis. If you cannot see to your own health you are more of a hindrance than an asset."

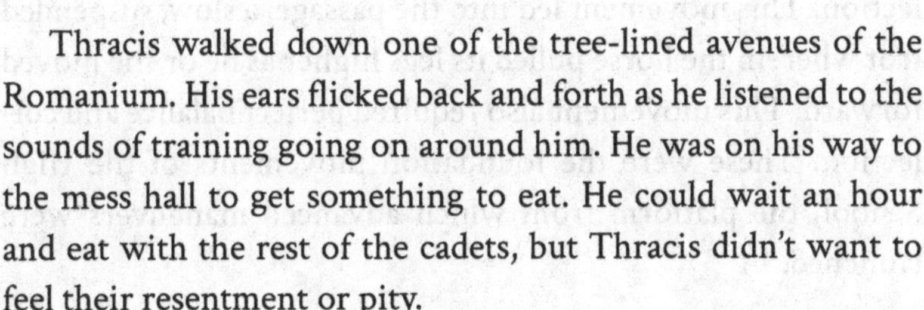

Thracis walked down one of the tree-lined avenues of the Romanium. His ears flicked back and forth as he listened to the sounds of training going on around him. He was on his way to the mess hall to get something to eat. He could wait an hour and eat with the rest of the cadets, but Thracis didn't want to feel their resentment or pity.

His thoughts chased and tumbled over each other. Why had Phrenicos been exiled? That seemed an extreme punishment for a difference of opinion. Thracis tried to contact Pyrios, but encountered the mental wall his brother employed when focusing his thoughts. He also used this wall in the council chamber to discourage eavesdroppers. Thracis tossed his head and decided to try again in the evening when Pyrios would be at Lord Kantaka's stable.

As he walked, he passed a mural that showed the advancement of the combat maneuvers. On the cadets first day the ilarches had positioned them all in front of this mural and described the different maneuvers and the sequence of training. It gave the students an outline of the weeks to come. The mural even showed the piaffe and passage, movements of the High Dances that the ilarches no longer taught.

The mural began with the cadence of the collected trot. This was how an Equine learned to collect him or herself together so that they were pushing forward with impulsion from their hindquarters. From the collected trot, the mural moved into the rapid, up and down diagonal movement of the piaffe. This was a movement in which the horse's legs moved up and down diagonally as the horse trotted on the spot. It was checking of forward impulsion and forced the horse into deeper collection. This movement led into the passage, a slow, suspended trot wherein the horse pulled its legs higher as he or she moved forward. This movement also required perfect balance and collection. These were the foundation movements of the High School, the platform from which advanced maneuvers were launched.

The actual combat maneuvers began with the mastering of the pesade and levade. They were the introduction to the more difficult movements. The pesade, the first and most basic movement, was completed when the horse raised its forelegs off the ground while remaining on its hindquarters, forming a forty-five-degree angle. The horse's forelegs must be tucked, if it strikes out the movement is a simple rear.

Once the pesade has been achieved to the ilarches satisfaction, the student is taught the levade. The pesade and levade are similar, with one exception. The levade must be lower. This is a difficult maneuver to perfect as the Equine must hold all his or her weight on their back legs while keeping low to the ground in a near-squat. This was used to condition the muscles for the rigors of extended fighting and was not often used in combat except to evaded an attack to the forelegs.

Thracis had little trouble with the pesade and levade if he didn't think about them. He had performed the levade often when under pressure. He was frustrated to no end that now that he had to duplicate the maneuver under the supervision of his instructors, he was unable to do so. His pesades were still too wobbly for him to move on to the levade. Until he mastered these movements, he could not hope to move on to move advanced maneuvers.

As he imagined his dreams of becoming one of the Hippeus slipping away, Thracis' foot stumbled over a stone and he nearly went sprawling. He recovered as quickly as possible but not before hearing a snicker to his left. Rolling his eyes, Thracis looked at a shaded alcove.

Othello Iago, the top student of the Romanium, stepped forward. His thick black Andalusian mane was braided to keep it off his neck in the summer heat and his brown coat glistened in the sunlight. With his muscled torso and above average intelligence, Iago was exactly the kind of stallion the Romanium wanted to promote. It was whispered among the cadets that Iago might become Asapatish one day. Thracis galled at the thought. The two stallions had shared an animosity from the moment they met.

Iago may be strong and cunning in the eyes of the ilarches, but in Thracis' humble opinion the Andalusian stallion was a pain in the tail. His silver tongue and submissive posture when dealing with his superiors hid a shrewd and calculating predator. After the first week, Thracis had tried to keep much distance between himself and Iago, having decided he had problems enough. But the Andalusian refused to give Thracis peace, openly taunting the Calabrian at every opportunity.

"I would think you would be in the practice rings, trying to keep up with everyone else." Iago's voice was a sneer.

"I've been instructed to do otherwise." Thracis began to walk away. He did not want stand here and listen to Iago's current list of Thracis' shortcomings.

Iago blocked Thracis' retreat. "That does not surprise me. The ilarches have been talking about you. They say you are poor example of the Romanium's ideals."

"I'm surprised they allow you to listen to their private council."

Something flickered in Iago's eyes, but it was gone before Thracis could identify it. "As the top student I am granted certain liberties."

Iago looked at Thracis' shabby coat. "You should be ashamed to walk these streets with a coat like that. And your hooves." Iago tisked. "Not only do you struggle through the simplest tasks, but you have no respect for the image of the Romanium."

Thracis was beginning to get angry. He was aggravated enough with his own failings. He did not need this strutting peacock to point them out. "I am trying my best." His voice was dropping in temperature.

Iago noticed and goaded Thracis further. "Perhaps your best is good enough in a backward province like Calabria, but here at the Romanium your best is not even mediocre. Maybe you should scamper back home and leave the fighting to the real stallions."

That was it. Thracis didn't pause to think. He threw himself forward, colliding with Iago's shoulder.

Iago, anticipating Thracis' lack of control, braced himself. The shock of the impact went through both stallions but Thracis was less equipped to deal with it. He staggered backward, trying to regain his balance. Iago followed Thracis, bringing his head down to clamp his teeth at the base of Thracis' neck. He bit hard, while at the same time striking Thracis foreleg with his own.

Thracis squealed in surprise and pain and tried to pull away. A month ago, he would have been able. Now, his body and mind were at the end of their endurance, Thracis lost all hold on his cognitive thought and panicked. He reared, twisting toward Iago, and striking with his front legs.

Iago released Thracis' neck and reared as well. He was intending to push Thracis back and flip the other stallion onto his back. Thracis, already light-headed, had reared in a desperate attempt to get away and therefore did not set himself correctly on his hind legs. He didn't so much attack Iago as fall forward onto the Andalusian. This threw Iago backward and the stallion couldn't balance himself. Both horses tumbled into a heap on the packed dirt of the street.

The two Equines became a tangled ball of flailing legs and biting teeth. They rammed their heads against each other as each attempted to get back on his feet. Every blow Thracis took felt like a hammer on an anvil. Iago wasn't getting much leverage but in Thracis' current state, the Andalusian didn't need it. Thracis was being pummeled. Finally, Thracis decided his best course of action would be to just hold still and stop struggling.

Iago was on his feet in an instant, backing away from Thracis, who lay shuddering on the ground. The Andalusian looked around to see if they had been discovered. The street was still deserted. Iago was shaken. He had thought himself invincible and yet even in his weakened state, Thracis had managed to get the upper hoof for a brief instant.

Iago watched as Thracis drew one breath and then another, trying to calm himself. Iago took a moment to fix his mane and mentally brush the dust from his coat. Then he advanced on the prone stallion. He stood next to Thracis' head, looking down at the other horse's face.

"The rest of us at this institution have put up with you long enough." His voice dripped with loathing. "Today I will see that you are dismissed not only from the schooling rings but from the entire Steppe."

Thracis closed his eyes and listened to Iago's retreating hoofsteps. Even Commander Dias would not be able to keep him in the Romanium after this incident. Fighting among the cadets was accepted as long as it did not interfere with the training. The ilarches knew that when this many stallions from different regions and social structures came together, fighting was inevitable. However, many of the ilarches were looking for any excuse to get rid of Thracis. They would see this as the perfect opportunity.

In his agony at being dismissed from the one place on all Equus where he wanted to stay, Thracis reached out to the one horse who would give him comfort.

17

CHAPTER 17

Now is not a good time. Calypsa's weariness could be felt through the mental link. She was trying to rest after giving birth to a healthy, dark coated filly early that morning. The filly, Aquina, was sleeping in a ball at her dam's feet and Calypsa was taking a moment to relax. Much as she loved all her foals, Calypsa wished she could take ten minutes for herself.

I am sorry, mother. I will contact you at a more convenient time.

Calypsa sighed. She could feel the hurt and loneliness in her son's mind. *It is alright. We will not be able to talk once your sister is awake in any case.*

A flicker of delight from Thracis. *Is she all you and sire hoped she would be?*

Calypsa's joy warmed the link the way a sun warms spring flowers. *She is perfect. And already showing she will follow in her brother's hoofprints.*

I hope she is following Pyrios. My steps have faltered badly as of late.

Calypsa's maternal instincts flared. *What has happened?*

Nothing that I did not bring on myself. Thracis told Calypsa of all that had happened since coming to the Romanium. She felt his anguish at the loss of a dream, he explained that the ilarches would not overlook his skirmish with Iago no matter who was at fault. His fear of what would become of him. Pyrios had found his path and now Thracis' way was barred. Where now could he turn? Even Calypsa knew that Thracis had been born a warrior, though she had tried to convince herself otherwise.

Calypsa waited a moment after Thracis had finished speaking. She chose her words carefully, knowing how vulnerable her son was at this moment. *All is not lost, Thracis. There are others who can teach you what you wish to learn.*

Those teachers will not grant me the respect graduating from the Romanium would. They cannot make me a Hippeus in the Imperial Cavalry.

A true Hippeus cares not for titles, Calypsa replied.

I know, but I wish to be looked on as though I have value.

Is that what bothers you? That you will not be respected?

Thracis was silent.

You are a grown stallion and capable of making your own decisions. Now you must make a fundamental one. You must choose between respect and envy.

Graduating would grant me respect. Thracis refused to be pulled out of his mulish position.

Do your fellow classmates respect this Iago or envy his position?

Thracis had no reply. In truth he hadn't paid enough attention to be able to answer the question.

Position does not automatically garner respect. Calypsa's voice held a hint of irony.

It often seems to.

Do not confuse respect with fear.

You sound like someone else I've met recently. The thought was out before he could stop it. He hoped his dam was sufficiently distracted and wouldn't notice.

Mare or stallion?

Thracis knew he could not lie. Not to his dam anyway, she always knew. *A mare.*

He felt his dam's interest. *Is she from a respectable herd?*

In a way. Thracis kept his mind vague. *She is a princess.*

The Princess Salia? I had thought Queen Helena was more interested in Pyrios.

She is not of the Mykenian Stable.

Then who is she? Calypsa's voice was a whip crack command.

Thracis took a deep breath. *She is a daughter of Queen Hippolyta.* He braced himself for the tirade he knew his dam was about to launch. This was one more headache he didn't need. But as usual, his dam surprised him.

Calypsa laughed. *That is interesting news indeed. Your sire will be most intrigued.*

You are not angry?

It is not the type of mare I had in mind, but I think you would be suited to a lady of Diomedean heritage. She will certainly be more capable of dealing with you than a society mare.

I thought they only viewed stallions as breeding stock.

Calypsa tossed her head. *Some surely do, but not all. How does she feel about your interest?*

I have not told her.

Why not? Calypsa sounded curious, not angry as Thracis had expected her to be. His dam thought very little of Pyrios' treatment of the mares he fancied.

I am not sure she would accept my courtship. She has given me no clear signal.

Calypsa weighed that statement for a moment. Even though he tried to hide it, she could feel her son's longing in the link. It delighted her that her younger son had found someone to hold his interest. While Pyrios spent a great deal of his time entertaining the local mares, Thracis only courted a few and they were very far between. *Would you take the advice of a mare who has not been courted in quite some time?*

You know I value your opinion.

Treat this mare with respect and patience. As confused as you are I can tell you that she is even more so. Give her time to gather her courage and do not pressure her. Be wary, I think any sign she gives will be subtle.

Were you nervous when you first met my sire?

Thracis felt the warmth of his dam's love for his sire. He wondered what it would feel like to have a love like that. *I felt like a gangly filly at my first formal occasion. Zephyros was so handsome, not like any of the other young stallions I had met. He was so confident. I thought surely he could hear the pounding of my heart at our first meeting.* Her voice softened. *If he did, he's kept it to himself all these years.*

Thracis was feeling more himself. He rose to his feet and squared his shoulders. *I should be getting back to my barn. I'm sure the ilarches will be looking for me by this time.*

Good luck. Remember that whatever the decision, your sire and I will stand by you. You will find your position in this herd, Thracis. Growing up just takes time.

Thracis bowed his head. *Tell sire all that has happened and tell my little sister I love her.*

Thracis felt a whisper of affection pass through his mind as his dam broke the link. Taking a deep breath, Thracis shook the dust from his coat and began walking back to his barn to learn his future.

18

CHAPTER 18

Thracis stood before the council of the Romanium. The council formed a formidable line along a raised dais at the front of the assembly hall. The Headmaster stood in the middle, flanked by Commander Dias and a high-ranking ilarches. Other members feathered out from those central three. All the council members wore stern, unreadable expressions.

The assembly hall was filled with the Romanium's current cadets and ilaraches. Behind and to the left of Thracis, standing in the front row for the best vantage point, was Iago. The Andalusian had at least enough sense not to smirk as Thracis' punishment was announced. To Thracis' right, Aeos stood with outward calm but his insides felt as if they were twisting themselves into knots. The dun stallion was finding it hard not to fidget. Thracis himself was motionless, patiently awaiting his dismissal.

"Cadet Thracis," the Headmaster began, "it has come to the attention of this council that you are not qualified to experience the rigors and discipline of the Romanium at this time. Therefore, it is the council's decision that you are to be dismissed immediately. Perhaps you may begin training again at a later time when you have matured more and have passed the Romanium's requirements for acceptance. You are an example as to why we do not accept students based on political connection. That is all."

With a pointed looked at Commander Dias, the Headmaster turned and walked down a hallway leading back to the main offices of the Romanium. The council members filed out behind him, each giving Thracis' a disapproving glare before turning away. The cadets stood for a breathless moment before being herded back to their exercises by their ilarches. The chamber filled with the echoes of retreating hooves and whispered voices until only Thracis was left to stand in the silence.

As the main doors shut behind the last cadet, Thracis looked around to make sure he was alone. Seeing no one, he dropped his head and took a shuddering breath. For all his anxiety, Thracis hadn't imagined his dismissal would be so abrupt. He had thought he would have at least a chance to defend himself. He had not been allowed to speak at all.

He had never been so alone or ashamed. That he would let his temper flare at such blatant instigation. Thracis shook his head. Nothing to be done about it now. The council wouldn't even entertain the idea of his return to the schooling rings until he had at least a year's experience in the cavalry. He would also have to pass the traditional entrance exams the next time he attempted to gain acceptance into the Romanium.

Thracis turned to leave. He was already wearing his armor harness and had packed his few belongings. They hung from various pouches on the harness. He had known he was being dismissed, the gathering was only a formality, an example of what would happen to any other cadets who followed in his hoofsteps. Thracis would have much rather taken his things and left without the embarrassment of being dismissed in front of the entire training facility, but he wasn't given a choice in the matter.

He walked slowly down the tree-lined streets to the main gates, savoring every last instant he would have inside this hallowed place. The schooling rings of the Romanium. The gateway to becoming a Hippeus. From the time he was old enough to spar he had dreamed of training in the practice rings. He had trained with anyone who could teach him to fight, pushing himself to the limits of his endurance, stubbornly repeating the same exercise over and over until he reached perfection. Now it was this same obduracy that had cost him his goal.

Thracis stopped just outside the main gates of the Romanium. He turned to look over his back at the words written across the gates. Honor, loyalty, and strength; the creed of the Hippeus. How far the Romanium had come from those three simple words.

Thracis sighed. A choice lay before him: should he go left or right? Right was the obvious choice. That branch of the road would take him back to Lipizza where he could live with Pyrios and Lord Kantaka. The representative had already extended the invitation. Thracis looked in that direction. Pyrios would not look down on him and Lord Kantaka would be polite but Thracis couldn't take the risk that his brother would be shunned simply because Thracis had been dishonored. Pyrios was working too hard to become a political influence. And Thracis was tired of living in his brother's shadow.

Thracis supposed he could do as his dam wished and enroll in the University. His parents would send the necessary funds for board and tuition and he was sure he could find some course of study to hold his interest. That route would keep him in Lipizza and close to the Romanium in the event of his reacceptance. He knew many of the stallions at the Hippikon enrolled at the university while they waited for positions to open in the military. His ears flicked at the idea of days and weeks spent on the university campus, discussing ideas and theories. He would expire from boredom within a month.

What, then, to do until he 'matured'?

The stallion looked left. This branch of the road would take him south into Courbettania and farther on to the country of Diomedea. A shiver of excitement scurried through his body at the idea of traveling to Psyche's homeland. The borders of Diomedea weren't closed, exactly, but it would be difficult for a lone stallion to gain entrance. Perhaps Kamuzu or Alcander could put in a good word for him with someone in authority, allowing Thracis access to Diomedea.

"I would be happy to join you if you wish to venture into the warrior mares' lands."

Thracis spun at the sound of the amused voice behind him. The movement made his head spin and he had to take a moment to settle himself before looking up to see who was following him.

Aeos stood with ears pricked. Thracis felt mental bands around his legs and shoulders, holding him steady. He nodded his gratefulness. "You startled me."

"I had thought you heard my hoofsteps."

"You do not wish to continue at the Romanium? You've risen so high in the ranks."

Aeos twitched a shoulder and released his mental straps from Thracis. "Rank is not that important to me." An ideal held by a true Hippeus, according to Calypsa.

Thracis cocked his head. "But you were enjoying the training."

"Like you, I felt something was missing." Aeos tossed his head. "Besides, I do not care for Iago's company. I was to be assigned to his herd for group training." The disgust was clear in Aeos' voice. "That stallion does not respect the discipline needed to learn true combat and he cares little for the welfare of others."

They were quiet for a moment. Thracis tilted his head at the left branch of the road. "I did not know you had any interest in Diomedea."

"I have a little. And Kamuzu did tell me I would be welcome if I chose to journey there."

"Do you think that invitation could be extended in my favor?"

"I think it could."

They tossed their heads at each other. Aeos walked forward and inspected Thracis' armor and supplies. "We will have to stop at the first village we pass to get ourselves properly equipped before continuing on such a long and arduous journey." He looked up at the cloudless sky. "At least it's summer. That should make the weather easier to contend with."

The two of them began to walk down the road. Having no distinct destination, they were in no hurry. The summer day was warm and pleasant. Birds sang in the high grass of the timothy fields. A gentle breeze rustled the leaves in the few trees they passed. Thracis didn't want to disturb the midmorning tranquility, but his curiosity burned.

"Why are you so interested in Diomedea?" Aeos, unreadable as always, flicked an ear in Thracis' direction. "I am interested in the healing arts. Diomedea is reputed to have some of the best teachers on all Equus."

Thracis snorted. "A good excuse but not the only one. If you wanted to learn more about healing you could have inquired about classes at the university. I'm sure the professors there are adept at their instruction."

"Fairly observant for someone who couldn't tell that Iago and his followers wanted you out of the Romanium from the first day you stepped into the ring." Thracis pinned his ears. This was typical of Aeos. The dun stallion would always change the subject as soon as Thracis began digging at something Aeos was not ready to reveal. And it was always a subject that was too tempting for Thracis to ignore.

"What are you talking about? I didn't even meet Iago until the second week."

"A clever student is always aware of his competition."

"But I was half-dead when we first arrived. I would not think of myself as competition."

Aeos tossed his head. "Are you so blind you do not see your own potential? Even exhausted physically and mentally, you were making headway. The very fact that you could comprehend what the ilarches were trying to teach you spoke of your natural talent. A trained opponent is daunting enough; couple that with raw aptitude and Iago knew he would have formidable competition."

"Are you suggesting a conspiracy was set in motion to ensure my dismissal?"

"I am stating that many of the students and ilarches will not mourn your absence."

Thracis walked on in silence. He had no idea that he had been so disliked for simply trying to keep up with everyone else. This knowledge did not sit well with his idea of what a Hippeus was supposed to be. Aeos kept peace for several heartbeats before trying to console his friend.

"Do not think to poorly of them. They have been conditioned to believe that anyone who stands out above the herd is a potential threat."

"Plenty of others stood out."

"But all those, with the exception of myself, know how to manipulate others around them."

Thracis rolled his eyes. "I've seen your gift for manipulation."

"Yes, but I manipulate for the good of all."

Thracis snorted laughter at Aeos' feigned pious demeanor. "If what you say is true than I guess I am better off for having been dismissed."

"For the time being anyway. I have no doubt that one day you will return."

19

CHAPTER 19

"This does not look promising."

Aeos stopped at the edge of the small copse of woods he and Thracis had been walking through. In front of them, across a field several hundred yards long, was a fortified stone gate. The gate had been carved into the rock face of the cliff beyond. This was the Andromedan Gate. It was the only passage into Diomedea from Courbettania. It led directly into the province of Artemia.

Artemia was the only province of Diomedea that directly bordered on another country. Having the most interaction with the other countries of Equus, Artemia was by far the most open-minded of all Diomedea's provinces. The mares in this region were even beginning to form family herds that included stallions. This was a monumental step in Diomedean society. The mares still held all the authority, but the stallions were at least being looked at as more than studs to be used once and discarded.

The Andromedan Gate, usually open for merchants and travelers, was closed. Armed guards stood on the battlements and Thracis could made out several ballistae as well as more technological weapons within easy reach of the sentries. The mares, as sentinels of Diomedea they had to be mares, looked ready for a war. The sunlight gleamed off retracted armor harnesses and Thracis could see sparkling glints high up the cliff face, leading him to ascertain that more armed sentries looked down on the gate from above.

"Let's hope they don't run us through before we get close enough to identify ourselves." Thracis looked at Aeos as they began walking forward. "Did Kamuzu tell you anything helpful when you spoke with him last evening?"

Aeos and Kamuzu had been in contact every night since the two stallions had left the Romanium. Kamuzu had been delighted with the news that Aeos was traveling to Diomedea in search of the Felisian city of Sanctuary. Sanctuary was close to the Diomedean capital of Ruffiana, in the province of Amazonia. Kamuzu had told Aeos that he would inform others of the stallions' arrival to smooth their entrance into Diomedea.

For his part, Thracis had tried, unsuccessfully, to contact Psyche on several occasions. The mare wasn't ignoring him, exactly, she just didn't have the time or energy to hold a mental conversation over a great distance. Or so she said. Worried that she may be in trouble, Thracis pestered Aeos until the other stallion asked Kamuzu to check in with the mare. The lady was perfectly fine, Kamuzu reported in a sly voice, and wished that Thracis would stop acting like an idiot and give her some peace.

"She didn't really say that, did she?"

Aeos twitched a shoulder. "I'm only relaying the message. If you want to know more, contact Kamuzu ourself."

"I'll wait." In truth, Thracis didn't want to contact Kamuzu. The Felisian was very talented in the psychic arts and Thracis had no doubt that Kamuzu would discover the stallion's feelings toward Psyche as soon as Thracis and Kamuzu made mental contact. It was all well and good for others to speculate on what was going on between Thracis and Psyche, but it was entirely different for Kamuzu to know exactly how deeply Thracis felt about the mare. Especially since Thracis was still trying to find out if his advances would be welcome.

"In our conversation last night, Kamuzu told be that he had informed the Andromedan guards that we would be arriving today and that he could vouch for our integrity."

"That's comforting, but do you think they believed him?"

"I have an idea that humble as he may seem, Kamuzu holds a high position in Ruffiana. Something to do with his mother."

They were getting close to the gate. Thracis could see that the ballistae were armed with wickedly barbed missiles. The memory of his attacker's barbed armor flared and Thracis' neck gave a painful twinge.

In the time since leaving Romanium, Thracis had replaced all the weight he had lost. His coat, nourished from full meals and restful nights, was back to its copper gloss. His muscles were back in tone as well and his mind was sharp. He felt better than he had in months and was beginning to think the effects of the poison were finally behind him. Aeos had watched the slow improvement and had begun Thracis' drills again now that the other stallion could keep up.

Aeos' first teacher, the same stallion who had trained Aeos' sire, taught Aeos the importance of proper balance. Night after night, the dun stallion made Thracis practice pulling himself together in proper collection. All impulsion should come from the hindquarters, according to Aeos' long ago instructor, therefore a horse must have perfect balance. Thracis complained at first, his back and haunches were not used to such hard work, but as time passed and his muscles became more and more conditioned, the movements smoothed out. Now Thracis could hold his collection for an hour without overly taxing himself. It was a significant improvement. Aeos could tell that Thracis was ready to learn the movements of the High Dances; the piaffe, passage, and canter pirouette, but they had not had the time to start. These movements required patience and practice. Aeos was hoping that in Diomedea they might find an instructor who was willing to train he and Thracis in this dying art.

"Halt and state your names and purpose." This command came from a dapple gray mare standing on the battlement directly above the gate. Far from the nervous university sentry, this mare looked down at them with dark suspicion.

"I am Zephyros Thracis of Thetis Stable. This is Quintus Aeos from Acadia Stable. We are traveling to Diomedea in search of knowledge in the healing arts and combat training."

I though we may as well be honest, Thracis thought to Aeos.

"We had received word that you would be arriving soon, stallion of Thetis Stable. Lady Hippolyta has said that we are to grant you passage and give you leave to wander our lands. But know this: if you cause any trouble, you'll learn that the mares of Diomedea can finish any fight."

Thracis and Aeos bowed their heads. "We want no conflict." Aeos kept his head lowered to hide the amused glimmer Thracis knew was sparkling in the other stallion's eyes.

The gray mare said something to the other guards above the gate and Thracis heard the grinding of machinery as the massive iron grillwork lifted. The gate was only raised high enough for the two stallions to walk under. As soon as they had stepped into the small indoor courtyard, the gate was lowered behind them. It closed with a finality that made Thracis shudder.

Thracis and Aeos were standing in a small chamber that had been burrowed out of the stone of the mountain. This was a sort of foyer where travelers could have a few moment's rest before heading down the two-mile tunnel that had been bored through the solid rock of the mountain. On the left was a warren of stalls where the guards were housed. On the right was a water fountain for drinking and half a dozen bedding boxes where travelers could spend the night.

A sorrel mare approached them. Unlike her comrade keeping watch on the gate, this Artemian looked at least civil. "We have grain and hay if you wish to eat before continuing on your journey."

"We're fine. A drink would be most welcome though." Aeos had regained his composure by this time.

The mare nodded at the fountain. Thracis and Aeos took their time at the fountain. Their ears flicked back and forth as they listened to the shifting hooves and swishing tails of the mares patrolling the gate. They could hear them even through the stone. The sorrel was still waiting when they finished getting their drink.

Tossing his head at the gate, Thracis said, "I thought Artemia was open to commerce and travelers."

The mare bobbed her head. "It usually is, but we've been having trouble of late."

"What kind of trouble?"

"Those Baroquian mules won't take no for an anwer." This came from the dapple gray mare. She was walking across the courtyard, the weapons of her armor harness twinkling in the light thrown from the globes placed around the ceiling. She stopped next to the sorrel. "Queen Hippolyta has been dealing with the Baroquian Pact for months now."

"Why would the Pact be interested in Diomedea?" Aeos kept his voice humble, the gray's ears were already part of the way down. "The mares here are exceptional fighters but even the Pact would not allow you to join the military. And, while rich in natural resources, Diomedea would have little to offer a cavalry on the move."

"But you forget that the reason Lady Cassandra and her followers settled in Diomedea was because of its defensible position. Diomedea is bordered on two sides by water and on one by the Natarian Desert. The only way a cavalry may pass through the Pleiades Mountains is this gate."

Aeos, who had a much firmer grasp on geography than Thracis, saw the Baroquian strategy. "If they have leave from Queen Hippolyta to occupy Diomedea, the Baroquian cavalry will have the perfect staging area to invade Lipizzania."

"Exactly."

Thracis looked from Aeos to the gray mare. "The two of you speak as if war is unavoidable."

"You know it is not." Aeos kept his attention on the mare. "How does the queen feel about the Pact, if I may ask?"

The gray pinned her ears. "Diomedean memories are long. We have not forgotten that it was Zaxas who imprisoned our foredams as slaves. We will not side with those of his lineage, no matter how they sweeten their promises."

"But you have strained relations with others in the Registry as well."

"Not so strained as one might think. A lot can be done under the guise of camouflage."

Aeos nodded. He looked at Thracis. "I think it's best we be on our way. We want to cover several miles yet before nightfall."

The dapple gray tossed her head. "If you want a good stable at a decent price, try to reach the town of Medea. There is a boarding stable on the main street called the Dancing Filly. My sister owns it. She will see you are made comfortable."

Thracis and Aeos bowed to the gray, she had thawed considerably since first sighting them walking across the field. Thracis inclined his head at her. "Thank you for the information about the Pact."

"I felt you should know our stance if you any sympathies toward the Baroquians."

Thracis pinned his ears. "My herd is descended from Lord Bucephalus. The Baroquians have obtained an even colder reception from my sire's lands."

"We are all in good company then." She and the sorrel stepped out of the way to allow Thracis and Aeos passage.

Thracis and Aeos walked down the long tunnel that would lead through the mountain to emerge in the province of Artemia. The tunnel was lit every ten feet with globes. The Artemian mares had also seen fit to have an intercom system installed that would allow travelers to contact help in case of emergency. This use of technology was smart as most Equines did not willingly let outsiders contact them telepathically.

"Forgive me for sounding like a simpleton, but I paid little attention to my history lessons as a colt," Thracis' voice sound loud, yet hollow, inside the tunnel, "but how did the country of Diomedea come to be?"

Aeos gave Thracis a sidelong glance. "It is wise for you to know the history of your lady's herds."

Thracis ignored the obvious tease. "I'm only curious now that we are here."

Aeos sighed. "Very well, I will tell you how the warrior mares of Diomedea came to be."

20

CHAPTER 20

Zaxas was a shrewd ruler, he knew the easiest way to obtain loyal followers was to grow them. During his reign it was well known that Zaxas encouraged his generals to keep the mares of conquered regions as slaves. This practice became so common that many generals had herds of twenty mares or more that they kept as harem slaves. Zaxas himself was reputed to have over forty mares at his disposal.

One such mare was Cassandra. She was part of a harem kept by the general Agamemnon. Young and strong, Cassandra quickly showed that she was more trouble than she was worth. In anger, Agamemnon sent her among his soldiers to be a relief for their needs. None now speak of the horrors she must have endured, but rather than be crushed to dust, a fighter arose in the mare's battered frame.

During the months she spent in the cavalry's encampment, Cassandra created a following of mares who would stop at nothing to be free of their captivity. They made their plans of escape in secret and carefully selected others to join their cause. They knew they could never hope to overpower their captors with physical force, but Cassandra culled her mares with care; she only harvested those with the strongest mental powers.

Months passed until Cassandra made her move. Mentally joined together as they were, the hundred or so mares that she had brought into her coven had little trouble destroying the minds of the stallions who had abused them for so long. Knowing Zaxas would seek revenge, Cassandra led her herd into the Natarian Desert, where no cavarly would follow. The shifting sands and endless sun were a death sentence to any Equine.

The mares were presumed to have perished until a decade later when rumors began to circulate that the southern peninsula of the Mesohippos continent, long thought to be the dwelling place of uneasy spirits, was being claimed by a curious herd of Equines made up of only mares. The southern peninsula, a dense, tropical region virtually isolated from the rest of Equus, had never been inviting to Equines. The humidity, jungles, and treacherous mountain ranges were an unwelcoming landscape to the four-footed horses.

Those first rumors were quickly followed by tales of a warrior queen named Cassandra who had decreed that the southern peninsula would be known as Diomedea and that all stallions would enter at their peril. This claim was further solidified as groups of weaned colts were found wandering the borderlands of Coubettania. Of course, with such open boasting by a herd of combative mares, several stallions thought to investigate and learn if the rumors were true. None ever returned.

It was after his nephew disappeared that Bucephalus himself led a contingent of soldiers to this new country. What he found astounded all of Equus.

Diomedea was indeed ruled by a warrior queen. Lady Cassandra had risen from slave to ruler in grand fashion. While in their chosen exile in the Natarian Desert, the mares of Cassandra had captured several stallions with flawless military training. Cassandra's subordinates had set their mental abilities to learning all the stallions knew. The stallions were also kept for several years as breeding stock before being subsequently executed.

Over the years, the mares of Diomedea had treated other stallions in the same fashion. Stealing all the information their captives had to offer before disposing of them. If a stallion was of thought to be capable of producing strong and intelligent offspring, he may be kept for a few months to mate with those mares who wished for a foal. In this manner, the herds of the Diomedean mares grew. If a filly was born, she was kept to be raised by her dam in Diomedean society. If a colt resulted from a mating, the foal was raised until he could be weaned and it was established that he could defend himself and he and several other colts were sent through the Andromedan Gate to find acceptance among the other herds of Equus. It was soon discovered that these colts were physically and mentally stronger than other youngsters they encountered.

At the time of her meeting with Bucephalus, Cassandra herself had two daughters, Clotho and Lachesis. It was widely rumored that her third daughter, Atropos, born almost a year after their fateful meeting, was a filly of Bucephalus. Cassandra, as queen, only carried the foals of the most dominant stallions.

During his audience with the Diomedean queen, Bucephalus proposed a compromise as he knew he could not route the mares from their territory. Nor did he want to. Having been born of a slave, Bucephalus was sympathetic to the followers of Cassandra. He suggested that Cassandra send representatives to the Registry of Breeds where her territory would be recorded as a legitimate country. She would be treated with the same respect of any king, as at that time there were no other queens, and her mares would all be seen as free Equines. For her part, he requested that Cassandra stop detaining stallions and executing them. These stallions should not be punished for the wrongs others committed. He also opinioned that rather than send colts out into the world to fend for themselves, the mares should contact the foals' sires and request that the offspring be accepted into the sire's herd. Cassandra agreed to the terms and that was the beginning of Diomedea.

The mares continued to be superior and very few stallions stayed in the family herds. The mares, guided by Cassandra and her original followers, remained particular in the stallions they mated with. They primarily chose stallions who were strong in the psychic arts. Even before the Felisians established the city of Sanctuary after they arrived on Equus, Diomedea was known for its strength in otherworldly powers. It was said that the darker the mare, the more powerful her mental abilities would be. It was unknown how the colts born to Diomedean mares fared. Logic would suggest that they would be talented with their mental abilities as well, but Aeos had never heard of a black, or even a gray, Diomedean stallion. He supposed that colts born with Diomedean heritage were a different color than the fillies.

"I have it on good authority that color is directly related to psychic power in Diomedean society," Thracis mumbled when Aeos was done speaking.

"Was the mare you met in Iliad a dark horse?"

Thracis shook his head. "Yes and no. She is a patchwork of black and white. She told me a gray would have more power than she."

"I doubt it," Aeos said dryly.

"Why would she lie?"

"Perhaps she didn't want you to ask questions she did not want to answer."

"In that case, you and she should stay away from each other. The two of you would hardly be able to complete a conversation."

Aeos nipped Thracis' shoulder. "It would do you good to learn to keep your mouth shut at times."

"Now you sound just like her."

"I think I would enjoy meeting her."

Thracis pinned his ears.

"Don't be so jealous, Thracis. I am well-aware of your claim to this mare even if the lady in question might not know of your interest."

"I think she has an inkling."

"Then what is the problem?" They were walking out of the tunnel and into the late afternoon light. The tunnel had opened into a long valley. Smoke rose lazily in the distance. That was the location of the town of Medea. Aeos and Thracis should reach the settlement before nightfall with little trouble.

Thracis sighed. "She has not given me any clear signals. My dam says I should be patient, that this mare is just as nervous as I am about making the wrong impression, but it's hard. Especially now as she is too busy to make contact with me."

"And you wonder what she's so busy doing."

Thracis twitched his shoulders as they walked. "I can't help it. I've never felt this way."

"I'm ashamed to admit it, but I have even less experience with mares than you do. At least mares I care about. The demands of my sire's stable keep me too busy to pursue any mare on more than a provisional basis."

"It is different now that I care what this mare thinks of me. In the past, if one mare didn't care for my company, I could find another readily enough."

Aeos rolled his eyes. "That must run in the family."

"I have not spoken of this mare in any detail to my brother," Thracis said sharply. "I would ask that you not say anything as well."

"I have not had contact with Pyrios since we began our journey together. Besides what you say to your brother is between you two and none of my business."

They were silent for several moments. The column of smoke was getting closer. Aeos sniffed the light breeze that flowed through the valley. "Kamuzu has told me a little about this mare. She is the youngest of Lady Hippolyta's daughters. She has a talent for seeing and healing." He looked at Thracis. "As was apparent in the talisman she gave you."

"Has Kamuzu told you where she is?" Thracis tried to hide the eagerness in his voice.

Aeos shook his head. "He has only told me that she is safe. Come on, let's get moving. I don't want to arrive at sunset when all other travelers in the area will be looking for board."

21

CHAPTER 21

Pyrios bowed his head as yet another dignitary was introduced to Lord Kantaka. Pyrios, Phlegon, and Lord Kantaka had been at this engagement for most of the evening and after a week of heated debate in the council chamber, Pyrios was weary of political intrigue. He had not heard from Thracis in some days and was beginning to worry about his younger brother. This worry was also keeping him from focusing on the problems in the council.

Pyrios had understood Thracis' decision to leave Lipizzania and try to find his own place in the world, but hadn't agreed with it. Pyrios, as well as his sire Zephyros and his dam Calypsa, believed Thracis should stay in Lipizza and attend classes at the university. This would keep Thracis and Pyrios close together. Pyrios did not think it was wise for them to be separated by such distance. Especially since Pyrios did not agree with Lord Kantaka's deductions that the Baroquians were more interested in Pyrios than Thracis.

Since they were foals, Pyrios had suspected Thracis was destined for greatness. He never had any proof of this suspicion; it was just a feeling. From the time he was young, Thracis had an air about him, something that made other horses want to be near him. This power was daunting at times and often caused problems for Thracis with those who craved Thracis' self-confidence. Because of these few individuals, Thracis often found himself alone with no one to turn to but his brother. And his parents of course, but no stallion wanted to rely on them his whole life. Of the two sons, Thracis was fated to have the harder road.

Much as he wanted to be the older brother and protect his sibling, Pyrios understood that Thracis had to find his own way. Hopefully, this journey he was taking with Aeos would answer some of his deepest questions. Pyrios regretted that Thracis was, for the time being anyway, barred from becoming a Hippeus, but he knew his brother was resourceful. Thracis would find his place in society, Pyrios was certain of that.

"And this is Lord Dimitri Alexi, lead stallion of Kigeria." A steward informed Lord Kantaka, presenting a dun stallion.

Pyrios bowed his head, but not before noting the red dun mare standing to the left of Lord Alexi. She was like nothing he had ever seen. Unlike the other ladies at this gathering, she was bare of all adornments. Her red mane, more a dusky roan than an actual red, was cut short so that it only fell to the middle of her neck, rather than flow to the front of her shoulder as was the style among most mares. Her forelock was long though, falling to just above her roan nose. She stared back at him in open challenge.

Lord Alexi bowed to Lord Kantaka, then inclined his head at the dun mare. "This is my lady, Stephanos Nerissa."

The three stallions bowed to the Kiger Lady. Pyrios fought hard to drop his gaze from hers. To bow his head and retain eye contact would be viewed as a challenge. Not to mention impolite.

"I am pleased to meet you, Lord Kantaka. My mate has told me much of Lipizza. I understand you were once a professor at the University of Piber."

Pyrois felt the hair on his rump stand on end at the sound of that deep, gravelly voice. He had never met a mare with such a voice. All thoughts of Thracis fled in light of this new conquest. That she was the mate of Lord Alexi was of little consequence. In the months Pyrios had been standing as Lord Kantaka's aide, he had witnessed multiple acts of infidelity among the aristocrats in Lipizza. With the way Lady Nerissa was looking at the other stallions in the room, Pyrios doubted she would hesitate at the thought of a clandestine affair.

His eyes shifted to Lord Kantaka. It would be the ultimate insult to Kantaka's stable if one of his trusted associates was caught in such an unethical situation. Pyrios had never had to weigh such consequences before. His pursuit of that mare or this never had an effect on anyone else. At least he didn't think it had.

"You speak the truth, Lady. I was head of the history department at one time. Now my obligations to the Registry keep me far too busy to teach."

"A shame. You sound as though you truly love to instruct." Her eyes flitted across Pyrios and Phlegon before settling back on Lord Kantaka. "I envy the position of your aides. I'm sure they will learn much while in your stable."

Pyrios' ears flicked at the light conversation that seemed to have hidden undertones. He couldn't believe that this striking mare was that interested Equine history.

"Perhaps I could stop by for a history lesson. If my mate has no objection," she added with a quick look at Lord Alexi.

Lord Alexi flicked his ears. "I think it would be good for you to learn the history of the area if it interests you."

"I think a lesson or two could be arranged. May I also suggest that you sit in on a few lectures at the university? My old friends at Piber would have no objections, I'm sure." Lord Kantaka and Lady Nerissa moved off into the rest of the partygoers with Lord Alexi following behind. Pyrios and Phlegon exchanged a look.

"We've enough headache dealing with politicians day and night. That mare is going to be nothing but trouble," Phlegon grumbled.

"It might be nice to have a mare around the stable once or twice a week. Besides the maid, I mean."

Phlegon flicked an ear at Pyrios. "You've less sense than a two-day old foal if you're thinking of pursuing her."

Pyrios watched the Equines throughout the chamber. "It seems to be the thing to do around here. I'm beginning to think every union aristocrats make is for some sort of political gain."

"Maybe not all, but certainly most. You cannot insult Lord Kantaka in such a manner."

"Are stepping in as my sire in his absence?"

Phlegon shook his head. "There are plenty of mares in this city who would be more than willing to spend an evening or three with you. What ever happened to that pretty spotted sentry at the university?"

"We shared a pleasant week or two before deciding to go our separate ways."

"How can you move on from mare to mare with no guilt?"

"I am always honest with them. They know I have not intention of being loyal."

"Does Thracis share this same theory on courtship?" Phlegon wasn't paying much attention to the conversation any more. For all his jiving, he had shared plenty of female company since coming to Lipizza. He had just noticed a quietly pretty mare standing in an open doorway leading to one of the many terraces that opened off the main chamber and was seeking a way of excusing himself for a few minutes to speak with her.

"I have no idea what Thracis' does with the mares he meets. He's very private about such matters."

"Probably a wise decision."

Pyrios pinned his ears and was about to ask Phlegon what made him so high headed, when another young stallion approached.

"Well, look who it is? Lord Kantaka's latest charity cases."

Pyrios rolled his eyes as Favory Demas, oldest son of the Hapsburg Stable, strode through the crowded room. His sire, Favory Alexander, was the current king of Lipizzania. In a nutshell, this meant that Demas was the fair-haired foal and everybody spent an inordinate amount of time worshipping the ground he walked on. If asked their opinions, Pyrios and Phlegon would have said they thought Demas was a spoiled colt with a very high opinion of himself and an arrogant demeanor.

Demas came to stand next to Pyrios so that he could observe rest of the hall. "A lot of eligible mares in attendance this evening. Perhaps one of you could win favor with a lady from a prominent herd."

"We've better things to do with our time than flatter society ladies," Phlelgon said dryly.

"Like play secretary?"

"Haven't you anything better to do than dazzle us with your charming company?"

Demas flicked an ear at Pyrios. "Indeed, I do not."

They watched the horses mingle for a little while before Demas spoke again. "I've heard that your brother has gone back to your home stable with his tail between his legs. Such a disgrace. To have so much promise only to be dismissed from the Romanium. He'll be lucky to recover from such an incident."

"The Myrmidons do not place such import on their reputations as the Lipizzans do." Pyrios was speaking through gritted teeth.

"Good thing, that." Demas smiled at one of his Conversano acquaintances. Pyrios had seen this stallion around the Registry and did not care for him. He was older, for one thing, and even as a Conversano he should not be spending so much time with those of the younger generation. As yet Pyrios and Phlegon had been unable to find out the Conversano's name or family stable. As Lipizzans carried the name of their bloodline rather than their sire or dam, it was hard to pinpoint their herd lineage. Lord Kantaka only knew that the stallion had shown up a few weeks prior to Pyrios' arrival in Lipizza.

The Conversano struck Pyrios as being a shady sort of horse. He always spoke in soft, lilting tones and spent a great deal of time ingratiating himself to anyone he thought was in a position of power. So far, he had avoided any close contact with Lord Kantaka or any of the Mongolean stallion's colleagues.

"Who is that Conversano stallion? I've seen him in the Registry but have not had the opportunity to introduce myself." Pyrios spoke on the off chance that Demas would do the polite thing and begin a round of introductions. He was mistaken.

"Oh, he's only an associate of my herd. I don't know him well enough personally to make an introduction."

An obvious lie, but not one that Pyrios could call the other stallion on. He was trying to find another topic to discuss, one that Demas would find too boring to be a part of, when Demas spoke again. "Funny that your brother has not returned home yet. Perhaps he stopped for a little holiday before facing your sire?"

Why was Demas so interested in Thracis? Pyrios was about to say that far from returning to Thetis Stable, Thracis was on his own expedition to find his purpose when a feather-light touch probed his mind. Pyrios immediately erected the psychic wall he used to block unwanted communication. The touch returned, more insistent. Knowing he couldn't deal with the psychic probing and the verbal sparring, Pyrios turned to Demas.

"Forgive me, but I have to excuse myself for a moment. Perhaps we can continue this conversation at another time?"

Demas looked startled that Pyrios would end the conversation so abruptly. Not wishing to create a scene, he said, "Another time, Pyrios. Phlegon."

Phlegon bowed his head at Demas, then waited until the other stallion was out of earshot before turning to Pyrios. "What's the problem?"

"No problem. I really have to excuse myself. Tell Lord Kantaka that I'll be back directly."

Phlegon nodded and watched as Pyrios wove his way through the guests. Pyrios was almost to the halls that would lead him to the servants' areas and privacy, when Nerissa stepped out of an alcove. She deftly crossed in front of him, halting his progress.

"And where are you off to in such a hurry? Going to meet a doe-eyed maid in the servants' quarters?"

She couldn't have caught him at a worse time. The psychic touch on his mind was becoming more adamant. Pyrios struggled to focus his mind on Nerissa, sensing that she was the more dangerous of his two problems.

"I just need to step out for a moment."

"Perhaps I'll join you." She stepped closer. She wasn't wearing any perfume to mask her natural scent and Pyrios' nostrils flared at her proximity. He could smell her excitement and eagerness. He was sure there would be an empty stall close by. They would only be away from the party for a few minutes.

He tossed his head. What in Pandemonium was he thinking? To fantasize about having this mare in the coming weeks was one thing. It was another entirely to be contemplating taking her here at this party where her mate was only a few yards away.

Nerissa, enjoying his indecision, stretched her neck to nuzzle the underside of his jaw. "No one will be the wiser. My mate is talking politics. He won't miss me for hours yet."

Giving in to her advances a little, Pyrios said, "One of the servants might see us."

"I'm sure they can be discreet." Nerissa was lightly biting the bottom curve of his neck. Her breath was warm on his gray coat. He reached out and nipped the top of her shoulder. She responded by pressing close to him and rubbing her cheek against the topline of his neck.

Giving in completely, Pyrios tossed his head in the direction of the servants' quarters. Swishing her tail provocatively, Nerissa led the way to a vacant stall that looked like a closet of some kind. As the literal door shut behind him, Pyrios slammed a mental door on his mind, shutting out the persistent touch for good.

22

CHAPTER 22

Damn stallions and all their incessant urges.

So thought Psyche as she paced around the small stable she shared with Moirae, the Felisian prophetess who had taken Psyche in for instruction of the psychic arts. Moirae was out in the garden meditating and Psyche was supposed to be practicing opening her chakras. Halfway through the mantra she used to center herself, Psyche had seen a vision of Pyrios talking with a gray stallion at a party.

Psyche didn't like the gray stallion at all. His aura was wrong for one thing, too dark. And he was goading Pyrios into giving up information about Thracis. Even though Thracis was safely behind Diomedean borders, that wouldn't stop a strong psychic capable of aural projection. The Baroquian Pact couldn't know Thracis' whereabouts. Not until Thracis had undergone mental training to learn how to protect himself from psychic onslaughts.

Psyche didn't like the stallion Pyrios was looking at either, the older one with the wandering eyes. She was certain he had something to do with Thracis' ambush. Knowing Pyrios was close to losing his temper and telling the gray stallion all he wanted to hear about the younger Thetis stallion, Psyche tried to contact his mind.

At first Pyrios seemed interested in her attempt to garner his attention. Psyche saw him excuse himself from the conversation with the younger gray stallion and then head off on his own after speaking with Phlegon. Pyrios was searching for a quiet place where he could open his mind to her in privacy. He had almost found one when that red dun wench walked out of the alcove. As soon as Psyche saw the mare, she knew Pyrios was lost to her. She tried to contact him more forcefully, but in the end Pyrios shut her off completely.

"Damn them all to Pandemonium," Psyche hissed. She struck a box containing yarn with a foreleg. Bright colored skeins of yarn, material she used for weaving as she relaxed in the evening, flew in every direction. Psyche pinned her ears. "Stupid, ox-brained, *males*."

"I would guess by this show of temper that you've been in contact with your mystery stud."

Psyche's ears flicked toward the door and the bay mare who stood leaning against the frame. "What do you want? I thought you'd be buried in your lab until you succeeded in your venture."

The bay flicked her ears and cocked a back leg. "Even I need a break. My theory is sound. I just have to figure out how to make the solar sails light enough that they can be carried with little trouble."

Pysche's ears pinned at the technical babble. "If your sire knew how close you are to achieving your goal, he'd put a stop to your tampering."

The bay tossed her elegant head. "He wouldn't. He is a stallion of his word. If he says the mares may have the sky, he means it."

"Eno, if horses were meant to fly as Lord Pegasus does, He would have given us wings."

"Spoken like a true oracle."

"That's a laugh. I'm having more difficulty than a first-year student."

Eno, used to Psyche's false modesty, rolled her eyes. "You and I, and everyone else who comes near you for that matter, know that you are the most talented mare in your whole herd. It's a natural talent, yes, and you haven't learned how to focus it yet, but you will. And when you do, the Pact with have an entirely new problem."

Psyche gritted her teeth. "I can't even get a single stallion to pay attention to me."

"Your mystery stud? I thought he was pestering you to distraction."

"Not him. His brother."

Eno cocked her head. "His brother? Flirting with two stallions at once doesn't seem like you. It can be fun, though, if you do it right."

"Only you would jump immediately to the wrong assumption. I think it's because you grew up among the bachelor herds of the Equine military."

"Maybe. My sire always tried to keep me away from the young stallions. Bad influences and all that."

"Too bad he didn't realize you would become the bad influence." Psyche's voice was arid.

Eno laughed. "I'm sure he had an idea. Come on, let's go find something to eat. I want to enjoy some sun before I go back to my self-designed dungeon."

Giving the yarn a passing glance, Psyche followed Eno down the hall and out the back door. The afternoon was warm and fragrant with the scents of Moirae's summer flowers. Psyche breathed deep as she and Eno walked along the mulched path that led to the timothy field behind the stable.

"Such a beautiful day." Eno looked up at the sky. "One day, Psyche, I promise. One day."

Psyche tossed her head, not in negation of Eno's claim, if any Equine was going to learn to fly without spacecraft it would be her, but at the sound of grim determination in the bay mare's voice.

Eno and Psyche had been friends since early in their marehood. They had met at the University of Piber where both had been sent by parents desperate to have a few months peace from their constantly querying daughters. They had shared a stall together and despite differing interests and class agendas, had gotten along from the very first moment.

Eno was the only foal of Commander Talos Dias. Her dam had passed on when Eno was barely a yearling. Even though she had an aunt who would have been more than happy to raise another daughter, Eno had been raised by her sire. Dias had loved his mate deeply and couldn't bear the thought of being separated from his one living link to her. He had tried to raise her as much a lady as he could, but Eno's fundamental nature had soon proved stronger than her sire's determination. Eno was a fighter, through and through. It irritated her to no end that mares were forbidden to enlist in the Equine military. On top of being a capable warrior, Eno was very intelligent and a better strategist than most of Commander Dias' military council. This caused considerable upheaval in Commander Dias' stable.

As a compromise, Dias had made a deal with his quick-witted daughter. Mares, he said, were forbidden to enter the military. On land anyway. If Eno could find a way to give mares wings and allow them to fly as Lord Pegasus did, Commander Dias would sign a decree that the mares could form military ranks in the sky.

Eno had argued that most of the space fleet's pilots were mares already to which her sire had replied that the use of spacecraft in battle on Equus was also forbidden. Eno had seen the loophole her sire was providing. While mares could not engage in military combat on land, there was no law anywhere that said they couldn't fight in the sky.

Aware that she would get no peace from heckling if she began her project in the Hippikon where her sire was the current Asapatish, Eno had spent the last year in Amazonia. With the help of Queen Hippolyta, who was a strong supporter of Eno's proposal, Eno had built a fully equipped laboratory on the outskirts of Ruffiana, the Diomedean capital. It was only a mile or so from Moirae's home, in a secluded meadow with plenty of room for the trials of Eno's many experiments.

Eno had only been in Ruffiana for a year and so far she had made considerable progress. At least in Hippolyta and Psyche's humble opinions. But Eno was a mare with big ideas and little patience. She was also her own worst critic. She had already designed several prototypes, but was finding flaws with each. She had figured out how to use thrusters with circular cooling systems that would grant the mares lift-off if there wasn't a cliff anywhere handy. The cooling systems kept the metal from getting hot where it pressed against the mare's skin. Psyche had been ecstatic with the progress, but Eno had been disgusted that the thruster development had taken so long.

This was another trait Psyche and Eno held in common. Both were intelligent and talented but neither saw their own worth. Eno was building things other horses couldn't even begin to design. Psyche could mentally contact horses all over Equus with minimal discomfort, a feat only the most disciplined psychics could claim. And yet, neither mare was satisfied with her own progress.

Psyche and Eno grazed their way through the middle of the timothy field, the sun warm on their backs. Psyche found herself wondering if it was sunny where Thracis was. Summer was the wet season in Diomedea and dark clouds were already building in the west. She should take some time this evening to contact him. She knew he was hurt by her new aloofness, but she really did have to concentrate on her studies. Well, if Eno was willing to allow herself a break, then Psyche could have a quick conversation and not feel guilty.

"So," Eno said around a mouthful of timothy, "why are you trying to contact your suitor's brother?"

"He's not my suitor. He's just a friend."

"Uh, huh. Why are you talking to his brother?"

Psyche shook her head. "Because he's surrounded by Equines who bear both Thetis stallions ill intentions."

"Stop talking like Miorae and be straight."

"He's a simple-minded idiot that doesn't have the good sense to know that the Baroquians are searching for Thracis' whereabouts."

Eno sniffed. Psyche looked away, shoulders hunching. "Thracis is it? Not the same Thracis who was dismissed from the Romanium?"

"The same and how would you know about that anyway?"

"My sire keeps me well-informed. Besides, no one has been dismissed from the Romanium in years. He must have done something really naughty."

"No. He just didn't have enough sense to pace himself." Psyche's voice held a hint of sorrow. "He has been trying to find his place. A little faster than was prudent."

"Sounds like the two of you have a lot in common."

Psyche pinned her ears. "As do the two of us."

Eno ignored the bait. An argument about who was more driven between the two of them was exactly what Psyche wanted. "My sire agrees with that sediment. He was sorry to see Thracis leave. He also told me that another promising student left the Romanium as well. A stallion named Quintus Aeos."

Psyche nodded. "Thracis' friend. He is interested in the healing arts and has frequent contact with Kamuzu and Alcander."

"Will they be returning soon?" Eno liked both the Felisian and the miniature and had missed their company in the past months.

"Soon enough."

"Did the simple-minded idiot keep his mouth shut?" Eno was referring to Pyrios.

"Yes, but only because a mare intervened."

Eno's shoulders twitched. "Catastrophe avoided."

"Not exactly. She has a union with a stallion already. A stallion of importance given the way she carries herself. I think Pyrios is bolting toward disaster."

"Perhaps he is, but that's none of your concern. You have your own studies to see to. Not to mention this Thracis will likely come looking for you once he gets to Ruffiana." Psyche had told Eno of Thracis' journey to Diomedea.

"I'm not worried about that. He will be stopped in Artemia and with the Baroquians starting trouble with my dam, I'm sure both you and I will be called on to fight."

"I have never fought against warriors in open combat. Have you?"

"In Diomedea society all mares are trained as soldiers. My dam is a firm believer in mock battles. If the Baroquians insist on occupying Diomedea they'll have to invade. That will give my dam all the pretext she needs to begin a full-on assault."

"You sound almost gleeful at the thought of fighting a contingent of heavily armored stallions." Eno felt her own excitement beginning to build.

Psyche turned gleaming eyes on Eno. "It is what I was bred for."

23

CHAPTER 23

"The countryside is very pretty, but do we have anything resembling a plan? Other than going to Sanctuary, I mean."

Aeos flicked his ears at Thracis. The Calabrian was in an exceptionally irritable mood this morning. Not that Aeos could blame him.

Psyche had contacted Thracis last night only to begin a meaningless conversation and then abruptly end it, stating that she had things to do. Annoyed, and not a little bit hurt, Thracis had then tried to contact Pyrios only to be told that he was busy as well and couldn't devote any concentration to the conversation. Furious, Thracis had stomped out of the stall he was sharing with Aeos, slamming the door behind him. Aeos hadn't seen him again until breakfast. He had no idea where Thracis had been and didn't ask. Sometimes it was better not to know.

"Once we reach Sanctuary and I find someone who is willing to take me on as a healing apprentice, I thought I'd ask around and see if there is anyone in Diomedea who would be willing to continue your combat training."

"I didn't think the mares around here would deign to teach a stallion how to fight."

"Approach them with that attitude and I doubt they will."

Thracis pinned his ears and tossed his head. Aeos hoped that would be the end of the conversation, but he was wrong. "Why do we have to go all the way to Sanctuary? I'm sure you can find a teacher here in Artemia."

"Stop whining. You sound like a spoiled colt." Aeos had meant the remark as a flippant attempt to get Thracis to close his mouth. He was stunned at the wounded expression that crossed Thracis' face before the other stallion trotted on ahead down the road.

Aeos sighed. He and Thracis were about the same age, but Thracis seemed so much younger at times. He was still raw from his dismissal from the Romanium and because of that, this was, in Aeos' opinion anyway, the most inconvenient time for Psyche and Pyrios to leave Thracis on his own. Thracis liked Aeos and had shared a lot with the dun stallion, but this bond was nothing compared to the bond he had with Pyrios. Thracis also felt closer to Psyche because she was the one who helped him the most after his poisoning. To be more or less abandoned by them at this moment in his life was something Thracis was having difficulty coping with. As a result, he was becoming sullen and moody.

Aeos trotted up alongside the other stallion. "I'm sorry."

"Don't be. You're right. I've been spending a lot of time feeling sorry for myself."

"Understandable."

"But not acceptable."

"Are you always this hard on yourself?" Aeos thought this was a rhetorical question, but it gave them an avenue.

"Usually."

"That is why you were having trouble learning the combat maneuvers."

Thracis stumbled at that statement, coming to a stop in the middle of the road. "What are you talking about?"

"I'm talking about you. I have to admit, I was as stunned as anyone that you were having such difficulty with the simplest of exercises. After spending this much time with you without any distractions I've figured you out."

"And what conclusion have you reached?"

"That you have too much going on in your head that has nothing to do with you."

Thracis cocked a back leg, perplexed. "I thought we just agreed that I've been feeling sorry for myself."

"We did."

"Wouldn't that be hard if I wasn't thinking about myself as well?"

Aeos swished his tail at a fly. "Did you see that fly? That is a good representation of what I am talking about. Your thoughts are like flies filling your mind with their endless buzzing. What you need to learn is how to swish them away."

"You cannot simply 'swish away' important things."

"Like what? So, Psyche is too busy with her own endeavors and Pyrios is learning the corruptions necessary to be a successful politician. Those are their issues, not yours, and have no reflection on their relationship to you."

"What about my inability to keep up with the rest of the class? That was my issue and mine alone."

"That's not true either. You were weakened from your poisoning and did not have the foundation training you would have gotten if you had already been enlisted in the military."

Thracis' ears flattened. "Neither did you."

Aeos tossed his head. "No, but my teacher at home stable was fluent in military tactics and taught me as he had been taught."

"I should have been able to progress in the training."

"If you had been healthy and sufficiently prepared you would have. As it was you made a heroic effort."

Thracis sighed. "Those just sound like excuses to my ears."

Now it was Aeos' turn to lower his ears. "They are not excuses. They are explanations. And they were aspects out of your control, you must let them go."

"Swish them away?"

Aeos began walking again. "Exactly. A good warrior must have a clear mind. That's what my teacher always said."

Thracis fell in step beside the dun stallion. "So, you don't think I've been a jackass for the last few days?"

"Oh, you've definitely been a jackass. The point is, now you need to get over it."

"You sound like my dam."

"Well, someone has to save you from yourself, Thracis."

They walked on in silence for a few minutes. The day was promising to be hot and sticky, with rain likely in the late afternoon. Sweat was already darkening the stallions' coats where their harness tracings rested. They would stop traveling in an hour or so and rest during the hottest part of the day, making up the lost time in the early evening.

"If I play the meek and humble stallion do you think you could find me a teacher even here?"

Aeos looked sidelong at Thracis. "I think if you just be yourself I can find someone who would be willing to put up with you."

"Psyche did give me a name back in Iliad. She seemed to think he was at the Romanium, but Commander Dias told me that instructor had been exiled."
"Sounds like you already."

Thracis reached over and nipped the top of Aeos' shoulder. This caused Aeos to pin his ears and toss his head in retaliation. Ignoring the threat, Thracis bit Aeos again, harder this time. Aeos returned the favor by swinging his rump around and giving Thracis a quick, painful kick in the hock.

"Ow. That hurt."

"It was meant to."

Thracis snorted and returned to the topic of instruction. "Anyway, his name is Alois Phrenicos. Psyche described him as being 'accustomed to dealing with one such as you', meaning me. I haven't decided if that was a complement or an insult." Thracis was continuing to walk and chatter, oblivious to the fact that Aeos had stopped and was staring after him.

Regaining his composure, Aeos hurried to catch up. "Psyche has met Alois Phrenicos?"

Thracis, still unaware of Aeos reaction, twitched his shoulders. "She didn't say. I would guess she has since she thought he could help me."

"You have no idea who that stallion is, do you?"

"Commander Dias told me he was the Headmaster of the Romanium once."

Aeos snorted. "He wasn't just the Headmaster. He was the descendant of the great Podhajsky who trained under Xenophon, who was instructor to Bucephalus. Xenophon is praised as being the stallion who developed the High Dances and advanced combat maneuvers. You should know this."

"I know all about Xenophon." Thracis ducked his head. "But I didn't really pay much attention after the historians stopped lecturing about Bucephalus. I wasn't a very good student in the academic arena."

"I hadn't noticed."

"If Phrenicos came from such a noble lineage, why would they exile him?"

"Politics most likely," Aeos mused. "I do know that Phrenicos believed in the traditional methods of training. That a student should learn balance and impulsion before moving on to the more complicated movements of combat."

"Balance as in the piaffe and passage?"

Aeos nodded. "And canter pirouettes."

"Why don't they teach those at the Romanium?"

"I was under the impression they did. I was confused by the lack of attention in those areas. But, as you've discovered, balance and impulsion take time and patience, two things seriously lacking at the Romanium. You can't be expected to graduate dozens of warriors a year if you take the time to build their foundations."

"Then why don't they cover balance and impulsion in basic training?"

"Not enough qualified instructors? I don't know. You should have asked Commander Dias."

"He wasn't interested in continuing the conversation," Thracis mumbled.

"I'm sure he wasn't. Exiling Alois Phrenicos could not have been an easy decision."

"Where do you think he went?" Thracis meant Phrenicos. They both knew where Commander Dias resided.

Aeos twitched a shoulder. "Maybe you should contact Psyche and find out. The lady seems to be able to pinpoint the horses we need to find."

"Maybe you should contact her."

Aeos looked at Thracis, startled. Up until now Thracis had been guarding Psyche with open aggressiveness. This was a complete change in attitude. And not one Aeos found reassuring. "Where did you go last night, Thracis?"

Thracis looked away to the field they were passing. "I went for a walk."

"Until morning?"

"What does it matter to you where I went? I'm not a foal who needs minding." The anger in the words masked another emotion.

Aeos proceeded with prudence. "You do know you have no obligations of loyalty to Psyche, don't you?"

Thracis gave Aeos a sharp look before turning back to the field. Aeos sighed. Thracis was going to beat himself for months for one night's indiscretion. And all over a mare who might have no more interest in him than that of a friend or an older brother.

Aeos reached over and nuzzled Thracis' withers. This was a supportive gesture accepted among stallions. "Don't whip yourself too hard. You needed some kind of release, Thracis."

"The same justification Pyrios would use."

"And he would be right in this case." Aeos took a deep breath. "It is not uncommon to seek out the company of a mare for an hour or an evening, especially when a stallion is single and traveling."

"She will never forgive me."

Aeos assumed Thracis was speaking of Psyche and not whoever he had spent the night with. "If she is as wise as you seem to think, she will understand and forgive."

"Why should she?"

Because it's partly her fault you were with that mare in the first place. Deciding Thracis would start kicking at any disrespect to Psyche, Aeos said, "Because she has not given you a clear signal as to her feelings toward you. Besides, she may have other suitors herself."

Thracis pinned his ears at the mention of unknown stallions vying for Psyche's attention, but Aeos felt some of the tension flow out of his friend. Thracis was a grown stallion after all and knew how the game was played. "How do you sug-gest I proceed?"

"I think you should contact her about Phrenicos, but noth-ing more. Give her some space, some time to wonder what you're up to."

"Ignore her, in other words."

"Not ignore. Right now you're available for her whenever she decides to talk to you. Make her think you're unavailable. At least some of the time."

Thracis nodded. "That might work."

"It would also give you insight as to how hard *she's* willing to work to get your attention."

Thracis relaxed even more. He shook his whole body, then turned to look at Aeos. "I think we need to go for a run. A short gallop before it gets too hot to even walk."

Aeos bobbed his head. "You go on. Find a place to eat some-thing and doze the afternoon away."

Thracis nodded and took off at a canter that quickly turned into a gallop. Aeos continued at a fast walk. He was in no hurry to catch up with Thracis. He thought both of them could use some time apart. Thracis had a lot to think about and so did Aeos.

Like the mare that Thracis had spent the night with for in-stance. Was she a black and white pinto? Aeos was willing to bet she was. He was as sure of that as he was that once she and Thracis had gone to her stall, everything that happened after had gone on in the dark. The better for Thracis to imagine he was with someone else.

Would Psyche forgive him? Aeos thought she would. Would Thracis forgive himself? That was a much harder question and one Aeos didn't have a ready answer for. He hoped Thracis would.

Sighing, trying to follow his own advice about not worrying about other horses' problems, Aeos broke into a light canter in search of Thracis.

24

CHAPTER 24

Psyche settled herself on her feet. She was in her stall, preparing to meditate for a few minutes before going to bed. She found she slept better if she took this time to clear her mind. In the past weeks, sleep had become more and more elusive for the young mare.

It had been two days since Eno's visit. Psyche had spent that time refocusing on her studies, much to Moirae's delight. The prophetess was eager for Psyche to move on to more challenging psychic exercises, but understood the need for balance. Psyche needed to learn to quiet her mind before trying any mental calisthenics.

The mare was just slipping into the twilight of meditation when an unfamiliar mind touched hers. Unlike another Equine who was not adept at protecting their innermost selves, Psyche opened the first layer of her mind to this new presence. This was a safe way to contact an unfamiliar touch as the mind was constructed in a series of layers. Each layer wrapped around a

central core that housed the host's inner self. The more profi-
cient the host at the psychic arts, the more layers an intruder
would have to breach to cause damage, expending large
amounts of mental energy. This in turn left the intruder open
to attack.

Who is contacting me? Psyche could tell the presence was
Equine and male, but that was all.

It is Quintus Aeos, Thracis' friend.

Psyche's heart beat faster. She hadn't contacted Thracis
since Eno's visit and that conversation had been short and, she
had to admit it if only to herself, curt. Since then she had been
trying to find a way to contact Thracis and mend any feelings
she may have stomped on, but she had yet to find the right
words.

Is Thracis' well? In her panic to find out about Thracis' health,
Psyche forgot to shield her feelings. She felt Aeos pause before
speaking and could have kicked herself for such a blatant mistake.

Thracis is fine. Caution filled the link between them. *He is
practicing some training maneuvers.*

Her relief was palpable. She sagged on her feet. *Why are you
contacting me?*

*I am curious about your opinion. As you may be aware, I am
traveling to Sanctuary to study the healing arts with the Felisians.*

Among other things. Psyche couldn't hide her amusement.

Yes, but Thracis does not know about those yet.

How prudent.

Tired irritation in the link. *Anyway, I was hoping you might
know the whereabouts of a suitable instructor for Thracis. He has in-

formed me that you have suggested a celebrated instructor and may know where to find him.

I do. I also think you should stay with Thracis. For the time being anyway. I feel it would be wise.

Then I will.

Psyche tossed her head. She liked this stallion who had the good sense to know when to yield. *You will find Alois Phrenicos in the town of Boudica, on the southern coast of Amazonia.*

Thank you, good lady. A pause, then, *Did you know of Phrenicos' exile before we traveled to Lipizza?*

Sometimes the road we must travel has many sharp stones. This wasn't really an answer, but Psyche thought Aeos was smart enough to understand her meaning.

Is this road something you have seen?

No, it was something my instructor has seen. Psyche allowed some emotion into the link. *She has been helping me decipher the things I have seen regarding Thracis and those around him.*

That's good. I would imagine her view is a little more objective.

Psyche started and prepared to throw her own mental dart, but before she could formulate a satisfactory retort, the link was broken. Stomping a foot in frustration, Psyche stood in her stall, fuming. No way in Pandemonium was she going to sleep well tonight.

That was an informative conversation, Aeos thought as he watched Thracis canter in a slow tempo in a large volte. Thracis was progressing well with his collection and was more than ready to try a piaffe.

Aeos couldn't believe the cautious way Psyche and Thracis were stepping around each other. Their mutual attraction was obvious. They would save each other a great deal of headache if they would just admit their feelings. After his contact with Psyche, Aeos didn't fault Thracis in the least for seeking out female company. The *ammoni* mare was enough of an enigma to drive any stallion to distraction. He wondered if she had ever made the same emotional slip with Thracis. Aeos shook his head. She couldn't have, if she had Thracis would have never even looked at another mare.

If Psyche had any problem with Thracis sharing a night with another mare, Aeos would be quick to point out that Psyche had brought that pain on herself by not letting Thracis at least think his advances would be welcome. Aeos wondered if all Diomedean mares were so careful with their emotions. He thought maybe. In their society, where formal unions with stallions were still frowned upon, most mares had probably been conditioned to keep their hearts closed. A shame, for them and the stallions they were turning away.

Thracis completed the volte and walked toward the tree Aeos was standing under. Thracis hung his head low to stretch his neck and back muscles. Ten feet from Aeos, he removed his armor harness and dropped to the ground for a thorough roll. Getting up, Thracis shook bits of grass from his coat and put his harness back on. Since the ambush, neither he nor Aeos took off their armor for more than a few minutes when they were out in the wilds and never at the same time.

"I have had words with your lady," Aeos said mildly. It had been Thracis' idea for Aeos to contact Psyche after all, but that didn't mean he was comfortable with such intimate communication.

"And did she give you the information you wanted?" The tone was neutral.

"She did. We are to circumvent Sanctuary and move on toward the southern coast of Amazonia until we reach the coastal town of Boudica."

"We? I thought you wanted to learn about stitching and bone mending." The neutrality was giving way to anger, but not a hot anger. Aeos thought it was more a frustrated anger. Maybe because Psyche was more agreeable with him instead of Thracis.

"She thought we should stay together for a little while longer. I was under the impression that things are a little tumultuous around here."

This was a topic Thracis was willing to discuss. "The mares at the Andromedan Gate said the Baroquian Pact is trying to establish a military force in Diomedea. I would guess things are going to get way passed tumultuous before the Pact takes the hint to find another stationing point."

"Have you spoken to Pyrios lately? I wonder how the trade agreements are fairing in the council chamber."

Thracis shook his head. "Pyrios keeps pushing me away. In my experience that means my brother is pursuing a chosen mare. He'll be focused for a few days more or even a week and then he'll lose interest until the next lithe female crosses his path." If Thracis had any idea about the mare his brother was currently pursuing, he wouldn't have been so quick to make such a claim about Pyrios' attention span.

"In that case, maybe we should push a little harder to get to this town. My guess is the coastal towns will be the first to engage the Baroquians if they intend to force their way into Diomedea."

Thracis nodded. "A good idea. Whatever their feelings toward stallions, even the mares around here would welcome an extra set of hooves in a fight."

"Or maybe they'll use us as bait."

For some reason, that comment didn't strike Thracis or Aeos as being especially amusing.

25

CHAPTER 25

A tired but contented Thracis stopped at the top of a gentle rise that looked down at the town of Boudica. The town was not directly on the water, as some were, but about a mile from the ocean. It was more of a hamlet than the sprawling towns of Lipizzania and Myrmidonia. The buildings were both large and small with delicate crosswalks connecting many of the roofs. It was in this way that Thracis and Aeos learned that Boudica had just as many Felisian inhabitants as Equines.

This was common among coastal towns. Equines did not eat fish but did enjoy soups and salads made from kelp and succulent seaweeds. Felisians could do without the plants but loved fish. Both species benefited greatly from these symbiotic settlements. As Felisians were also adept sailors, the ports of these towns and villages were centers for trading between ocean-bordered countries. Equines could and did sail, but preferred not to. If the Baroquians planned to invade Diomedea, the sea would be their best approach. If and when the battle ensued, the Felisians' prowess on the water would be invaluable.

"That must be the place. It's the only town we've seen for days." Aeos tossed his head back the way they had come. "I was beginning to think that Felisian trader had sent us on a squirrel hunt."

"He did have a strange scent, didn't he?" Thracis replied. They started toward the town.

"Yes, but that could have been a mixture of the assorted herbs he was peddling."

Thracis snorted at the memory.

The Felisian, a short, tubby tabby, had been pushing a cart filled to bursting with various fresh and dried herbs. Singly, some of the plants smelled rather nice, Thracis did see several species he recognized, but strewn together as they were made a noxious fragrance that brought tears to the eyes. To make matters worse, the Felisian wasn't content to merely give the two stallions directions. No, he wanted to sit and gab about Diomedea's current politics, while his merchandise baked in the sun releasing even more pungent fumes.

"There had to have been something wrong with his nose," Thracis opined.

"Maybe he burned all his scent glands from inhaling too much of his product." Aeos cocked his head. "He had a healthy amount of dried alfalfa under that curtain around the cart's lower half."

Alfalfa, the Equus miracle plant that was the cause of the Baroquian strife, had a great many practical uses. It also had a great many recreational attributes depending on what it was mixed with.

"I'm beginning to think that it's not the alfalfa itself that so important," Aeos mused. "I thing the plant is simply a catalyst of sorts. Or maybe an intensifier."

"But we use pure, concentrated alfalfa as an energy source."

"True, but it works much better if it's mixed with other compounds."

Thracis nodded. He didn't know much about the science of alfalfa, but he was basically aware of how it worked. Since Thetis Stable's technology was solar powered, Thracis didn't have much experience with alfalfa. Alfalfa compounds were mostly used as energy for spacecraft where solar and wind power couldn't be utilized. He wondered if the Caprians were interested in the plant's technological or recreational qualities.

"Have you ever used alfalfa for recreation?" Thracis didn't really expect an answer. It was the kind of question Aeos habitually evaded.

"A couple of times. It's effects are very different depending on what other plants it's been cut with."

Thracis was speechless.

Aeos turned his head slightly to look at Thracis. "Surprised?"

"A little. A lot actually. You don't strike me as being much of a risk-taker. And you seem much to, to..."

"Disciplined?"

"Reserved."

Aeos laughed. "I'm not always reserved. I like to relax and be stupid from time to time. Unfortunately, with you around somebody has to be mature."

Thracis tossed his head. "I don't believe you ever relax."

"If we ever stop moving for more than a day or so and in a place where even you can't find any trouble, I'll find the chance to unwind."

"I'll believe it when I see it."

They had reached the entrance posts for Boudica. The town's name was displayed on a long piece of driftwood decorated with colorful seashells and whimsical drawings.

"Are you sure this is the right place?" Thracis sniffed the sign. It smelled like someone had doused it with flowered perfume. He sneezed.

"Psyche said Boudica."

"Seems a little more artistic that I had imagined."

Aeos twitched a shoulder and continued into town. The town itself was a collection of expressed creativity. Every building was covered with bright colors painted in various mosaics. Primitive, quirky sculptures adorned storefronts and walkways or peered down from the catwalks that crisscrossed overhead. The smells of smoked fish and drying kelp were thick in the air. They mixed with the scents of herbs in a complementing fashion that had been present on the Felisian peddler's cart.

A gang of foals, the oldest perhaps eight months, cantered through the center of town, Felisian kittens clinging to their backs with mental straps. One of the foals, a dark filly, nearly collided with Thracis before swerving away. The kitten on her back slid sideways before righting itself.

"You youngsters stop tearing around here like a pack of heinas." This shrill cry came from a Felisian female sitting on a burlap pedestal and weaving a net.

With a look at Thracis, Aeos approached the Felisian.

"Can I help you colts?" The female's voice was cool, suspicious.

"We certainly hope so." Aeos tried to sound as pleasant as possible. "We are looking for Alois Phrenicos. We were told he resides near here."

The Felisian's dexterous paws halted in their weaving. "That he does. But he doesn't train anymore. Sorry."

"I think he will make an exception. This stallion," Aeos nodded at Thracis, "was sent here by the Lady Hippolyta Psyche. It was she who told us to seek out Phrenicos."

The Felisian's almond eyes regarded Aeos for a moment before switching to Thracis. Thracis felt a strange fluttering in his mind, as if a butterfly had gotten trapped in his head. He mentally recoiled from that touch. The Felisian smiled. "You speak the truth." She nodded down the street. "Go on down to the tavern and have a drink. I'll see if I can locate Phrenicos."

The two stallions followed her directions. Thracis looked back over his shoulder, but the pedestal was empty.

That was strange, he thought at Aeos.

You've never had your mind probed before?

Not like that.

Aeos tossed his head. *The Felisians are much more subtle in their psychic endeavors than Equines.* He led the way into the tavern.

The tavern was set to both Equine and Felisian standards. High round tables dotted the lower floor. The second floor was an open balcony fashioned with smaller tables surrounded by the short pedestals Felisians favored. Three discreet ramps led to the second story, all far too small for any Equine. The tavern was empty at this time of day with the fishing boats still out on the water and farmers still out in their fields. A couple of ceiling fans paddled the salt-laden air.

Aeos and Thracis walked across the room to the bar. A gruff Clydesdale with a patch covering her left eye was restocking the liquor shelves. Sitting on the Clydesdale's rump and taking careful inventory on a pawheld electronic device, was a calico Felisian. The Felisian was wearing a bandana that covered the top of her head but had holes to allow her ears to protrude. Familiar with it as he was since Thetis Stable was home to several Felisians, Thracis just couldn't get used to their habit of wearing articles of clothing.

"What'll you have?" The Clydesdale's voice was a deep rumble.

"Two gallons of mead if you please." Aeos produced his bag of creos and lay it on the counter. The bag was considerably lighter than it had been at the start of this journey, as was the one Thracis carried. If they planned on staying in town for any length of time they would have to mind a way to make money. They could contact their parents and ask that they send them some money. Equines did have a carrier service that used technology to move parcels about the planet and Thracis was sure their parents wouldn't mind the request, but it was important to both stallions that they do as much on their own as possible.

The Clydesdale shifted slightly to look farther down the bar. Two buckets floated just below a huge barrel of mead. The Clydesdale opened the spigot and filled first on bucket and then the other before floating them over to set them in front of Aeos and Thracis.

"Four creos."

Aeos paid the barkeep then secured the pouch back to his harness. During all this the calico watched the two stallions with undisguised curiosity.

"See something green?" Thracis flicked an ear at the calico. The Clydesdale had resumed her stocking but her ears were pointed back in the stallions' direction.

"That harness is pure achillium. We don't see much of that around here."

"It was a gift."

"Was it now?" Her orange ears flicked back and forth.

"From my sire." Thracis was aware that he and Aeos were no longer alone in the tavern. A group of four mares had walked in and were standing between the stallions and the door.

"We didn't come here to start trouble. We're just looking for someone." Aeos shifted his weight back on his hindquarters. He was looking at the Clydesdale, but his words were directed at everyone in the tavern.

"So we've been told." The voice came from behind them.

"We don't get many strangers through here anymore." A second voice joined the first.

"Especially not ones with such expensive equipment." This third voice was edged in sarcasm.

Not liking the idea of having the Clydesdale and Felisian behind him, but needing to face the newcomers, Thracis turned around. Aeos continued to watch the barkeep and sip his mead.

The four mares had spread out and were forming a semi-circle in the center of the room. They were all wearing armor harnesses. Thracis would bet that their armor was equipped with plenty of weapons as well. All the mares looked ready for a fight.

Thracis tried to be diplomatic. "Listen, we're from Myrmidonia, not from Baroquia. We're only looking for Alois Phrenicos."

"How are we supposed to know you're telling the truth? Kebi searched your mind and knows you're hiding something." This came from a palomino on the left.

"What right she have to poke about my mind without my consent?" Thracis felt his temper rising.

"Every right given the spies that have been frequenting the countryside as of late," the gray mare next to the palomino snarled.

Thracis felt the tension in the room edging ever closer to the breaking point. Trying to avoid a conflict, he spoke more evenly. "I would have been willing to let her search me if only she had asked permission."

"As if a stallion ever waits for permission." Until that moment, Thracis had been focusing more on the palomino than any of her companions. The pure fury in that sentence had him swinging his head around to face the diminutive black mare on his right. Too late he remembered that a Diomedean's color was directly proportional to her psychic ability. He didn't need to see into her mind to know that this mare had been hurt. Badly. And she was just looking for someone to vent her rage against.

Bowing as low as he could without dropping his eyes from the black mare, Thracis said, "I apologize if I said anything out of turn. If you wish to know the truth of why we are here, I invite you to check my mind."

Thracis heard Aeos' sharp intake of breath behind him. The other mares were exchanging shocked glances, but Thracis never let his gaze fall from the black mare's. Thracis knew he was taking a risk by allowing this mare, the *ammoni* mare, to use the Felisian term, access to his mind. He would be leaving himself open to a psychic assault that he had no hope of combating.

The black mare shifted her feet. "Very well. If what you say about knowing Psyche is true, then you know the danger you are putting yourself in."

At that, Aeos turned around. The sudden movement made all the females in the room pin their ears. "Don't do this, Thracis. Let her search my mind. She can tear you apart."

Thracis flicked an ear at Aeos. "If she is honorable, she will not."

"What would you know of my honor?" The mare's voice was a challenge.

"Fine, I'll speak in practicality then. I do know Hippolyta Psyche and if you destroy my mind on a whim, she will retaliate against you."

For the first time, the black mare looked uncertain. "I will only search as much as I must to ensure you are telling the truth."

Thracis nodded. He forced himself to relax. He immediately felt her mind brush against the first layer of his own. He withdrew more out of habit than reaction. The black mare pinned her ears. Thracis took a deep breath.

The mare brushed against the first barrier again. Thracis allowed her access. He could feel her mental hooves sorting through all the thoughts at the front of his mind. Not finding what she sought, the black mare pushed against the next barrier. Fighting his instinct to strengthen against deeper invasion, Thracis opened the second barrier. This was as deep as he ever let anyone get, even his parents.

The black mare sensed his discomfort at having her this deep within his mind. She realized that he did not understand that a mind had many more than three or four layers and that he could add or subtract layers at will.

Part of her, the wounded, angry part that she kept hidden, wanted to rip through his barriers and violate him as she had been violated. She was sure she could mend any broken fences with Lady Psyche should the other mare become angry. Another part of her, the part that was trying to heal itself and follow the teachings of her mentors, told her to remain polite. This was not the stallion who had hurt her, he was just a horse counting on her to do the right thing.

She stayed in his mind a little longer, finding out that his friend had spoken the truth. The mare also found the memory of the ambush, still fresh in Thracis' mind as well as the shame of his dismissal from the Romanium. This was something she would not share with her herdmates. She found his memories of speaking with Psyche but did not inspect the conversations.

While connected to him, she took the opportunity to speak privately. *While you are here it would do you good to learn some basic psychic defenses from a master.*

She withdrew then and turned to her companions. "He truly is looking for Phrenicos and is not associated with the Pact. The Baroquians have already tried to kill him in point of fact, and on Levadian soil at that."

This statement drew startled murmurs from the other mares. The Felisian behind Thracis raised her voice to be heard above the excited chatter. "Are you the one who intrigues the *ammoni?*"

Thracis twitched his shoulders. "I guess. I haven't spoken with any other seers besides Psyche."

"You'll meet plenty now that you're here," the Clydesdale commented in her rumbling voice.

The black mare tossed her head. "I am Alcina. This is Dysis, Echo, and Haidee." Each mare bobbed her head in turn. Alcina nodded at the bar. "That is Titania the barkeep and her friend Neema. You may as well start learning who your neighbors are since you plan on staying around for a while."

"Whether we stay or not will depend on Phrenicos' decision as to whether he will teach me anything. I am Thracis and this is Aeos." Thracis followed Alcina's lead in keeping the introductions informal.

"Oh, he will train you. The *ammoni* of Boudica will see to it." Neema examined her curved claws.

"Do the *ammoni* know why Thracis is so important to the Pact?" Aeos had turned back to the mead now that the threat was over.

"That is something you will have to ask the dephae, the head of the *ammoni* coven in this village." Neema was watching Thracis with amber eyes.

"I will want to speak with her," Thracis said between sips of mead. "But first I want to meet Phrenicos."

"After you finish your drink I will show you his home." Alcina settled herself at a table where she could watch the stallions at the door. The other three mares, knowing a dismissal when they heard it, walked back out into the sunlight.

"You seem more at ease," Aeos commented.

"I've nothing to fear from the two of you. You are not the ones who threaten our shores."

26

CHAPTER 26

"Well, isn't this a pleasant surprise. And what do I owe for the honor of a visit from the Lady Alcina?"

Thracis stared at the stallion destined to be his instructor. He felt his heart sink.

Alois Phrenicos, far from being the tall, muscular, dominant stallion Thracis had been picturing, was a small, compact, and almost mincing individual. Phrenicos wore the pure white coat of most older Lipizzans, with a few strands of white mane still sprouting from his slender neck. His chest was adequate, his back short, his stocky legs almost straight. Thracis wondered if their slight crookedness was a result of genetics or injury.

Alcina tossed her head at Aeos and Thracis. "I've brought you something, Phrenicos. A couple of colts in search of discipline. They are Thracis and Aeos." She introduced them as they had been introduced to her, without their sires' names.

Phrenicos turned his attention to Thracis and Aeos. He looked at them with measuring eyes, spending significantly more time on Thracis. His gaze wandered over Thracis' neck and the shadows of scars under his copper coat. "What happened?"

"I was attacked by a warrior in barbed armor. We were locked together and I could not escape."

"You obviously did."

Thracis tossed his head. "It was an act of desperation, not calculation."

"Many of the maneuvers trained at the Romanium were born of desperation." Phrenicos shifted his eyes to Aeos. "How is it that you were unharmed in the attack?"

Aeos shifted his feet. "I was fortunate enough not to face a combatant with superior armor. I also have more experience than Thracis, though only marginally."

"Will you teach us?" Thracis tried to keep from sounding desperate.

"Perhaps. First, I will hear why one who has such talent was dismissed from the Romanium." Phrenicos shifted to stand hipshot.

Thracis' eyes slid to Alcina. He did not know that she had seen his dismissal clearly in his mind. Alcina cleared her throat. "If you can handle these two, I really should be heading back to Boudica. We've had word that fishercats have spotted Baroquian ships."

Phrenicos pinned his ears at the news. "Very well. Contact me once you have more information."

Alcina bowed her head. She nodded at Thracis and Aeos before turning and cantering back the way they had come. Thracis waited until her hoof beats faded before beginning his story.

"I was dismissed because I could not keep up with my fellow students." Thracis heard Aeos shift beside him, but the dun stallion kept silent.

"And why could you not keep pace?" Phrenicos voice was mild, almost uninterested.

"Because I did not train hard enough."

Thracis jumped back as Phrenicos' head snaked toward him. "Wrong, foolish colt. You were unable to keep up because you did not give your body the respect necessary for proper healing before whipping yourself to exhaustion."

Thracis stared at Phrenicos. Did everyone he meet think he was an idiot? He didn't have to turn an eye to see the smug look of satisfaction on Aeos' face.

Phrenicos was shaking his head. "You'll have to learn a fair amount of patience before moving on to combat training."

"We've been working on that," Aeos said in his customary arid tone.

"Have you made any progress?"

Aeos sighed in dramatic fashion. "He's getting better, but you know how these Calabrian's are, think they know it all."

This elicited a short, snorting laugh from Phrenicos. "Perhaps you are not a lost cause after all, young Thracis."

"Does that mean you will give me a chance?"

"I will teach you until you give me reason not to."

"I thank you."

"And I as well," Aeos interjected. "I've seen Thracis in combat. He has talent, but needs guidance. It would be a shame for him not to fulfill his potential."

"And what of you? Do you wish for instruction as well?"

Aeos waited a moment before answering. "I do, but I warn you, my true interest lies in healing."

Phrenicos looked at Aeos a little too long before tossing his head and giving his body a thorough shake. "Well, since it looks as though the two of you will be staying with me for a little while I'd best get you settled."

He turned and began to walk along a path lined with driftwood. They had met Phrenicos on the beach as he was gazing out over the water. Thracis assumed that this path must lead to the old stallion's stable.

The path wove through a grove of tall pines, their needles a dark, almost blue-green color. The grove was free of underbrush and Thracis could see glints of the teal ocean beyond the white beach. He felt a pang of homesickness. He wondered what his herd was doing, how his sister was faring.

The three horses crossed a sunlit meadow with a few summer flowers. Late butterflies fluttered from blossom to blossom. The grass had a green smell, warm against the cool scent of the dark earth in which it grew. The whole area projected a sense of peace and tranquility.

Phrenicos led them to a modest stable with several stalls. On the roof were half a dozen solar panels, leading Thracis to believe Phrenicos enjoyed the convenience of electricity. A field on the left side of the stable was rich with timothy and orchard grasses. The right side of the stable boasted a water garden. Like the stable it was modest. Thracis counted three wind chimes hanging over the gurgling streams and still pools. He wondered where the training arena was.

Phrenicos guided them to the door and invited them inside. The interior of the stable was spacious and decorated with humble but elegant furniture. Dark-wooded bookcases and tables, simply carved lamps holding light globes. The floor was the rubber textured footing favored by Equines. This floor was a combination of dark and light browns worked together in an eye-catching pattern of swirling geometric shapes.

The main room was a combination living room, dining room, and kitchen. Thracis could see plenty of lights, but they wouldn't be necessary until the sun went down. Three large windows, open to let in the summer warmth, allowed the sun to bathe the room in golden light.

"The guest stalls are down this hall." Phrenicos led them down a short hall to two stalls separated by a wash stall. The stalls were identical. Both were large with one dresser, a bedding box, a small table, and two large windows. Thracis chose the stall on the right that overlooked the back of the stable and the large training arena.

Aeos inspected the small table and the top of the dresser in his own stall. "Someone has burned sage here and often."

"A lot of my guests come here to find the peace they need for meditation." Phrenicos tilted his head. "I have an herb garden and drying room on the far side of the water garden. You are welcome to choose and dry your own herbs and flowers if you wish."

Aeos bobbed his head. "I would like that very much. I will need something to burn the mixtures in, however."

"I can take you down to the beach during the low tide so that you may harvest your own abalone shell. You can purchase these shells in Boudica, but the *ammoni* believe it's better for you to dig in the sand to find the shells which call to you."

Lowering his voice so that Thracis wouldn't hear, Aeos said. "Will you teach me?"

Phrenicos shook his head. "That is a task for the *ammoni*. They can teach you all you wish to know. I will see that you meet the *dephae*."

"Thracis does not know of my…interest in the psychic arts."

"Don't worry. I will keep him so busy in the coming months that he won't have time to wonder about your whereabouts."

"Why do you not cover at least part of the arena?" Thracis had come in to stand behind Phrenicos.

Phrenicos turned his head. "Because I view a rainy day as a gift from Lord Pegasus to relax and reflect." He gave Thracis a shrewd look. "Besides, do you think battles are only fought on sunny days with pleasing winds?"

Shaking his head, Thracis went back to his own stall. Aeos sniffed his bedding box. "You have bedding available or do we have to get some from town?"

"I can have a load of shavings sent up from the village if you like, but I use fresh grasses in the spring and summer and hay in the fall and winter. I find those materials more inviting than wood chips."

"I do as well."

Thracis had left his stall and was inspecting the books lining the shelves of the living room. Aeos joined him. Phrenicos walked into the kitchen and opened the pantry. "I'll have to go into the village tomorrow and buy some more grain. If there is anything special either of you need, I suggest you come with me. By tomorrow everyone in town will want to get a good look at you."

Aeos nodded. "I do want a few things."

Thracis was still looking at the books. "May I read some of these?"

Phrenicos came to stand in the center of the three rooms. "If you are careful. Many of them are first editions and very old."

"It's an impressive collection." Aeos spoke with true admiration.

"It's taken me years to assemble. I enjoy a good read in the evening. It eases the mind."

Thracis turned from the bookshelf. "So, when do we begin? Do you want me to show you how much I already know?"

The older stallion gave a slight smile at the youthful impatience. "We begin now. Follow me."

Phrenicos led them out of the stable via the back door. The arena, while uncovered, was surrounded by tall sprawling trees that kept the shade all day with the exception of an hour before and after noon. The footing was heavy sand, not too deep, that would help keep feet from slipping while building muscle. The sand was a mixture that gave it a taupe color that wouldn't reflect the sun's glare. The perimeter was designated by long, twisted pieces of driftwood laid end to end.

Thracis trotted out to the center of the arena, getting a feel for the footing. Phrenicos stood at the arena's edge and watched Thracis trot a few circles around the perimeter before speaking. "Nice texture, isn't it?"

"It's exquisite."

"I'm glad you like it. Now I'd appreciate if you would get your tail out of there." The white stallion didn't raise his voice at all, but it still carried a whip crack command.

Confused and embarrassed, Thracis walked to the edge of the arena with his tail drooping. "I apologize for any offense I have committed."

Head high, looking down at the copper stallion standing with lowered head, Phrenicos finally resembled the Headmaster he once was. "You, Thracis of Calabria, have not yet earned the right to set foot in a master's ring. To work in this, my arena, you must first prove your worth."

Thracis lowered his head even more.

"Come this way, foolish colt, and see where you will be training."

Without lifting his head, Thracis fell in step behind Aeos as Phrenicos walked a path that led alongside the arena. They passed the drying room, Aeos gave it a speculative glance but didn't pause for fear of reprimand, and stopped at a much less grand arena more or less hidden under years of leaves, brush, and stomach high grass.

This arena was set out in the open where the summer sun would bake on the back and withers. The footing was the same heavy sand, but it was much deeper and more white than gray. The lighter color would make the sun's light shine bright, dazzling the eyes and skewing perception. The perimeter was designated by rectangular cement beams.

Clip those with a hoof and you'd be lame for a day, Thracis thought as he surveyed the ruined schooling ring with a sinking stomach.

Phrenicos stood at the arena's edge. He tossed his head expansively. "This is where you will earn respect."

Aeos and Thracis exchanged a look. The schooling rings in the Romanium were a luxury compared to this wreck.

Taking a deep breath, Thracis said, "Where would you like us to put the refuse from the cleaning?"

Phrenicos' laughter was rich and came straight from his stomach. "You see, young Thracis, you are learning already."

CHAPTER 27

Thracis stood in one corner of the water garden. Phrenicos was out walking along the beach and Aeos was sorting herbs in the drying room. Thracis would have much rather been in the training ring perfecting the trot patterns he and Aeos were learning, but Phrenicos had ordained that each stallion spend at least one hour a day in meditation. This was an exercise Aeos embraced with enthusiasm. Thracis viewed it as slow punishment. It chafed him to have to stand in one place and force himself to relax when a hundred different things he'd rather be doing galloped through his mind.

He sighed and shifted his feet. He hated it, but this was his hour and he would get through it.

They had been with Phrenicos for almost a month and Thracis liked to think he was making some headway. Phrenicos had set the pace to be abominably slow, but any time Thracis raised the possibility of speeding things up a little, it resulted in the instructor slowing the lesson even more. Phrenicos refused to allow Thracis to race through his exercises, stating that perfection takes time and patience.

Aeos was quite agreeable to the relaxed atmosphere and enjoyed taking the time to make sure his voltes were the exact same size and his canter changes flawless. Thracis was finding that Phrenicos was pleased only if an exercise was performed correctly. He was quick to chastise if Thracis sped through a lesson in his urgency to complete it.

The problem was, Thracis *wanted* to perform the exercises in the correct manner, he just couldn't seem to corral his mind long enough to focus on one thing at a time. Thus, the daily hour of meditation had begun. Phrenicos believed, as did Aeos, that a good warrior needed a clear mind. He told Thracis that before he could continue with the training, he must learn to calm his bolting thoughts.

Over the past month, Thracis had learned the foundation he had been seeking at the Romanium. Every morning after breakfast, he and Aeos spent twenty to thirty minutes stretching and limbering themselves before beginning their trotting drills. They then spent as long as they wished trotting at various speeds, making sure to warm their muscles before starting to hold themselves in collection. From this point, Phrenicos insisted they focus on their balance and the patterns he had described to them.

The patterns, all performed at a collected trot, were meant to drill the stallions in forward and lateral work. Voltes, serpentines, renvers, travers, zigzags, and half-passes. Thracis' mind danced with the graceful movements. His body moved from side to side, his front and back legs leaving identical parallel lines in the heavy sand. His neck, the wounded muscles stretching and loosening with the lateral movements, was becoming limber and strong. From the simple shoulder-in wherein Thracis' neck and head were bent in the opposite direction than the one in which his curved body was moving, the Calabrian stallion had graduated to the renvers. This movement was like a shoulder-in or half-pass, but instead of looking to the inside curve of his body, Thracis' head was turned in the direction he was moving while his body remained in a gentle curve. This was a difficult movement and had taken days to learn correctly. It still pained Thracis if he performed too many renvers but his muscles were slowly limbering.

Once he was satisfied with their progress on collection and lateral movements, Phrenicos took each of them in turn and began to instruct Thracis and Aeos in the first steps of the piaffe.

At first glance, this movement looked as though it should be easy to accomplish. To Thracis it simply looked as though Phrenicos was trotting in place. How hard could that be? To his dismay, Thracis found that checking his forward impulsion, keeping his collection, and making sure to move his legs up and down in a fluid movement was tricky to say the least. It was also very tiring. When they first began, Thracis found he could only manage a few steps at a time. Phrenicos told Thracis and Aeos that they must first be able to perform the piaffe for five minutes at a time without stopping before he would move them on to the slower, but more difficult passage. At this point, neither Thracis or Aeos could piaffe for more than thirty seconds without losing their focus. After beginning the piaffe, both stallions were happy to return to soothing patterns and rhythms of the trotting patterns.

To be honest, Thracis found it easier to clear his mind as he moved through the established trot patterns. If he were working alone, Thracis could easily lose himself for an hour or more. His feet followed the patterns without his even being aware of it. As he let his mind and body relax, his movements became less strained, less forced. Thracis glided across the arena as if he had wings on his hooves. Of course, neither Aeos or Phrenicos had brought this solace to Thracis' attention for fear the Calabrian would become self-conscious. This was another reason Phrenicos insisted on a quiet hour of meditation in the garden.

Thracis' ears flicked back and forth as he listened to the everyday sounds of the water garden. The bubbling streams and twinkling wind chimes created lilting music. Birds chattered in the trees, insects buzzed in the high timothy, the distant sound of the ocean, all these stirrings rounded out the natural orchestra. The whole scene was perfectly serene, if listening to the voices of nature was his thing, Thracis would have been in Tranquility, the land where all the gods that ever were resided and all good Equines would travel after their passing. However, it wasn't and Thracis' felt as though he were in a forgotten corner of Pandemonium.

You haven't spoken to me much as of late.

Thracis tossed his head. *I've been busy.*

Too busy for a quick hello? The link held a resonance of Psyche's anger.

It seems you have been. Thracis quipped. He was unused to her temper. He had never encountered it before without its customary amusement.

An image of Psyche appeared in his mind. Her ears were lowered but not pinned. She raised her head and tilted it, her forelock falling to partially cover her left eye. *I have, but that doesn't mean you can't tell me what you've been doing?*

Thracis felt his skin tingle. This didn't seem like the Psyche he knew. She had never pried before. She had always seemed to know what he was up to.

The mare dropped her head and looked up at him from beneath her lashes. *Why don't you imagine yourself here?* The voice in his head was coy, flirtatious. *I can show you a few things about mental linkage that I'm sure no one has shared with you yet.* She swished her tail.

Thracis was stunned. Psyche had yet to give him permission to court her and now she was practically throwing herself at him. Aeos must have been right; some mares must like a stallion who behaved with a certain amount of aloofness. Thracis almost imagined himself in the mist with the black and white mare, but something in the back of his mind, far from the psychic link, told him to wait.

Psyche fidgeted. *Something the matter?*

You seem very...playful for someone who usually keeps her distance.

I've been talking with some of my friends. They suggested I should explore other possibilities with you than simple friendship. She turned slightly, giving him a wonderful view of her muscled flank.

Thracis felt his resolve to be cautious start to waver. She looked so appealing, so close and welcoming. He had just begun his meditation; Aeos and Phrenicos would give him privacy for at least another three quarters of an hour.

Psyche felt his longing through the link. She turned back to face him and lowered her head even more. *I'm waiting for you, Thracis.*

It was the use of his name that snapped Thracis out of his near trance. He shook his head, not breaking the link but trying to ground himself. This wasn't Psyche. Thracis didn't know who or what it was, but it was not the black and white mare from Iliad.

The mare, feeling his refusal through the link, pinned her ears. She snapped her teeth. *Don't think you can escape me, stallion of Thetis Stable.*

Thracis recoiled, trying to break the link. Too late he realized that he was tangled in some kind of mental net. His own mind fought to free itself. It was a terrible sensation, this scrambled feeling. Even as his mind struggled to get away from the mist and the creature that hid in Psyche's guise, Thracis could feel cold sweat breaking out on his body despite the warmth of the summer sun. It was like being stuck in a nightmare from which he could not wake. Panic soared through him.

What are you? Thracis could feel his panic broadcasting through the link.

The mare cocked her head. *I am anyone you want me to be.*

Thracis felt her lust and yearning through the mental connection. It sickened him. *I don't want you.*

The mare snapped her teeth at him again. Thracis felt a sharp mental stab that made his mind quiver. *This could have been a pleasant experience for you, stallion of Thetis Stable. Now I will take pleasure in hearing your mind shriek as I find all the information my superiors require.*

Thracis redoubled his efforts to free himself. The mare laughed, delighted by his tenacity. Thracis felt her mental hooves hammering the barriers at the first layer of his mind. Thinking of Alcina, Thracis immediately began putting up as many layers as he could between his core and the thing trying to rip him apart. In desperation, he tried to contact Aeos or Phrenicos.

The mare smiled. Her image kept wavering, as if was difficult for her to remain disguised. *Cry all you want, little rabbit. No one will hear you.*

Thracis ignored her taunts and reached for his body. It was still standing as before, a husk basking in afternoon light. Thracis tried to make his limbs do something, anything. They refused to obey his commands, the mare had blocked him somehow. Thracis had never encountered this kind of battle before, he felt helpless. All his weeks and months of physical training were useless in a mental battle.

The mare had bulled her way into his first layer, Thracis could feel her ripping through his mind as if she had claws instead of hooves. Gritting his mental teeth, Thracis tried another tack. He couldn't just stand here and wait for her to demolish every barrier in his head.

Snaking out a mental tendril, Thracis made a loop and threw it around the mare's head. The mare, not expecting him to fight back in such fashion, reared at the invisible lasso. Thracis felt the tendril pull in his mind as if he were physically attached to the mare. Intrigued, Thracis pulled back, tightening the loop.

In her surprise and subsequent panic, the mare forgot that all she had to do was dissipate the image of herself in his mind. Without that image, Thracis would have nothing to focus on. Instead of reacting as she had been trained, the mare pulled and pulled, trying to free herself.

Gasping from the mental strain of holding the mare, Thracis tried again to call for help while the mare was distracted. This time he thought he felt a response from Aeos but couldn't be sure. The mare had finally regained her senses and her image vanished from his mind. The mental lasso closed on air.

At a loss as to what he should do, Thracis retreated behind his mental fortress. The mare's harsh laughter filled his mind, everywhere at once. He felt a horrible ripping sensation. Thracis screamed inside himself at the mental pain. It felt as if his whole body was being stabbed by long metal spikes. The pain disrupted his focus. Suddenly, he realized the mare was standing just outside the last barrier between her and his core.

A valiant effort, stallion of Thetis Stable, but all in vain.

Thracis sensed her gathering her strength for this final assault. His mind shuddered in anticipation, unable to produce token resistance. Then his mind was suddenly his again. The mare's retreat was so sudden Thracis' head swam. He reached for his body and found that he was in control again. He shook his whole body and took a shaky breath, then his legs buckled and he fell into a heap in the garden.

Thracis looked up through squinted eyes and saw Aeos cantering toward the garden, his dun coat shiny with sweat. Thracis could hear other hoofbeats as well and understood that Phrenicos was returning from the beach at a gallop.

"Thracis? Thracis, can you hear me?" Aeos' voice was heavy with panic.

Thracis tried to answer, tried to give his friend some kind of assurance that his mind was his again, that he was more than an empty husk. All he could do was blink his eyes.

"Do not worry, young Calabrian." Phrenicos' voice as deep and soothing. "We'll see to the things that need seeing to."

Confident in the abilities of his companions, Thracis permitted his trembling mind to find solace in unconsciousness.

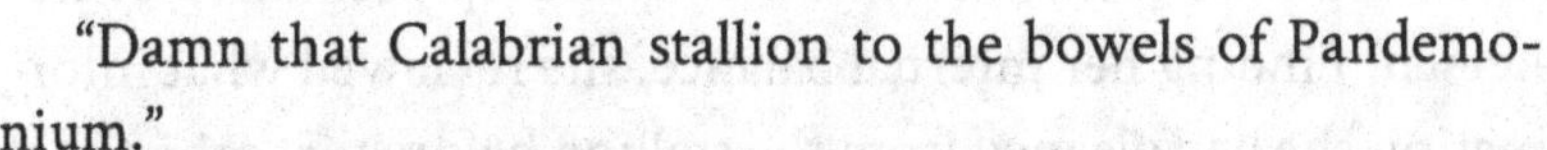

"Damn that Calabrian stallion to the bowels of Pandemonium."

Zeva, exiled daughter of Queen Hippolyta, stomped her front feet and snapped her teeth at the other mares in the large circular room in which she stood. Her black coat was damp with sweat, the edges of her eyes showed white with her fury. Uttering a shrill whinny of frustration, Zeva whirled and kicked, her foot connecting solidly with a smaller mare too slow to get out of the way. The other mare made a timid sound of distress and danced backward, away from flailing hooves.

"Out," Zeva yelled, "all of you. Get out and stay out."

The other mares, used to the frequent outbursts that characterized their leader, pushed and shoved each other in their haste to put distance between themselves and Zeva. The chamber filled with a cacophony of hooves at the mares' exit. The silence that followed after they shut the heavy metal doors behind themselves was deafening.

Zeva began to walk around the perimeter of the room, cooling her body and slowing her racing heart and bolting thoughts. How could he stand against her, this untrained colt from Calabria? He hadn't the experience or the talent to fight against a mare as adept in the psychic arts as herself. Zeva cursed her own stupidity. This failure was her fault; she had underestimated her opponent. This was a grievous offense among her ranks and one that assured swift and harsh punishment. As the lead mare, she would escape reprimand but her subordinates might secretly question her abilities. Well, she'd deal with that issue if and when it arose.

Calmer, her coat dry of sweat, Zeva moved to stand in the center of the room. She took a couple deep breaths to center herself. Finding her internal balance, she reviewed what information she had gleaned from the stallion before that other, that dun, had blindsided her and severed the link she had formed. She would do well to keep an eye out for that one.

The information she found was little more than she already knew. She did learn that the stallion was called Zephyros Thracis. She had known that he was the younger of the Zephyros colts, but now she knew that he was still using his given name. He was aware that he was of interest to the Baroquians, but someone had him nearly convinced that it was his brother, Pyrios, who held higher importance. That meddling filly, Psyche, had told him what she had seen, but Thracis was too dull-witted to understand the significance of the vision. Zeva had also underestimated Thracis' feelings toward the Diomedean mare. That information would most certainly be pertinent in future engagements.

Psyche. The youngest of Queen Hippolyta's foals and the closest in age to Zeva. The one over whom Zeva had been exiled. She had grown to be a powerful *ammoni*. Zeva shook her head slowly from side to side as a sly look painted her face. How Zeva would love to tell Psyche of Thracis' fate after the Calabrian was destroyed. With any luck, Zeva would be able to tell her little sister of her lover's death, while looking down into Psyche's dying eyes. The thought filled Zeva with a tingling warmth, making the hair on her rump stand on end. Delicious.

Opening her mind, Zeva requested contact from her commander. It was several moments before she felt his mind, a steel mouth with razor teeth, touch her own.

Has he been eliminated?

Zeva bowed her head in the empty room. *I am sorry, my lord. I failed in this attempt.*

Anger, fierce and hot, burned through the link. Zeva winced at the mental pain. *I was under the impression that you were the best of your herd.*

Zeva kept her voice submissive. *I am the best of my herd. It was my own fault. He is stronger than I would have believed.*

All the more reason to end his existence now, before he can gain any more experience.

I agree entirely, my lord.

Her commander paused, musing. Finally, he said, *Perhaps this is not as much of a disaster as I feared. We have learned that he has some psychic prowess.*

It was not he alone who cast me out. He had assistance from his companion.

That one, too, should be eliminated.

After a few moments of silence, he said. *We will move on the western coast of Diomedean in the next week. Lady Hippolyta as foreseen this action and fortified her coastal towns. It will be a hard battle but I feel we will be victorious. It has been long since the mares of Diomdea have engaged an enemy. They have grown lethargic.*

Zeva kept her opinion on that subject to herself. She felt it was too soon to march on Diomedea, the Baroquian fleet not yet strong enough. Of course, her commander was not sending the entire fleet to assault Diomedea, but Zeva did not feel this was his wisest course of action.

The Baroquians had chosen to invade Diomedea on an open stretch of beach north of Boudica and south of the port of Persephone. It was about a mile in length and protected on either side by sheer cliffs with no place for archers to gain purchase. The beach led into an open plain that stretched for miles in either direction. It was the one place on the western coast on Diomedea where an invading army would have the greatest chance of success.

If the Baroquians could construct a hasty camp and ensconce themselves on Diomedean soil, Queen Hippolyta and her subjects would have a hard time removing the intruders. This occupation would be the distraction necessary to ensure the coastal towns would be left defenseless. The rest of the Baroquian fleet would then be dispatched to move up and down the Diomedean coast, leaving nothing but death and ashes in their wake.

It was a good theory, but Zeva had been born and raised in Diomedea and she knew Queen Hippolyta would never leave any of her horses open to attack. The black mare had been exiled many years ago, but she still remembered the doctrines of Diomedean training. One of the very highest was the knowledge that you never left your flanks unprotected. Zeva felt her commander was going be in for more of a fight than he bargained for.

Zeva cleared her throat. *And what of my mares and I?*

You will stand down from this battle. Let someone else bring me the Calabrian stallion's head. You and your mares have a much more important purpose. You must stay your course.

Zeva bowed her head. It was no less than she had expected. *As you wish, my lord.*

The presence in her mind vanished. Zeva shook herself. She respected her commander because of his battle prowess and the many promises he had given her and her followers. But she never liked sharing mental contact with him. He was not right, his voracity for power overshadowing hers until Zeva's will was nothing more than a dim flickering light.

Pushing these thoughts from her mind, Zeva walked to the chamber's door. Her mares did indeed have much to do to prepare for the coming war. Zeva's skin prickled in anticipation of the coming battles. Yes, her commander was right, she must stay her course.

CHAPTER 28

Thracis shifted in the bed box, his eyes fluttering open. He blinked in the dim stall, his gaze finding and focusing on Aeos. The dun stallion, his mane disheveled and his expression worried, came forward as soon as he saw the light glinting off Thracis' eyes.

"How are you?" His voice was soft and Thracis was grateful. His ears felt sensitive; the smallest sound was a roar.

"I feel as though someone has scooped out my mind and left only pudding."

"That is what a mindreaper leaves behind in the wake of an attack."

Thracis' eyes rolled to see Phrenicos standing in the corner of the stall and looking out the window. Phrenicos turned to look down at Thracis. "The Baroquians must feel threatened indeed if they are falling to such a devious level."

"Why did you let her into your mind to begin with? You know the dangers of granting an unknown Equine access to you thoughts." Aeos sounded like a worried dam. Thracis would have kicked him if he'd had the strength.

"She sound and looked like Psyche."

Phrenicos pricked his ears and came to stand over Thracis. "How much did she resemble Psyche?"

"Identical in looks. It was her character that was flawed."

Phrenicos and Aeos exchanged a look. "That is usually what happens when a mindreaper takes the guise of someone they know only slightly. Or knew a long time ago." Phrenicos inclined his head at Aeos. "How would she have known of Thracis' involvement with Psyche to begin with?"

Aeos twitched a shoulder. "I have told no one. Did you tell your brother about Psyche?"

Thracis shook his head. "I can't remember. I did tell him I had met a mare in Iliad. I told my dam as well." He looked from Aeos to Phrenicos. "But I gave neither a description of what she looked like."

Phrenicos tossed his head. "You wouldn't have had to. It would not have been hard work for a Baroquian spy to learn about Psyche once they had a place to start. Perhaps your brother said something in passing to someone he thought was trustworthy. He may have learned her identity from Kamuzu and Alcander. They would not have seen any reason to keep her a secret." He sighed. "I do not believe your brother realizes the precariousness of his position."

"Should I warn him?" Thracis hadn't contacted Pyrios in weeks, perturbed by his brother's constant brusque demeanor.

"Tell him to keep his mouth shut where you are concerned. Unfortunately, if a mindreaper has found you then the Baroquians are aware you are in Diomedea."

"Do they know our exact location?" Aeos queried.

"Doubtful. My guess would be that they know you are somewhere in Amazonia." Phrenicos went back to the window.

Thracis and Aeos waited several moments in silence. Interested as he was in the conversation, Thracis only wanted to sleep for another few hours. "Aeos, can you contact Psyche and make sure she's alright? I can't even focus on a simple sentence."

Aeos nodded. Before he could even begin to locate Psyche's mind, Phrenicos spoke. "That will not be necessary. We will be seeing her in the flesh shortly."

That roused Thracis from a semi-doze. "She is coming here?"

Phrenicos shook his head. "We will be going to her."

"We will?"

Phrenicos turned from the window. He looked at the two other stallions, one standing and one lying the bed box. "We will be traveling north toward Persephone. There is a stretch of beach between there and Boudica where the Baroquians will have to come ashore. Queen Hippolyta has amassed a force of Equines and Felisians who will meet the Baroquian invaders. We should be there to lend aid."

Thracis felt renewed energy flow into his muscles at the prospect of battle. He struggled to push himself to his feet. Phrenicos set his nose on Thracis' neck, pushing the other stallion back down onto the fragrant grasses. "No need for you to get up just yet, young Thracis. We won't be leaving until tomorrow. Take the rest of today and tonight to regain your strength."

Thracis sank back down into the bedding box. Phrenicos nodded at Aeos and the two stallions left the stall, closing the door behind them.

Phrenicos led the way through the stable and out the back door to the training arena. He often spent the evenings here alone, listening to the wind and trotting to the cadence of the twilight creatures. If he were in a more meditative mood, Phrenicos would walk around the sand, creating whimsical patterns that helped clear his mind.

Aeos stood at the arena's perimeter, respectful of his master's privacy. Phrenicos spent a few minutes trotting in various patterns to clear his mind before slowing to a walk. He addressed Aeos as he passed the other stallion.

"That was brave thing, coming to Thracis' aid in such a way. Reckless, too. You'd no idea what you were opening your mind to and you have yet to meed with the delphae."

"I was hoping to have the element of surprise."

Phrenicos stopped in front of Aeos. "You won't have it again."

Aeos hung his head. "I know."

"Come and walk with me Aeos. We have things to discuss away from prying ears." Phrenicos inclined his head at the stable.

Aeos followed the other stallion to the path that led down to the beach. He felt his anxiety rise as he tightened the defensive walls he kept around his innermost self. He knew the time had come for him to tell someone what it was he was seeking in Diomedea, but that didn't make the telling any easier. He had hoped to keep his silence until he met with the delphae of Boudica, bu the *ammoni* were busy with their own battle preparations and as yet had not cleared time to meet with him.

Phrenicos proceeded forward until he was knee deep in the salty waves. He turned left, away from his stable and Boudica. "The salt water is good for working muscles."

Aeos drew alongside the white stallion. He waited for Phrenicos to ask his endless questions; questions for which Aeos had few answers.

Instead, Phrenicos appeared to have a history lesson in mind. "Do you know why only Diomedean mares wear the dark coats that proclaim their psychic powers?"

Aeos shook his head.

"It is said that black is the color of Lord Pegasus' escort, the Lady Selene, Lady of the Moons, when she is at her most mysterious. Selene's coat is said to change colors in variance with the cycle of the moons. She is gray when the first sliver of lunar light appears. As that glowing orb grows, Selene's coat brightens from gray to sparkling white, and the lighter she becomes, the more of her mysteries she reveals. But when the moons are new and dark, that is when Lady Selene is at her most shrouded and powerful."

"I have never heard that story."

Phrenicos tossed his head. "That does not surprise me. Most of Diomedea's history is kept here and not taught on the rest of Equus. The ladies here enjoy their secrecy."

"Does this story describe male Diomedeans?"

"It does not, but I will tell you of them as well. For reasons unknown, Diomedean mares birth many more fillies than colts. These fillies all have psychic talents above that of the average Equine. The colts, while strong and intelligent, are mediocre at best. Their strength lies more in their physical attributes. They can contact other Equines and species as we all can, but they have little mental endurance. With few exceptions.

"It is said that as Selene is the Lady of the Moons, her brother, Helios, is ruler of the sun. His coat is said to be the many colors of the sun, from dawn's silver to twilight's gold, the most flattering to the mares of Diomedea. It is said that every few generations, a colt is born with this same dun coloring. Unlike a palomino, these colts have a dorsal stripe of a darker color. This is said to be where Helios ran his muzzle down the colt's back, granting his blessing. These stallions are said to be as psychically strong as the blackest of Diomedean mares."

Aeos said nothing. The wind blew his dark, tarnished silver mane back over his light, tan coat, the dark stripe down his back clearly visible in the sun's rays.

"Not all duns are psychically talented of course," Phrenicos continued. "Only those born to Diomedean mares." He looked at Aeos. "As you must have been."

"I did not know my dam. She passed on even as I came into this world."

"Your sire would have told you of her."

Aeos shook his head. "He did not. The memory is too painful. He often says my silverish mane reminds him of my dam."

"I know she and my sire met during his journeys throughout Equus as a young stallion. He traveled across the entire planet. I know they were together long before she caught with her pregnancy."

Phrenicos tossed his head. "They did not wish for foals early in their union?"

"They never had a formal union. My dam was against it. As far as not wanting foals, my nurse said I may have been long in coming but it wasn't for lack of trying."

"It is common for Diomedean mares to not enter into formal unions with the stallions they choose as mates."

They walked on in silence for a few paces before Phrenicos said, "What made you suspect your dam was of Diomedean descent?"

Aeos flicked his ears. He listened to the sound of water made as it met the shore, the cries of the sea birds swooping in the sky, the soft sound of the wind in the trees beyond the white sand. Phrenicos was patient. Secrets harbored for so long were difficult to reveal.

Aeos' voice was a whisper, barely heard above the waves. "I have always been able to do things with my mind. Discover secrets, see things in the future, see things from the past. I can hear a horse's thoughts simply by being close to them." Aeos' words came faster and faster. "If I am in a room with another horse, I can tell everything about them that they try to keep hidden. In a room with many individuals, my mind becomes overwhelmed with dozens of thoughts and emotions."

He paused, catching his breath. "I can do other things as well. For instance, when Thracis was poisoned, I could touch his coat and follow the damage the poison was causing the way a mouse follows cheese. I could identify all the items used to make the poison and what I would need to counter its effects." He looked at Phrenicos. "I have never had any formal training regarding poison or antidotes."

"That is something we will have to remedy as soon as possible." Phrenicos stopped walking. He turned to face out over the water. "I do not know if you will be able to find out the identity of your dam. I am certain there are mares in Diomedea who cannot only discover who she was but who knew her personally. However, they keep their minds well-guarded. Here and nowhere else on Equus, you will have the opportunity to learn how to control your mental and healing abilities. Your training with me should be secondary to those."

Aeos nodded. He had hoped Phrenicos would come to this conclusion. The white stallion continued, "I have not been able to bring you to the delphae of Boudica, but in learning this about your heritage I feel you will have to travel on to Sanctuary, to be instructed by the Felisian *ammoni*. This journey will have to wait until after the current Baroquian threat has been dealt with."

"And what of Thracis?" Delighted as he was to be sent where he felt he should be, Aeos also retained a certain responsibility toward Thracis.

Phrenicos chuckled. "I will be looked after. He has great talent and I feel he will grow to be one of the greatest stallions I will ever teach, but this is a journey he needs to make on his own." His eyes shifted to Aeos. "Just as discovering your talents is a journey you need to make alone. It is the way of life."

He turned and they began walking back toward the path. "However, the two of you should keep in touch. I believe, as do the *ammoni* I have made contact with, that both of your destinies are entwined with each other, whether for good or ill. At the conclusion of your studies, the two of you will once again journey together."

"How can you be so sure of this?"

Phrenicos laughed. "Little colt, when you've been around as long as I have you learn that all coincidences serve a purpose. Understand that it was always in Lord Pegasus' design that you and Thracis would one day meet." He cast a shrewd eye in Aeos' direction. "And rest assured that there are others in this dance that have yet to reveal themselves."

"Hopefully, the others are of a female persuasion. I could use some feminine company."

Phrenicos laughed heartily. "Do not be so hasty. You have little experience when dealing with Diomedean mares."

29

CHAPTER 29

Psyche and Eno trotted along one of the many paths that led through the camp of Queen Hippolyta's cavalry. They wore identical armor harnesses, modified to accommodate the weapons favored by Diomedean mares. As mares could not hope to match the strength of stallions, their weapons were more devious than those preferred by their male counterparts. The Diomedean mares were especially fond of the barbed armor Thracis' attacker had worn. This was the reason Psyche had known beyond doubt which poison the ambusher had used. She had manufactured it herself on more than one occasion. One could never be too careful in times of war.

Eno herself had designed the harnesses and armor the two mares wore and Psyche had been pleased to see the modifications the other mare had created. Eno would have made more weapons and harnesses similar to the ones she and Psyche wore but there hadn't been enough time. Queen Hippolyta had underestimated how quickly the Baroquians could prepare themselves for battle.

Psyche and Eno entered the tented pavilion erected as a planning area for the queen and her commanders. Psyche, with Eno on her tail, slipped through the gathered mares and came to stand behind her dam. None of the other Equines paid the pair much attention.

Queen Hippolyta, her golden circlet replaced by a woven band of leather, stood behind a large table on which lay a map of the stretch of beach where the Baroquians would come ashore. "What have the birds seen?"

A gray and white Felisian, Queen Hippolyta's falcon master, Horus, stepped forward. Falcons, as well as many other birds, were used by the Felisians as remote viewing devices. The Felisians trained the birds by connecting to their tiny minds. Once trained, the birds were sent far and wide to investigate on behalf of their masters. After the birds returned, the falcon's master, would link with the bird's mind and see what the bird had seen.

Horus spoke loudly, so that his voice carried to all those in the pavilion. "The ships draw near, almost a hundred in all. They carry Equines and Felisians, heavily armored. We estimate their numbers to be between three and five thousand."

Mutterings from those gathered followed this statement. One of the commanders stepped forward. She was a bay mare with a regal head that bespoke of her Arab heritage. "I am Liana, lead mare of Argos Stable. I would suggest that we allow the Baroquians to reach the land. If their ships are even half as armored as Lord Horus believes, we will be as mice running to the Felisian."

Heads nodded all around her. Liana continued, "I suggest we attack after the soldiers have advanced up the beach as we have no structures along the sand which will give us adequate cover."

"A wise plan. We can better fortify away from the beach. They will be tired from trudging through the deep sand where we will have solid, level ground to charge across." This came from Lady Melantha. She was a close advisor to Queen Hippolyta, having been with the Augean Stable since before Psyche was born.

Lady Dendera hopped up on a burlap pedestal. The pedestal had been placed in the pavilion to allow the Felisians a high place from which they could address the assembly. "My good queen, my Felisians have devised equipment that allows them to travel underwater. They are excellent at rendering ships immobile, with the use of explosives." Her lips curved into a smile, revealing her sharp teeth. "Once the enemy is engaged on land, my cats will have little trouble making sure they have no retreat."

Grins and head tossings abounded all around the pavilion. The warriors here had no intention of letting the Baroquians gallop back to their home territory with their tails between their legs. The inhabitants of Diomedea were making a stand to let everyone on Equus know they were a force to be reckoned with. If that meant slaughtering every last invader, the Diomedeans were prepared to do just that. Diomedea was not known for its diplomacy.

"We will have to rely on strategy to win this battle as their forces far outnumber ours." Queen Hippolyta drew everyone's attention to the table.

"Larger numbers do not guarantee a victory," Lady Melantha reminded everyone. "Especially when one side is fighting for their homeland."

Eno inclined her head toward Psyche, keeping her voice low. "The numbers are not so different. Five thousand of them against twenty-five hundred of us. And we have the home field. We do not need to hear this."

Psyche nodded. "We must wait here until my dam tells us to which contingent we will be assigned."

"Where are your sisters? Should they not be at this meeting?"

Eno spoke of only two of Psyche's sisters. The tall and beautiful Alastrina, Lady Hippolyta's heir, and Lachesis, named for her distant foredam. Alastrina was out among her soldiers, having received her orders that morning. Her force was to remain hidden along the cliffs where they opened into the valley. This force was to flank the Baroquians after they had been engaged by Queen Hippolyta's primary contingents. It was up to Alastrina to see that the Baroquians could not retreat back to the beach. It was a duty to which Psyche's oldest sister was well-suited.

Lachesis, like her namesake, had risen to be the High Delphae of all Diomedea. She resided in the Temple of Consciousness in the Pleiades Mountains where the range dipped down into Athenia. Lachesis would not be present at this or any other battle. Having devoted herself to the otherworld, Lachesis had taken an oath to remain neutral in times of conflict. However, this neutrality did not extend to allowing harm to come to those who shared the Temple of Consciousness with her. The *ammoni* of the temple could and did defend themselves in times of crisis. The temple itself was a place of sanctuary that could not be defiled.

Psyche had one more sister, the second youngest and closest to Psyche in character and emotion. Zeva.

Early in foalhood, Zeva had shown herself to be almost as talented as her older sister, Lachesis. However, a darkness was harbored in Zeva, her sire's gift to her. Zeva's sire, a strong and fearless warrior, had first caught Queen Hippolyta's eye at the spring festivals. It had been five years since she had last carried a foal, and Hippolyta's body cried out to feel the growth of new life. Like her dam before her, Hippolyta was both warrior and devoted dam. She reveled in her body's ability to create a new being from a tiny seed.

Zeva's sire, as enamored with the queen as she was with him, immediately began to win her favor. Spring was the time of the fertility ceremonies, a time when a mare might choose a stallion for one night and never see him again. This was accepted and expected in Diomedea. It was said that a foal conceived during the spring festivals would have the blessings of Lady Selene and Lord Pegasus.

In the instance of Zeva, that blessing turned out to be a curse. Once Hippolyta was sure she was with foal, she left Zeva's sire with a memory of affection and nothing more. Zeva's sire, knowing how the affair would end before it was even begun, kept in his heart the knowledge that he had once held a queen's favor and would sire a foal that would grow to greatness under its dam's watchful eye. He left Diomedea and returned to his home territory, the province of Friesia. Had Queen Hippolyta even suspected the object of her adoration was from that ancient enemy of her horses, she would never had allowed him to even touch her. But she did not find out her suitor's origin until much later, after Zeva began to show glimpses of the darkness within her. Even then, Hippolyta had hoped that since Zeva was created in affection if not quite love, the filly would be able to overpower her darker self and embrace the goodness that flowed in her veins.

That hope was misplaced. The High Delphae had made a special trip from Athenia to Ruffiana to examine Zeva first hoof. What she had seen behind Zeva's eyes, buried even deeper than the filly knew, was a zeal for power and cruelty. With a heavy heart, the High Delphae had told the queen what she had seen. Queen Hippolyta defended her daughter with all a dam's fierceness, stating that Zeva would not be cast out until the filly gave her dam reason to do so.

That reason came six months after the birth of Psyche. Zeva, insanely jealous of her newest sister, had tried to rip young Psyche's mind apart in an attempt to kill the filly. Psyche had been saved by Lachesis, who had felt the animosity Zeva held for their youngest sister. A mental battle had ensued between Zeva and Lachesis that had left Zeva laying on her side, heaving, on the floor of Psyche's stall, while Lachesis braced herself against a wall, Psyche protected from danger by her sister's battered body.

After Zeva's true nature was revealed, Queen Hippolyta had but two options. She could either exile her daughter in hopes that Zeva would find her own place somewhere outside the borders of Diomedea or sentence her third daughter to execution. Even after witnessing the destruction Zeva had wrought, Hippolyta could not kill her daughter. So Zeva was exiled, never to return to Diomedea. It had been nine years since Zeva had walked out of her dam's court, but she had made her whereabouts known. She had ventured to her sire's herds. Of her sire himself nothing was known. Queen Hippolyta was well-aware that her black-coated daughter had allied herself with the Friesians.

Psyche shook her memories away and looked at Eno. "Alastrina is already in position and Lachesis, as High Delphae, will not attend this or any other battle."

Eno watched as Queen Hippolyta addressed first this commander, then that one. The pavilion was becoming emptier by the moment as everyone received their orders and went to prepare themselves and their soldiers. They expected to engage the enemy by dawn's light.

Eno wondered what her sire would think if he learned she would be fighting in open combat. As the forces of Diomedea were not considered members of Imperial Cavalry, the Registry could not object to mares fighting as if they were stallions. The military of Equus would be forced to undergo modifications in light of a civil war in any case. By simply talking about the prospect of inner turmoil, the military of Equus was going to be divided. However, the military faction controlled by the Hippikon and the Elysian Alliance would hold to their traditions and restrictions with more tenacity than those countries who would have to fall back on their own resources. While the Asapatish of the Hippikon was at least aware of what was going on in Diomedea, Eno highly doubted her sire would think her foolish enough to become involved. Then again, knowing her fundamental nature, Eno's sire might expect her involvement.

Queen Hippolyta didn't turn to speak with Psyche and Eno until only her personal advisors remained in the pavilion. The queen, her pewter coat glimmering in the noon's light, spoke to her daughter with both a dam's pride and apprehension. "I have given great thought to where you will be placed. I did not want the two of you at the front lines, as neither of you have adequate experience, but I also wanted you somewhere where you will gain the experience you lack."

The two young mares remained silent. Queen Hippolyta had been involved in several battles, most between rival stables. The Lady knew her soldiers and commanders as she knew the members of her home stable. She would make sure Psyche and Eno were placed where they could be supervised, but allowed to stand on their own legs. The two mares did come from a long line of fighters, after all.

"I have decided that you will be under the command of Lady Alcina. She will be orchestrating the collective forces from Boudica and the surrounding towns. It is a small group that will assist Lady Liana's contingent. I feel you will be most advantageous between those two groups."

Psyche and Eno bowed their heads.

"Go now and walk among your comrades. Learn who will be fighting at your sides."

Eno bowed low and left the pavilion. Psyche hung back and addressed her dam. "Will you be engaging the enemy, my queen?"

At times like these, surrounded by members of Queen Hippolyta's council, Psyche was profoundly aware that her dam had responsibilities that far outweighed her daughter's safety.

"I may. I must regretfully hold back until the final moments of battle."

Psyche bowed her head. "I hope that I will fill you with pride at tomorrow's battle."

Since the betrayal of Zeva, Hippolyta had always distanced herself from her youngest daughter. Ten years separated Psyche from Lachesis making Psyche more a tolerated cousin than a sister. These factors, though outside Psyche's control, had led the queen's youngest daughter to believe she was unworthy to be part of the royal herd at all. As a result, Psyche spent years of her life trying to attain some acknowledgement of pride from either her dam or her sisters.

Queen Hippolyta nuzzled her youngest daughter, a rare show of affection. "Do not let your desire to do me proud allow you to make a foolish mistake. I do not wish to weep at your passing when the battle has concluded."

Psyche, embarrassed that her dam would treat her as a foal in front of her entire council, bowed her head lower. "I will be careful." Not waiting for a reply, she trotted out of the pavilion to catch up with Eno.

CHAPTER 30

"You should not let your dam's hardened heart turn your own to stone." Eno spoke in a singsong manner that grated on Psyche's nerves. Eno knew nothing of what Psyche was feeling. Eno, who's sire had kept her with him when any other stallion would have left the foal with a female relative. Eno, who had been trained alongside her sire's soldiers, his pride and theirs. Eno, who Queen Hippolyta held in such high regard as of late.

Psyche shook her head. Now was not the time to dwell on the hurts of the past. She knew well her dam had hardened her heart against further agony after Zeva had been exiled. Psyche sometimes wished Zeva had shown her true self before Queen Hippolyta had begun pining for another foal.

Sensing Psyche's distress, Eno grew somber. "Come, let us find our comrades of tomorrow." Her voice grew more teasing. "Perhaps you will find an attractive stallion to share a few hours with. That will take your mind off further brooding."

"I only wish to spend this night with one stallion, and he is likely far from here," Psyche said quietly.

"Why not contact him and see?" Eno suggested. "You know he is training with Master Phrenicos."

"I do not wish to bother him. If I contact him he will feel my anxiety and think it has something to do with him."

"Of course, he will. Don't you know that all stallions automatically feel all feminine crises have to do with them?"

That, at last, coaxed a laugh from Psyche. "I don't know about all stallions, but Thracis surely does."

"It is only because he cares for you."

"I wish I could be as certain of that as you are."

Eno thought it better not to comment on that statement.

The two mares trotted passed several banners, each identifying various groups or herds. Not all the horses they passed were mares, they saw one stallion for every three or four mares. They also saw plenty of Felisians, sprinkled like exotic spices among the Equines. Though they headed for the banner depicting Lady Alcina's herd, Psyche and Eno were stopped when they reached Lady Liana's contingent.

"Your dam told me you would be joining me in the tomorrow's battle." Lady Liana approached Psyche and Eno at a brisk walk. She was honored that Queen Hippolyta would send one of her own daughters to complement her own ranks. That Psyche was initially promised to Lady Alcina was conveniently overlooked. Given Liana's exuberance and that Queen Hippolyta would have known Psyche would have had to go through Lady Liana's group to reach Lady Alcina, Psyche doubted that anyone had informed Lady Alcina that Psyche and Eno were even coming.

Lady Liana had no intention of letting Psyche get away. She had been vying for a position in Queen Hippolyta's court and babysitting the queen's youngest daughter was just the leverage she would need. "Come and join us, we've only just begun discussing the strategy your dam suggested."

At the mention of a strategy meeting, Eno immediately walked toward Lady Liana's encampment. This was also something Lady Liana had counted on. Eno's prowess at military maneuvering was no secret among the Amazonian herds. The Diomedean mares snickered at the arrogance of stallions who would not take the advice of one as talented in strategy as Eno.

Psyche flicked her ears at Lady Liana. "If it pleases you, I would prefer to walk around the camp a little more first. I will be back for the evening meal."

Lady Liana kept her disappointment from showing on her elegant features. "Of course. Do you wish for an escort?"

Psyche bridled under the implication that she was incapable of taking care of herself even while surrounded by Diomedean supporters. She did not let any of her anger slip into her voice. "Thank you for the offer, but I would prefer to walk alone."

Not to be put off, Lady Liana persisted. "Come now, the daughter of the queen should not be allowed to go about the camp like a common soldier." Lady Liana's ears flicked as she contacted a member of her group.

Psyche fought hard to suppress a sigh. She and Eno had come here to help and find acceptance as adults. Eno, it appeared, had found exactly what she was looking for. Psyche was still being treated like the six-month-old filly her sister had needed to rescue. Well, it was Psyche's own fault. Moirae had told her that she would not be accepted as anything more than Hippolyta's youngest daughter as long as her dam was present.

Lady Liana's face brightened as, surprise, surprise, the older of her two foals, Belen, came striding up to the two mares. "Lady Psyche, let me introduce my son Belen. I know he is only a stallion, but he is well-trained and strong. He will see that no harm comes to you."

And he will show every other stallion in this camp that I'm not available for courtship, Psyche thought sourly. It was on the tip of her tongue to insist that she was fine by herself, but then the idea of Lady Liana mentioning to Queen Hippolyta that Psyche had insulted her hospitality crossed her mind. Lady Hippolyta would not forgive her daughter for such a slight against an important ally.

Digging deep to find her princess manners, Psyche transformed her irritation into congeniality. "This is generous of you, Lady Liana. My dam will be most pleased to learn of your concern for my welfare."

Lady Liana beamed, delighted to have gained some small amount of favor with the Augean Stable. "I am glad you think so. Go and wander. Do not worry about returning for the evening meal. I am sure the two of you are resourceful enough to find something to eat."

Psyche bit her lip to keep from saying that perhaps Lady Liana should send a chaperon along as well. Instead, she bowed her head and requested that Lady Liana tell Eno where she had gone. With a look at Belen, Psyche turned and began walking away from Lady Liana's, and by association, Lady Alcina's, herd. Belen bowed his head to his dam and followed Psyche into the main camp.

Lady Liana watched the two horses move off. She felt as if some of her plans were finally falling into place. She was the lead mare of a strong stable, but her true ambition was to be part of Queen Hippolyta's chief council. This was a goal she had worked toward for years. By speaking up at the pavilion she had drawn the queen's attention. By sending Belen with Psyche, Lady Liana was giving a clear signal that Argos Stable was at least in the temporary favor of the Augean Stable. She was also hoping that perhaps Psyche would find some attractive qualities in Belen. A union between the two stables, even an informal one, would solidify Lady Liana's position in Queen Hippolyta's court.

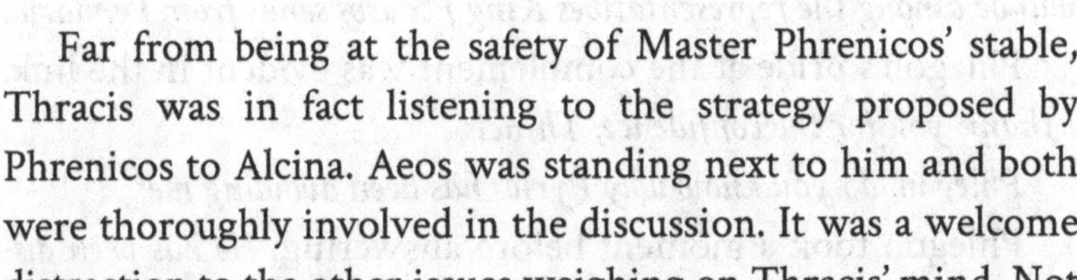

Far from being at the safety of Master Phrenicos' stable, Thracis was in fact listening to the strategy proposed by Phrenicos to Alcina. Aeos was standing next to him and both were thoroughly involved in the discussion. It was a welcome distraction to the other issues weighing on Thracis' mind. Not the least of which was his brother, Pyrios.

Following Phrenicos' advice, Thracis had tried to contact Pyrios on several occasions. Every time Pyrios had firmly shut his younger brother out of his mind. Exasperated, Thracis had contacted Phlegon. The Pendarian stallion had been delighted with the contact.

Have you found a trainer? Lord Kantaka was certain you would. Phlegon's excitement hummed through the psychic link.

I have and he is quite good. How have you been, Phlegon? Despite his urgency to speak with his brother, Thracis could feel the loneliness Phlegon was trying to hide.

I've been...busy. Lord Kantaka has many engagements. He and I are often at several different stables each week.

Thracis noted that Phlegon did not mention where Pyrios was during these gatherings.

The other stallion went on. *I am learning a great many things about political protocols and the importance of building a network of associates. I will also be taking informal combat instruction soon.* Phlegon was prattling on, but Thracis didn't mind. Hearing of the other stallion's duties was a reaffirmation that Thracis would not have been good at politics.

After several minutes, Phlegon paused to catch his mental breath. Thracis did not let the opportunity pass him by. *I am happy that you are finding your place in the world. Before long, you will be among the representatives King Pedasos sends from Pendaria.*

Phlegon's pride at the complement was evident in the link. *I thank you for the confidence, Thracis.*

Phlegon, do you know why Pyrios has been avoiding me?

Phlegon took a moment before answering. *He has been distracted as of late.*

With a new conquest?

The situation is a bit more complicated than that.

Thracis groaned. *What has he gotten himself into?*

I would prefer not to discuss it in this manner.

Thracis understood. Phlegon was concerned their conversation might be overheard by an eavesdropper. *Since he refuses to talk with me, can you give my brother a message?*

I will try. Pyrios has not been communicative to anyone recently.

Thracis closed his eyes. It was exactly the way his brother behaved when a mare ensnared his interest. *When you get a chance to speak with him alone, please tell him not to discuss my whereabouts to anyone. Tell him to keep his mouth shut about anyone I may have had contact with as well.*

Do you want me to tell Lord Kantaka also?

Thracis considered. *Yes, and have him inform Commander Dias.*

Has something happened?

I don't want to discuss it. Just know it would be better if I remained as elusive as possible.

I will see that they all get the message. Take care, Thracis. Tell Aeos to watch himself as well.

I will.

Three days had passed and Thracis had still not heard from Pyrios. He was more than annoyed at his brother. For the first time in his memory, Thracis was angry with Pyrios. It was just like the older Zephyros brother to focus all his attention on a mare and have total disregard for everyone else.

Aeos nudged Thracis. "I fear we will not get a chance to fight at all with all these mares around. Perhaps we should have stayed at Phrenicos' stable."

The comment jolted Thracis out of his brooding and he looked around the open tent to see that several more mares had joined their small group. Many of the newcomers were giving him and Aeos speculative looks that said they wouldn't mind company on the night before a battle. Remembering his wayward night a few weeks before, Thracis felt his stomach clench. Even though he and Psyche were more cautious when speaking to one another, he still felt loyal to her.

Aeos, on the other hoof, was returning every look he received. He inclined his head at Thracis. "It's been a long time since I've enjoyed any female company."

"That is one pursuit you will have to undertake alone. I don't feel like engaging in mindless banter. Or anything else," Thracis muttered.

"Fortunately for you I was not inviting you to join me in my prowling. I was merely stating that you will have to entertain yourself this evening." Aeos was talking to Thracis, but his eyes were locked with Dysis', the palomino that frequently accompanied Alcina.

"I had not thought Dysis was looking for a companion," Thracis observed.

"Not for the long term, but I think she could be persuaded to let her guard down for a single night."

Thracis tossed his head. "I wish you luck. I think I'll go for a walk."

Giving Dysis a wistful look and a wink, Aeos left the tent to follow Thracis. "I think I'll join you."

"I do not need a minder."

"No, but I want to limber up in case I find company later."

Thracis nipped Aeos' shoulder. "I'm not sure I agree with this new facet of your personality."

Aeos rolled his eyes. "When did you become so serious, Thracis? This new somber mood does not suit you."

"I should think you'd be glad that I've reached a new maturity."

"Being a killjoy does not equal maturity."

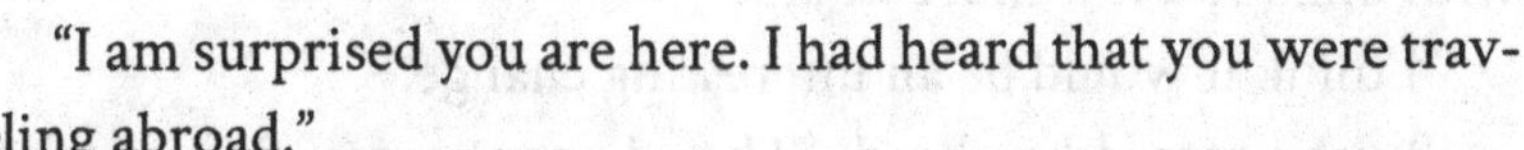

"I am surprised you are here. I had heard that you were traveling abroad."

Psyche suppressed a groan. This was yet another attempt by Belen to begin a conversation. Was he so dense that he did not realize she really had wanted to wander alone? She was frustrated beyond measure by the stupidity of stallions.

"I was, studying, other societies outside Diomedea." A half-truth, but she doubted Belen would notice. He had only one intention where she was concerned.

"Societies where stallions have more influence?" Belen was all but strutting alongside her.

"Societies where stallions and mares have equal influence."

"There is no such place," he stated.

How is it that a stallion with such arrogance was still breathing in Diomedea? Psyche thought it better not to ask. She turned down a path leading through a column of tents. She could feel Belen's eyes roaming over her rump but the path was narrow and there wasn't enough room for him to walk beside her. Psyche felt embarrassment heat her face.

She turned abruptly, cutting through two campsites to reach a broader walkway. Belen hid his surprise at her quick maneuvering and dutifully lengthened his stride to come up beside the mare. He walked on her right, the customary position for an escort though few outside the royal courts knew this protocol. To the horses they passed, the pair looked like a couple out for a stroll to ease their nerves before tomorrow's battle.

"Would you rather be in a place where the stallion has more dominance?" Psyche kept her tone light. She only had to put up with him for a few more hours.

"I think it would be an interesting change."

Psyche tossed her head. "Then I suggest you find another mare to spend your time with. I have no intention of compromising my independence."

Psyche had been walking with little regard for where her feet were taking her. She only wanted to put distance between herself and her 'escort' before her temper flared even brighter.

How dare this stallion openly brag about wanting more dominance. And to do so in the presence of the queen's own daughter. Did no one believe she was more than a brainless filly? Psyche tossed her head and walked faster. She could hear Belen trotting behind her to keep up.

She whirled to face Belen, disregarding any insult she might inflict to Lady Liana's stable. "Why do you still follow me?"

"My dam has instructed that I escort you. I have no intention of leaving you alone."

"I am perfectly capable of taking care of myself."

Belen's ears had been lowering with his tone. They were now pinned. "It does not seem that way to me. Have you looked at where you've led us?"

Psyche's ears flicked back and forth, the sounds of the camp were distant now, the voices of the other horses faint. She glanced around and noticed that they were standing in a field several yards from the nearest campsite. Out in the open, with the sun sliding toward the horizon, Psyche felt like a brainless filly indeed. She could have led them directly into an ambush without a second thought.

"My suggestion, Lady Psyche," Belen's voice dripped with his fury, "is that you and I return to the safety of the camp."

Angry more at herself than with him, Psyche tossed her head, her own ears lowering. "Why should we, so that you can foalsit in more comfortable surroundings?"

Belen snapped at the air. "Don't make me force you to return to camp. Even those mares ready to tear a stallion limb from limb in the morning light will agree that you should not be out here in the open with the Baroquians so close."

Psyche's ears flattened. "You would not dare touch me."

"If I must to keep you safe then I will."

Glaring at him, knowing he was right, Psyche stomped back toward the camp. She walked with her head lowered and ears pinned, a sign to any who crossed her path that she was in an aggressive mood. Belen followed along at a safe distance, out of range of her back hooves should she decide to kick.

She was so furious with the stallion behind her that she didn't see the one in front of her until she collided with him. The stallion, as startled by the collision as she, jumped back away from her. Psyche raised her head, ready to vent her aggravation on someone, when Belen pushed passed her. Before Psyche could say anything the two stallions began fighting.

Another stallion, a dun, was trying to intervene, to drive the two combatants apart. The four of them were still far enough into the field that they hadn't drawn any attention yet. The stallions, schooled in combat, had not voiced any challenging whinnies that would have alerted other horses to their conflict.

Catching the dun's eye, Psyche tossed her head to show that she would herd one opponent if he would fence the other. Moving at the same time, she and the dun forced their way between the fighting stallions, then dodged and darted to keep the fighters separated. It was hard as both stallions were intent on killing each other. Tensions had been running high in the camp and both horses had reached the breaking point.

"You should look where you're going. You could have knocked her down."

"Me knock her down? She's the one who rammed me."

"She was giving clear signs that she was upset."

"Maybe you should learn how to treat a lady then."

The lady in question, deciding she had had enough of male antics, stomped both her front feet and pinned her ears at Belen. "I can handle this myself. You're only making it worse. And you," she said, turning to the stallion she had run into, "You should..." Psyche stopped and stared. Thracis stared back. Aeos and Belen exchanged a look.

Thracis felt as if the ground had fallen out from beneath his feet. Psyche, here. He looked past her. Here with another stallion. He felt himself grow still. His eyes shifted back to Psyche. "Now I see why you haven't had time for me lately."

"What are you talking about? It is you who have been avoiding me."

"Only because you were cold to me first."

Psyche was stunned. She had never meant to appear cold. "I told you I was busy, foolish colt. I needed to concentrate on my studies."

Thracis tossed his head a Belen. "I see well what you've been studying."

Has every Equine on Equus lost their senses? Psyche thought. "I've been with my instructor. Learning the psychic arts." She glanced back at Belen. "I only met him a few hours ago and it was not my choosing."

At that, Thracis pinned his ears at Belen. "He has been harassing you, then?"

How fortunate I am that all these stallions wish to defend my honor. Psyche sighed. "It is complicated. He was assigned by his dam as my escort, as a favor."

Thracis snorted. "Why would you need an escort here of all places?"

Psyche kept her voice even. "As I said, it is complicated."

"Obviously the two of you have much to discuss." All three horses turned their heads to look at Aeos. "Might I make a suggestion? If the lady is agreeable, I propose that Thracis take over Belen's escort duties and Belen and I return to camp."

Belen pinned his ears. "I cannot disappoint my dam in such a manner. She is the lead mare of Argos Stable." This statement would have carried more weight had Aeos and Thracis known more about the herds of Amazonia.

"It will not be a disappointment. You can simply tell your dam that Psyche met a friend she hadn't seen in some time and wished to have privacy." Aeos lowered his voice. "You need not mention that friend is a stallion."

"My dam will find out."

Aeos twitched a shoulder. "In my opinion parents may wish much for their offspring but in the end we invariably make our own decisions."

Belen looked from Aeos to Psyche. The mare had made it quite clear she was not thrilled with his presence. He could find a more willing companion to spend the evening with. "I will agree to this if it pleases the lady."

"It would please me more to have no escort of any kind. Since that is not an option, I will accept the proposed compromise." Psyche felt her heart speed up at the thought of being alone with Thracis.

Belen bowed his head. "I will find a suitable explanation for my dam." He turned to leave, rebuffed.

Aeos called after him. "Wait." He trotted over to join Belen. "I am not from Diomedea and am not sure as to how to approach the mares here. Perhaps you could give me some advice?"

Advice on how to get a good kicking, Psyche thought but did not say.

Pleased that he now had an excuse to stay away from his dam's camp, Belen tossed his head. "I would be happy to show you what these mares expect." The two stallions trotted back into the main encampment. Psyche silently wished Aeos luck in his endeavor. For Belen she had no such kindness, the stallion was arrogant and vain. He would not find much female tolerance within that camp.

Left alone, as they had both wanted for so long, Psyche and Thracis fidgeted. Neither was sure how to approach the other without the excuse of some duty. Psyche wished she could talk casually with Thracis as she would any other stallion she met, but she had never been taught how to speak with a stallion she actually had interest in. All the other suitors she had met were of little consequence to her and therefore she did not care what they thought of her. Of those suitors none had ever been alone with her. Psyche had always made sure to have another horse present to discourage any unwanted male advances.

"Perhaps you would like to walk?" Thracis elected. "I know I find it easier to talk if my feet have something to do."

Psyche nodded. Thracis waited for her to choose their direction. Though it was safer in the camp, Psyche did not want to be examined by curious eyes. It was one thing to ignore the stallion she was with, the mares of Diomedea would give that behavior little notice, but if Psyche began an animated conversation with Thracis, the other mares would notice fast enough.

"Do you mind to walk a little farther from the camp?" She waited for him to chide her for leading them farther into danger, as if she were taking them straight to the Baroquian army.

Thracis tossed his head. "I would like that."

Startled that he would agree without convincing, Psyche led the way into the field. Thracis, aware that walking behind any mare made them uncomfortable, strolled along on Psyche's right side. Thracis, having been raised in a ruling herd, knew well that he was staking a claim to this mare in the event they crossed paths with another stallion.

Psyche noted Thracis' position and it caused a ripple of pleasure to run through her body. She was intrigued by the way he seemed to take charge while also appearing submissive. It was a strange paradox and one she was not used to, having spent most of her life in Diomedea. The stallions here, even the arrogant ones, always let the mare lead.

The moons were rising in the evening sky, painting everything in glimmering silver. The moonlight bounced off the horses' armor harnesses, making the achillium glow. In the distance, Psyche could hear the calls of owls as they readied for nocturnal hunting. She felt herself relax with every step, finding the ease she had been seeking.

Thracis felt the tensions of the last days falling from his shoulders as well. The past week had passed like a blur to the young Calabrian. Phrenicos had led Thracis and Aeos to the force being assembled by Alcina, who they learned was the unofficial lead mare of Boudica and small surrounding villages. From that point, the three stallions had traveled with the herd to this rallying place.

Thracis had never seen such a large grouping of horses in all his life. So many banners depicting the different stables. Most of the herds were composed of only mares, but some had the occasional stallion. Thracis and Aeos were openly accepted as being students of Master Phrenicos. They had spent the few days waiting for the Baroquian landing walking through the camp and becoming acquainted with various stables and herds. At every meeting Thracis felt as if he were being weighed and measured by the mares in attendance. This constant female appraisal of his physique, for none of these mares were interested in his mind, was exhausting and, at times, demeaning. He now understood a few of the frustrations mares had with stallions.

"How goes your training with Master Phrenicos?"

Thracis was nudged out of his reverie by the question. "It is slower than I would have hoped, but I like to think I am improving."

"'Things done right often take time.' Or so my own teacher often proclaims." Psyche slowed her pace, stepping a little closer to Thracis. "I am not advancing as fast as I wish either."

"Phrenicos says that my biggest fault is my lack of patience."

Psyche twitched a shoulder. "He should teach you how to meditate. It would help you to center yourself. Thracis? What's the matter?"

Thracis stood, trembling. His memory of the mindreaper still too fresh. Even with Phrenicos' and Aeos' encouragement, Thracis was still unable to open his mind and seek balance.

Psyche, distressed that she had caused him upset though she did not know how, turned to face him. She stepped alongside him and laid her neck across his withers, her head coming to rest against his mane. Thracis pressed his forehead to her shoulder, accepting her comfort.

"What has happened?" Psyche's voice was a whisper in the night air.

Taking a deep breath, Thracis told her what had transpired the last time he was in a meditative trance. He left nothing out, wanting her to know all there was, how the other mare had disguised herself as Psyche to win his confidence.

"I knew you would not be so forward with a stallion you had not yet accepted as a suitor," Thracis finished.

Psyche was quiet, digesting all he had said. A nagging possibility hooked itself in the recesses of her mind. Psyche knew of only a handful of mares who could launch that effective of a psychic attack from any great distance. And of that handful, only one would think to cause harm.

Not wanting to alert Thracis to the demons of her own herd, Psyche said, "I am sorry my intentions toward you are unclear. I am not very experienced when dealing with stallions."

Thracis raised his head to lay it across Psyche's back. He would move away at the slightest indication that his attentions were unwelcome, but as he felt Psyche relax against him, Thracis thought the two of them were finally becoming honest about their feelings toward each other. "I find that hard to believe. The stallion escorting you was more than willing to make a claim."

"A claim I would have rejected. I will only accept the attentions of one stallion. If he chooses to express them."

"I have been hoping for such an invitation." Thracis stepped away from Psyche a little so that he could turn his head and nuzzle the soft hair along her neck. He moved his head higher to brush his cheek against her silken mane.

Psyche rubbed her cheek against his shoulder, all thoughts of her dam, sisters, and Lady Liana's disappointment fleeing her mind. At this moment, only Thracis' view mattered and he did not see her as inadequate or inexperienced. He saw her for who she was and accepted that she was worthy.

31

CHAPTER 31

The shadowed pre-dawn light found Thracis and Psyche lying next to one another in the field where they had spent the night. Both were resting lightly, their ears flicking back and forth at the various noises about the camp as other horses prepared for the trek to the battlefield.

Knowing he was putting off the inevitable by lying here, Thracis got to his feet. He stretched languidly, rolling his shoulders and flexing his neck muscles to limber them for the battle to come. Next to him, Psyche rolled all the way over to scratch her back before getting to her feet.

After standing and shaking the bits of grass from her coat, Psyche looked at their harnesses, tossed casually on the ground near where they had been sleeping and uttered a short laugh. "My dam will have me whipped if she finds out I was stupid enough to sleep a night with no armor this close to a battle."

She tried to put a fair amount of bravado into her voice, but Thracis could hear the echoes of guilt that she had done something that might disappoint her dam. He reached out and nuzzled her cheek. "We were safe being this close to the camp." He tossed his head in the direction of the other horses. "And don't think for a second that every mare and stallion in that encampment spent the night fully armored and alone."

"I'm sure some did. My sister and dam would have."

Thracis lipped her ears, trying to lighter her mood. "Well, neither my sire or dam would have if they were our age. And they will not hold myself, my brother, or my new sister to rules they themselves would not adhere to."
Psyche pulled her head back away from Thracis' questing lips. "Your herd sounds much more forgiving than mine."

"Not really. My parents are realistic, however." He walked to his harness and began putting it on. His mind felt clear and energized this morning. Being with Psyche, learning she shared feelings for him, had settled his confusion and released much of his tension. As a consequence, he felt much more confident about the day's coming battle.

Shrugging into her own harness, Psyche turned to him. "After last night I should probably stand with Lady Liana's stable, as a sort of truce."

Thracis pinned his ears. "You should be next to me. I can't keep an eye on you if you are in the midst of another herd." He raised his voice to smother her angry protest. "And if I can't see you, you can't see me. Do you expect me to trust Aeos to watch my back?"

Psyche's tension drained away in her laughter. "I think you can handle yourself. As for me, I have a female companion much like Aeos who will need me to guard her flanks."

Thracis tossed his head but did not press his point. As the stallion who claimed her, he had every right to fight alongside his lady. It had become his duty to protect her. Watching as she deftly secured the buckles of her harness with hardly a glance, he wondered who would be protecting whom in a fight. Deciding Psyche would be insulted beyond measure if he insisted on standing with her in the coming battle, Thracis let the matter drop.

They walked toward the camp in the dawn's brightening light. If anyone thought their sudden appearance out of the field was strange, no one mentioned it. Psyche guessed she and Thracis were not the only pair that had spent the night outside the camp. Even Diomedean mares liked privacy.

She still couldn't believe she had done something so reckless. To give herself fully to a stallion was not the problem. The fact that she had not already done so was cause for speculation within her dam's court. It was unheard of in Diomedean society for a mare of Psyche's age not to have explored all the stimulation a stallion was capable of. That she had been with a stallion that no one in her herd had ever met or knew anything about... Psyche decided to play extra nice with Lady Liana to buy herself as much time as possible before Queen Hippolyta, or worse, Princess Alastrina, came to find out about the stallion Psyche was keeping hidden from everyone.

"Perhaps we should all group together and watch each other," Thracis suggested.

Psyche tossed her head and stopped a few feet from the camp. "It is too soon, Thracis. Today I would be a distraction for you, as you would be a distraction for me."

Thracis sighed. "I know you are capable of protecting yourself, but this is new for me. Other mares do not march into battle."

"After today you will see that perhaps other mares should."

"If that were the case, all the stallions I know would likely break their legs trying to rescue every female."

Psyche nipped his shoulder. "Have faith in our abilities, foolish colt. It is likely I have more training than you do."

Thracis dropped his ears in mock irritation. "I think you delight in frustrating me."

"I would think it keeps me interesting."

If they weren't already late getting to their respective camps, Thracis would chase her back into the field and show Psyche her mind wasn't the only thing that kept her interesting. Tossing his head to clear it, Thracis shifted toward Lady Alcina's banner. "I must get back before Aeos decides to come looking. And there comes your fearless escort, ready to herd you back into the fold."

Psyche groaned as she caught sight of Belen heading their way. "I hope he found an acquiescing mare to spend the night with. It might put him in a better mood."

"It worked for me," Thracis teased.

Blushing, still unsure about the situation, Psyche brushed her cheek against his neck. "Be safe, stallion of Thetis." She turned and trotted toward Belen, effectively keeping him from getting close to Thracis and starting another dispute.

"And you as well, my warrior lady," Thracis whispered. He watched until he lost sight of Psyche's black and white patches, then proceeded on to Alcina's camp to find Aeos and Master Phrenicos.

"Apparently you weren't the only one to find company last night," Phenicos said to Aeos as Thracis trotted up to the mess tent. A deep trough along one side of the tent was filled with grain, while an identical trough on another side flowed with fresh water.

Had the comment come from Aeos, Thracis would have ignored it. Since it was Phrenicos who spoke, Thracis stopped to speak with his instructor before heading to the grain trough to see if anything was left.

"I didn't realize I was under supervision."

Phrenicos tossed his head. "You weren't. I was simply making an observation."

"Did the two of you work out your differences?" Aeos was trying to sound casual and failing miserably.

"We reached an understanding."

"Good. That way I can count on you to remain focused as the day wears on." Phrenicos had adopted the stern voice he used when presenting a difficult maneuver that required concentration. It did little to hide his amusement.

Thracis nodded.

Phrenicos tossed his head at the grain trough. "Go have something to eat. Make sure you drink plenty of water as well. This day promises to be long and hot."

∪

"Where did you disappear to last night? Don't tell me you spent the night with that stallion you came back with, he's so conceited."

Psyche tuned out most of Eno's prattling as she headed first to get a long drink of water and then continued on to forage in the grain buckets. Belen had been full of questions during their walk through the camp, all of them centered around Thracis. Who was he? Was his herd influential? Was it true that he had been dismissed from the Romanium? What were her feelings toward him? As if Belen had any right to know Psyche's mind.

Psyche had halted the endless tirade by snapping that neither Thracis or she was any of Belen's concern. Belen had countered that as long as his dam insisted he follow Psyche around the least she could do is inform him of who she was spending the night with. The nerve she had, rolling around in a field like a common village filly. What would Queen Hippolyta say?

She would say rolling around in a field with a decent stallion was far better than spending the night with an arrogant fool. Psyche thought it best to keep this observation to herself. She had lapsed into a frigid silence and when they at last reached Lady Liana's camp, Belen quickly found an excuse to leave Psyche to her own devices.

"Did whoever you were with steal your tongue as well as your heart?" Eno teased.

"I was with Thracis, if you really must know."

"Thracis? He's here? And you didn't think to introduce me to him? I've only been hearing you complain about him for months." Eno bit Psyche hard on the flank.

Psyche spun and gave Eno a level stare. "I'm sorry I didn't think to put your feelings above my own."

Eno watched Psyche walked to the edge of Liana's camp. The black and white mare stood pawing the ground, fretting. Putting aside her usual sarcastic nature, Eno went to join her friend. "Did last night not go as you imagined?"

Eno saw a ripple go through Psyche's coat. "Last night was perfect. After we got rid of my brave escort." She glanced at Belen who was flexing his muscles for a couple of younger mares.

"Then what is the problem?"

"I am not sure. I just feel...unsettled."

"Probably a combination of things. I understand it is a lot for you to contend with."

Psyche nodded.

"So, if Thracis is here, why are we still in Lady Liana's herd?"

Psyche ducked her head and lowered her voice. "I thought it might be better following my insult of avoiding my escort's advances."

Eno snorted. "Psyche, you spend entirely too much time worrying about everyone else's problems."

"I have reason in this case. Once the battle is over and I return to Moirae's instruction, I have no intention of avoiding Thracis."

"This whole dilemma stems from your own herd, doesn't it?"

"It's just not a good time to introduce Thracis to the queen."

"You are afraid your dam will disapprove because he is not yet a proven warrior?" Eno had known Psyche for years and was aware of how the mares of the Augean Stable looked on stallions. Only Psyche seemed willing to view stallions as more than breeding stock. To have affection, or perish the thought, love, for an unproven fighter. Eno shuddered to think of what Queen Hippolyta and Lady Alastrina would have to say on the subject.

"I am afraid she will disapprove of many things. You see, I think that Thracis has been attacked by-" Psyche was cut off as a messenger approached.

"Beg pardon, ladies. Lady Liana has said that you are to join her. The queen has given the word that we are to march."

32

CHAPTER 32

The stretch of open ground where Queen Hippolyta chose to engage the Baroquians rumbled as with small earthquakes as the two armies prepared for battle. On one side, with the sound of the ocean and the deep sand of the beach behind them, stood the Baroquians. On the other, with plenty of open ground accessible in the event of a retreat, were the Diomedeans. Between the two was a vast stretch of open field that would soon be drenched with scarlet rain.

The Baroquians had spent the night on the beach, having landed late in the evening the night before. They had spent the better part of the morning trudging their way through the deep sands on their way to the flat fields that were more common to Diomedea. Their passage was made all the more difficult as they were weighted down with weapons and armor. Unaware that the mares of Diomedea had enlisted the help of their Felisian neighbors, the Baroquians had left their ships protected by only a handful of soldiers on each vessel. This would make the task given to Lady Dendera and her cats all the more effortless.

The Baroquian army was made up mostly of Friesians and Lusitanos, as both breeds were native to the Baroquian Peninsula and were the original breeds to enter into the Baroquian Pact. Other breeds were scattered throughout the army as well, including Andalusians and Trakenians. A fair amount of Felisians were also darting thorough the Baroquian herds. Like the Diomedeans, each herd or stable was depicted by a unique banner.

A bird flying over the battlefield would have seen the two groups, one substantially smaller than the other, as metal Equines of many colors. Very few of the assembly, and most of those few being commanders or officers, wore pure achillium armor. As a result, neither army had the uniform appearance witnessed when the Imperial Cavalry marched into battle. The armor covering the two armies varied in color and style depending on the metals used.

Thracis and Aeos stood well back from the front lines. The horses leading the charge would be those herds who had the most experience. Queen Hippolyta did not believe in using any Equine for mere fodder, each group was to be used to their best advantage. Off to the left, concealed behind a rocky ridge, Lady Alastrina's forces waited for the battle to commence. They had strict instructions to wait until all of the Baroquian army had engaged in combat. At that point Lady Alastrina's primary objective was to cut off any retreat by the Baroquians.

Thracis felt his first burst of adrenalin beginning to wear off. He had been more than ready to fight when Queen Hippolyta had led them out here over an hour previous, but now the waiting was giving way to boredom. On either side of him, Thracis saw other horse beginning to fidget. The lag in action was giving the Diomedeans too much time to consider the horrors of battle. Many looked as though they were losing heart.

"Why are we just standing here?" Thracis asked Phrenicos.

The older stallion turned his head slightly. He was standing a little in front of Thracis and Aeos. "We must wait until the queen gives the order to charge."

"Why is she waiting?"

"I am not sure. The longer we wait the more the resolve of those around you will falter."

Thracis stretched his neck to try and see over the horse in front of him. His armor, like that of the horses around him, was fully extracted. He was getting hot and the sweat gathering behind his legs and along his flanks was starting to itch. This wasn't what he pictured when his sire had told him of the epic battles of old.

Suddenly, a stallion's challenge shattered the quiet of the day. Thracis felt his mind focus immediately. The horses in front of him began to trot forward. As they moved, he could see that the lead horses were already charging across the field. They had formed a line, keeping their formation as tight as possible. Ahead of them, Thracis caught glimpses of the Baroquians surging forward. Their heads lowering as they extracted the forehead horns of their armor.

Adrenalin poured into Thracis' veins. He fought to keep his pace steady, the doctrines of Phrenicos pounding in his mind. A horse was only as strong as the rest of his herd. Their best attack was to fight as one and not get separated. Screams of rage and pain accompanied by the clang of metal, erupted ahead of him. The sound was horrible and exhilarating at the same time. All his training up to that point flowed through Thracis' mind as he slammed into his first opponent.

The stallion, a huge Friesian, spent no time being startled that his combatant was a stallion. He used his weight to push Thracis back. Thracis' feet slid in the grass, digging deep into the earth. Knowing he had no hope of defeating the Friesian by force, Thracis twisted away and spun to start kicking the other stallion. Once the Friesian backed off, Thracis spun again, lowering his head. The achillium of his horn sliced cleanly through the Friesian's inferior armor and into the soft belly underneath. The Friesian screamed in pain and tried to back away. Thracis followed, finishing the kill and whirling to face another opponent.

This was how it went, not just for Thracis, but also for Aeos, Psyche, Eno, and all the rest engaged in the conflict. At times, Thracis fought two or three combatants at once. Psyche and Eno, having frequently trained together, fought rump to rump, each using a variety of weapons Eno had specifically designed for them alone. Among these devices was a pair of razor-edged achillium hooks that swung out from the sides of the armor, puncturing an opponent's sides and dragging them forward to be impaled on the unicorn horn. Another design which made Eno's weapons unique was the ability of the wielder to retrieve any of their own projectile weapons with the activation of a magnetic system specifically designated to attracted certain metallic mixtures. It was a brilliant technique;

the projectiles not only caused damage when thrown but on their return trip as well. Psyche and Eno were able to inflict copious amounts of destruction with a minimum output of energy.

The sound of metal on metal, the screams of the wounded and dying, the challenges uttered by both sides, filled the air for miles around. The carrion birds, alerted to the promise of feasting, circled the sky above the conflict, gliding on warm drafts of wind and waiting for the quiet in which they would feed.

The Baroquians had brought a fair amount of launching equipment. However, the catapults and ballistae had become bogged down in the deep sand of the beach. They hadn't considered putting the catapults and ballistae on floaters because, as stallions secure in their greater strength and training, they hadn't really believed the mares of Diomedea would put up much of a fight. Now, some Baroquians raced back to the catapults hoping to get them loaded and fired before the mares discovered what they were doing. As they bolted back toward the beach, their retreat was cut off by Lady Alastrina and her contingents. Caught between the Diomedean forces, the Baroquians began to fight with shear panic, fragmenting their already splinted herds even more.

Relying on the catapults and ballistae was false hope in any case. Lady Dendera, in preparation for her cats to destroy the Baroquian ships, had ordered a small group of five cats to render all the projectile equipment useless. Their mission completed, these same cats fitted themselves with diving equipment and joined their comrades as they secured explosive devices to the hulls of the Baroquian vessels.

Lady Dendera, her black coat shimmering with water droplets, hid behind a rocky outcropping, watching to see that all her cats emerged from the water before setting the detonation device.

"Lady, the last group will be returning shortly." This came from Lisimba, Lady Dendera's second in command.

"Excellent. Make sure everyone is clear within five minutes." Lisimba bowed to Lady Dendera then his eyes glazed as he referred her orders to all his soldiers.

After a moment, he addressed Lady Dendera. "I have told them; they will be safe."

The combatants on the battlefield were not even aware of the destruction of the Baroquian fleet. The sounds of battle were too loud in their ears for them to hear distant explosions as the hulls were breached by the Felisian devices. Even if a few Baroquians managed to evade the Diomedeans and reach the water, their only recourse would be to swim back to Baroquia.

To Thracis the battle seemed to last forever. Every time a foe fell before him, two more were ready to takes its place. He was tired, his muscles aching. His head throbbed from all the stab wounds he had inflicted. His armor, while impermeable to punctures, was dented in several place from prolonged attacks by heavier opponents. He was suffering from dozens bruises and abrasions, as well as several shallow cuts along his legs where opponents had found the chinks in his armor. His throat burned from thirst.

He threw off his most recent opponent, a smaller stallion that had even less experience in combat than Thracis did, and released two spiked metal projectiles into the other horse's side. The other horse, his armor barely more than a leather cover, uttered a shriek before falling on his side in a convulsing heap.

Gasping, Thracis turned to face yet another combatant and was stunned to find no one stood before him. He staggered on his feet, his momentum thrown off. Seeing his weakness, another stallion several yards away charged at him. Thracis spun on his hind legs to face the stallion. Before the two stallions could engage, the charging stallion's feet were ensnared by a set of bolos. He crashed to the ground, screaming and struggling. Thracis was horrified to see that the wire of the bolos was sinking into the stallion's legs. Within seconds, the wire had reached the stallion's bones. Not wanting to prolong the misery, Thracis sank his horn through the other stallion's heart. He looked up to see who had thrown the bolos.

Standing a few feet away, Lady Alcina tossed her head. Her armor was streaked with blood and gore and she looked like she was favoring her right foreleg. She also looked like she was having the time of her life. "That will keep him from chasing down any unwary fillies." She turned and cantered back into the fray.

Thracis felt his stomach turn. War was not what he had expected. He didn't have time to considered its atrocities now, however, as another stallion was cantering toward him. His mind refocused, Thracis met the stallion head on, the two horses fencing each other with their horns.

Thirty feet away, Psyche was in similar combat with a new opponent. This opponent wore the barbed armor that Thracis was familiar with. The Diomedeans called this barbed armor, often tipped with poisons, Scorpio armor after the scorpions of the Natarian Desert. Only Baroquian crafters knew the secrets of forging this armor. The Diomedeans had learned the techniques by stealing the knowledge from captured stallions.

The Scorpio armor this stallion wore sparked with blue light every time Psyche's horn glanced against it. This was an indication that the armor was electrified. This stallion's combat technique would be to hook an opponent's armor with his own and then electrify them once they could not free themselves. Psyche had no intention of becoming ensnared by the barbs on that armor.

She backed away, giving herself room. The stallion, thinking she was retreating, advanced. As he took his third step, Psyche unleashed a net with strands had been coated with a corrosive acid. The net fell over the stallion's back, neither impeding or wounding him.

"That's all you've got, little rabbit?"

"Just wait. This weapon holds a surprise."

The stallion tossed his head and laughed. He began to advance again, but his steps faltered. The net's coating, not damaging on its own, was reacting to the heat given off by the electrical energy on the stallion's armor. The acid was eating its way through the armor and into the stallion's back. He shrieked and began bucking then threw himself on the ground trying to tear the net off. Psyche turned away, intent on finding another opponent. She needn't worry about this one. The net would not stop until it sank through the stallion's flesh and into the ground beneath. This weapon was not of Eno's design; the Deathshrouds were strictly woven by the mares of the Arachnae Stable.

Psyche fought her way back to Eno's side. They had become separated earlier in the battle. She was tired and thirsty, unsure how much longer she could go on. Looking at Eno, Psyche saw her friend was in the same state. Psyche reared back on her hind legs and looked out over the battlefield. What she saw lifted her heart. Despite their lesser numbers, the mares and Felisians of Diomedea were winning.

Psyche settled back to all four feet just as a Felsian bearing the colors of a house Psyche knew from Sanctuary raced underneath the black and white mare. The Felisian didn't give Psyche a backward glance as it launched itself at another cat several yards away. The two Felisians began rolling in an orange and black ball between the battling Equines, claws shredding and teething biting.

The Felisians had been combating just as ferociously as the Equines. They had their own weapons and armor in addition to their teeth and claws. Cats sprinted under Equine stomachs or over armored backs, sometimes colliding with their opponents in mid-leap. The air below the Equines' knees sizzled with hisses and angry howls as Felisians gave voice to their fury.

Lady Dendera's teams, their mission completed, bolted up the beach and into the battle. They had discarded their underwater equipment. It lay scattered across the beach, illuminated by the fires of the sinking ships. Placing explosives was all well and good, but now Lady Dendera and her cats were ready for a real fight.

The Baroquians, unprepared for such fierce opponents as the Diomedean mares, fought as well as they could, but the hard trek up the beach coupled with the mares' more devious weaponry, had the cavalry scattered into complete disarray. A few herds tried to fortify themselves by fighting rumps to rumps, but they were quickly dispatched. Queen Hippolyta had given the order that there were to be no prisoners.

33

CHAPTER 33

As the sun fell toward the west, Thracis stood with sides heaving. He and Aeos were in a clear area near the eastern edge of the battlefield. Thracis had no idea how they had gotten this far from their starting point. The last few hours were a total blur in his tired mind. Around the two stallions, other horses began to bugle triumphant whinnies and prance around, victory giving them renewed energy.

"It seems we'll live to see another day." Aeos' voice was cracked from thirst.

Thracis nodded. He felt elated that the Diomedeans had won, but even that knowledge couldn't ease the aches throughout his body. He scanned the immediate area for Psyche. He didn't see her.

Watching him, Aeos tossed his head. "Shall we go and look for your lady?"

Thracis nodded and turned away from Aeos, walking through the carnage of the battlefield. He could see pain and death on either side of himself. Several horses were walking along as he and Aeos were but with a far different purpose. They were finishing the kill on any enemy Equines or Felisians. Asklepiades and healers, both Equine and Felisian, rushed across the field as well, giving aid to as many Diomedeans as possible. The asklepiades' priority on the field was to stabilize the wounded as much as they could before the injured were moved to the medical tents erected in Queen Hippolyta's camp.

Aeos stopped frequently as they walked, offering reassurance to wounded horses as they waited for a healer. Thracis endured these pauses with as much patience as he could but he was anxious to learn of Psyche's condition. If he had given the matter much thought he could have simply contacted her mentally, but in his exhaustion and worry the idea never crossed his mind.

He was growing more and more desperate as he and Aeos slowly made their way across the field. Thracis did see several faces he knew, the light gone from their eyes. He saw some that would soon be passing from this world to journey to the peaceful fields of Tranquility. The Diomedeans had won but victory had come at a terrible price. Thracis' feet seemed to be shackled to heavy weights as he moved back and forth among his fallen comrades.

They stopped in their searching to aid Titania, the Clydesdale barkeep of Boudica. She had a nasty gash running down her neck to her shoulder. As Aeos worked on the mare a whinny caught Thracis' attention. He swung his head around, blinking away the dizziness the movement caused, and looked for the source of the call. He saw two horses, one leaning heavily on the other, stumbling toward him, Aeos, and Titania.

Unable to determine the identity of the newcomers but seeing that they needed help, Thracis left Titania's side and went to help the more wounded of the two other Equines. The horse collapsed before he reached it. Thracis could hear gasping within the armored shell.

Thracis investigated the armor box and located the switched used to retract the armor. The horse, a bay mare, immediately began to breathe easier as the armor slid away from her face and neck. Thracis checked her over, ignoring the encouraging mutters of her companion. Upon inspection, Thracis saw that the mare had incurred some nasty bruises and a cracked rib or two from the look of the swelling along her side, but her greatest danger was being overheated.

He looked up at her companion, still encased in armor. "Hail one of the water carriers, this mare needs water before she boils."

The companion nodded and began calling for a water carrier. A few moments later, a pony laden with waterskins and a bucket or two trotted up to Thracis. Ignoring the buckets for the moment, Thracis lifted one of the waterskins and emptied it along the mare's neck and shoulders. She shuddered as the water cooled her burning skin. Her breathing began to slow as she took deeper inhales. The pony removed a bucket and filled it to the brim, placing in front of the prone mare. Thracis walked around to the opposite side of the mare and used his head to help boost her up so that she could drink from the offered bucket.

"That's a good girl," the pony, a cream-colored Shetland, soothed, "careful not to drink too fast else the water will cause a colic."

The mare's ears flicked, indicating that she had heard. She sipped rather that gulped, taking her time in finding the bottom of the bucket.

The pony looked around, seeing that many more water carriers were coming onto the field. It would not do for the remaining fighters to die of heat stroke or dehydration now that the battle was over. The pony removed the other bucket and filled it, telling the other horses to drink. All sated themselves except Thracis who waited until the mare had drunk her fill before gently laying her back on the ground. Once she was comfortable, Thracis drank his share before helping the pony to repack its equipment so it could move on to another group of thirsty Equines.

"I hadn't thought you were so compassionate to strangers," the mare's companion mused.

"I hadn't thought you would stoop to the level of remaining anonymous," Thracis countered.

The mare's companion tossed its head. "If you had known who I was you would have spent all your time worrying over my bumps and scrapes while Eno suffered."

"I would have seen to her first," Thracis quipped though he thought Psyche was right in her assumptions.

"I'm sure." Psyche retracted her armor, tossing her head to free her dark mane from her sweaty neck.

Forgetting they were surrounded by dozens of horses that would run straight back to Queen Hippolyta with any information they could obtain about her youngest daughter, Thracis retracted his own armor then reached out to nuzzle Psyche's cheek. Titania's eyes widen but she remained silent. Alcina had told her that Thracis and Psyche were acquainted.

Psyche accepted the touch but backed away and went to Eno's side before Thracis' nose could venture further. Eno was watching the two with interest. She inclined her head at Aeos. "I'm sure he's told you as much about her as she has told me about him."

Aeos chuckled. "Given the political implications, I think I prefer knowing as little as possible. My name is Quintus Aeos, by the way. And this is Titania." Titania nodded at Eno as best she could without moving her neck too much.

"I am Dias Eno, yes the same as Commander Dias, and the story is too long for me to recite lying here on a battlefield."

Aeos chuckled at the mare's directness. "Then may I suggest we all go to the medical tents? Titania is in need of proper stitching and you could some more water. I also have skills that would be welcomed by the asklepiades and healers as well as the wounded."

Eno nodded. She rose to her feet with the help of Thracis and Aeos. Aeos inspected the swelling along her ribcage. "I would say at least two of your ribs are cracked. We will go slow to the tents."

"I can help you as long as you lean against my uninjured side," Titania explained. She moved to Eno's side and waited for the other mare to use her for support.

Aeos moved to Eno's other side, using mental bands to steady her. He looked at Thracis and Psyche. "The two of you are tired and bruised like the rest of us, but maybe you could help move the wounded. The faster we get them off this field, the better their chances for survival."

Psyche and Thracis nodded and moved away to see what they could do to help others. They spoke little as evening gave way to night. Felisians bounded across the field, distributing glow orbs so that the searchers could continue their hunt for surviving Diomedeans. As they bounced from one group of horses to another, the Felisians retold any news they had learned on their many trips back and forth from the camp.

The most significant information was that almost all of the battlefield had been searched and the injured removed. Queen Hippolyta was giving the order that most of the rescue groups could begin coming back to the camp where those who were able had put together washing stations and meal areas. Apprentice healers had been dispatched to look over those fighters whose injuries were not dire.

"We should go back to the camp." Thracis was helping a young mare, barely more than a filly, stand on three legs. The forth, a hind, was broken along the cannon bone.

Psyche was standing a few feet away with her head drooping. "We can send her with an asklepiade and continue on."

"Don't be stubborn. You can hardly hold your head up and I stumble over every rock and groove of dirt. We need to go back. If you insist on helping, you can aid the asklepiades in the tents."

Psyche pinned her ears, but knew Thracis spoke the truth. She was so tired she was seeing double. However, the thought that another mare would be hailed as having fought better, looked for injured harder, or offered aid until she dropped, haunted Psyche. That was just the sort of self-sacrifice Queen Hippolyta loved to reward.

"Please, Lady. I would be honored if you would accompany me back to the tents." The young mare's voice was soft, a whisper almost, but it caught Psyche's attention as Thracis' words had not.

"I would be honored as well."

Thracis watched this exchange and silently applauded the younger mare's tact. By asking Psyche to join her, she didn't sound as though she were telling Psyche what to do. He filed this information away for future confrontations between he and Psyche when the mare chose to be stubborn as a mule. The three of them began the laborious trek across the field to the welcoming lights of the medical tents.

Walking into the medical tents was like being thrown back into the midst of battle. Asklepiades, healers, aides, and anyone else with any medical knowledge darted up and down long rows of patients, some standing, most lying flat. Groans of pain and the tang of blood filled the air. The Felisians had rigged catwalks high up in the tents that allowed them to get from one patient to another without having to dodge around the Equines. The catwalks also gave them a bird's eye view of the rows of patients.

Thracis felt himself trying to gag, which was a feat in itself as Equines did not possess the ability to vomit. He and Psyche helped the young mare to an empty space and tried to make her comfortable. She would have a long wait as a broken leg was not life-threatening. Just being in the tent and off the field was enough to calm her nerves a little.

"Thank you. I will be fine now. I can already see a Felisian making its way to me." The mare tossed her head to the left where Thracis did see a gray Felisian wearing a harness laden with pouches coming their way. The mare ducked her head at Thracis. "You should go. The two of you need food and water."

Psyche was looking back toward the battlefield and not paying much attention to the younger mare. The younger mare lowered her voice. She spoke to Thracis but her ears were flicked at Psyche. "You might not have any major injuries but all those cuts and bruises must be taking their toll."

At the implication that Thracis was in need of medical attention, Psyche's head whipped around. "This mare is right. We should see to your wounds, Thracis."

Not understanding why they had to play this little game of ignoring Psyche's injuries and exhaustion, Thracis agreed to let Psyche look him over. She nodded to the younger mare, then led Thracis back through the camp. They passed horses that were not injured enough to go to the medical tents. These horses were either cleaning their shallow cuts and scratches or trying to rest. The Felisians in the camp were doing the same with the addition of cleaning their coats or sharpening their claws. These exercises were soothing to Felisians, the easiest ways for them to relax.

Psyche led them back to Lady Alcina's camp. Thracis was heartened to see many faces he knew. Phrenicos and Alcina had not returned yet, but one of the other mares told Thracis that Phrenicos was speaking with the queen and Lady Alcina was helping in the medical tents. Thracis and Psyche went into the mess tent to eat and drink before taking the time to clean the dirt and blood from their coats.

As they made their way to the wash areas, they saw Felisians standing with buckets and dripping sponges. These Felisians were little more than kittens. One of them, a tan female with black markings, walked up to address Thracis and Psyche. "We are here to clean you off so you will not have to strain your minds."

Thracis bowed his head to the Felisian. "That is very kind of you."

The Felisian smiled. "This allows us all to do our part."

Thracis and Psyche went and stood next to the buckets the Felisians had arranged. The Felisians used their nimble fingers to remove the Equines' armor harnesses. Thracis and Psyche both made a mental note to replace and clean all the weapons they had used at the first opportunity. After the Felisians had removed all the equipment, they dumped buckets of water over the horses' backs and used their sponges to wipe the dirt and mud out of any wounds they encountered.

Thracis sighed with pleasure at the feeling of cool water sluicing over his overheated body. He didn't even have the strength to twitch when a Felisian touched a particularly tender spot. He felt a soothing coolness as a Felisian slathered thick salve on any cut or scratch. Thracis hadn't thought he had been wounded that much, but after the Felisian was done with him, he looked like the spotted mare sentry at the university.

He looked over to see how Psyche was faring and saw that she was dozing on her feet. Knowing she would push herself to collapse if he suggested she rest, Thracis decided on another tack.

He reached out and nuzzled her shoulder. Psyche blinked slowly and turned her head to look at him. He could see by the careful way she was moving that stiffness was beginning to set into her strained muscles. "If you want to go back to the medical tents, you will have to do so alone." Thracis took a deep breath and tried to appear weaker than he felt. "I have to rest. I can barely keep myself on all four feet."

Psyche looked toward the medical tents, then back at Thracis. She took a deep breath. "I will stay with you; in case you should need anything."

Thracis kept his eyes downcast to hide the amusement in them. "That would be welcome."

They left the wash area and walked back to Lady Alcina's camp. The Felisians stored their equipment for later retrieval. Most Equine's were happy enough to lay on open ground in the camp but days of Equines walking back and forth through the camp had destroyed all the grass and left only cold, hard earth. As a rule, Equines stayed out of the sleeping areas but with the confusion of battle, some courtesies had been overlooked.

After inspecting the ground of the camp, Thracis tossed his head in the direction of the field where he and Psyche had spent the previous night. Besides being floored with thick grasses, the field was far enough away to mute the groans of pain coming from the medical tents. Understanding his meaning, Psyche followed him back into the high grass. Other Equines had gained this same insight and the field was full of dark masses outlining where horses were lying in the grass.

Finding an open space big enough for the two of them, Thracis and Psyche lay down and fell into dreamless sleep.

CHAPTER 34

The next morning Thracis was so stiff it took him several tries to reach his feet. Others in the field were having the same difficulty. Psyche was still sound asleep. Thracis looked out across the field. Mist was rising in a billowy curtain obscuring most of the camp, but Thracis could hear the sounds of others preparing for the day.

Rested, Thracis was eager to find Phrenicos and Aeos and learn how the Diomedeans had fared. He knew Psyche would be safe in this field surrounded by other warriors, but he thought it would hurt her to wake up and find him gone. Settling his weight and cocking a back leg, Thracis decided to contact Aeos mentally.

Did you ever find sleep? He asked when Aeos' mind opened to him.

Very little. We lost many as the night wore on.

Thracis was silent for a moment thinking of those that had fallen. *Did Eno survive?*

Amusement filled the link. *Survived and took every opportunity to complain about being forced to rest. The lady is quite headstrong.*

Something she and Psyche have in common. I didn't get her to rest until I suggested that I could not go on.

I must say, Thracis, you're learning all the time. Pyrios better watch out the next time you arrive in Lipizza.

I do not think Pyrios has to worry. Have you spoken to Phrenicos?

Thracis felt Aeos pause as he spoke to someone on his end. Whenever an Equine did this, the link felt slightly weaker. It was a sign that the individual's concentration was elsewhere. This practice also left the mind open to psychic attack.

After a moment Aeos was fully in Thracis' mind again. *I saw him late last night. We did not speak much, he only inquired as to our health and your whereabouts. He seemed pleased you were caring for Lady Psyche.*

Thracis' chest expanded at the compliment. *Does he wish to speak with us today?*

He said to meet him midmorning at Lady Alcina's camp.

Thracis thanked Aeos for the information and pulled himself back to the field. Psyche was standing next to him and looking at him with ears pricked. "You need to learn how to divide your attention when using your mind so that both your body and mind are safe."

"Phrenicos has said the same thing. I am sure that lesson is somewhere in my future."

"You should learn it soon." She turned her head to look around the field. "We should get back to the camp before everyone wakes up. It will be easier to find Eno and Aeos."

Thracis let her lead the way back to the medical tents. He was sure she had contacted Eno and knew exactly where the other mare was lying. In front of him, Thracis saw that Psyche was stiff on her right hind leg. He thought finding Eno would be a good thing. If the two mares wanted to catch up on the night just passed at least they would do so while being stationary. On their way to find Eno, they paused at Lady Alcina's camp to put on their armor harnesses.

Eno was waiting for them when Psyche and Thracis entered the first tent. She was standing with her back leg cocked to give her ribs some relief. She had a bandage that wrapped all the way around her torso in an attempt to stabilize the cracked ribs as much as possible. Her armor harness lay at her feet and Thracis didn't doubt for a minute that Eno's harness had weapons she could use whether or not the harness was on her back.

Psyche trotted to her friend and the two immediately began checking each other for injuries. They nuzzled each other's shoulders and lipped their manes. Thracis held back, giving the mares their privacy. He jumped when Aeos walked up beside him.

"They've been friends for many years, to hear Eno tell it." Aeos looked tired but content, having found his place in camp. Thracis was glad for him. Aeos had been distant as of late and Thracis had yet to decipher the reason why.

"I think they have a lot in common." Thracis tossed his head. "Have you eaten this morning?"

"Not yet."

Thracis whickered to get Psyche's attention. "Aeos and I are heading back to Lady Alcina's camp. Will you be joining us later?"

Psyche lowered her head to confer with Eno, then turned back to Thracis. "We have a few things to attend to first. We will find you later."

Thracis and Aeos nodded and left the tent. On the way to Lady Alcina's camp, Thracis saw several horses and cats stop and nod their heads at Aeos, many with bandages on their bodies.

"You've made a name," Thracis commented.

"I've been helpful."

"Will you leave Phrenicos now and begin your medical training?"

Aeos thought about it. "Not yet. Other things have come to my attention that I need to see to first."

"Why are you always so mysterious?" Thracis snapped.

"Why are you always so blunt?"

"One of us needs to be direct, else we'll all be talking in circles," Thracis grumbled.

They reached Lady Alcina's camp and ate and drank. The oats were beginning to take on a stale taste and the water in the toughs was getting low. Thracis and a few others would have to use some movers to go and get more water from the nearby streams and ponds. Grain could be purchased from area farms, but Thracis didn't think the cavalry would stay here much longer. He had already heard a rumor that Queen Hippolyta would announce today that horses and cats could begin returning to their home territories if they wished. Nothing was confirmed yet, but Thracis didn't see the point of keeping everyone here now that the battle was over.

Aeos ate enough for both of them and Thracis wondered if the other stallion had eaten anything since yesterday before the battle. He hoped some of the other healers had forced Aeos to eat at least something during the night. Aeos watched the flow of horses and cats as he ate, nodding to those he knew and auspiciously checking others for injuries.

Phrenicos arrived as Thracis and Aeos were finishing breakfast. He looked weary but far more spry than Thracis had anticipated. The white stallion was decades older than Thracis and Aeos but he looked ready to take up arms and march into battle at any minute. Phrenicos waited until he had the attention of all the horses and cats in the area before he began to speak.

"The rumors you have heard are true. After a sweep of the valley and beach this morning, Queen Hippolyta has learned that we have routed the enemy." He waited for the applause and shouts to die down before continuing. "She has stated that any who wish to return to their home territories may do so when they feel able. She has made arrangements for the wounded to be moved on movers as soon as they are stabilized. She does not want anyone to stay here longer than necessary."

This statement was met with general agreement. All around seemed to think their comrades would heal faster after they were moved to a proper hospital.

"If she has need of you in the coming months, the queen will summon you once again." Phrenicos watched as this news settled in. "Do not think the Baroquians will not retaliate once they have fortified their remaining forces."

"Surely if that happens, the capital will send the Imperial Cavalry to help us." This came from someone in the group.

Phrenicos nodded. "The queen has already sent messengers to the Hippikon and contacted the Registry of Breeds. They will now deliberate as to how the Baroquians will be dealt with."

Murmurs filtered through the group. Phrenicos spoke again. "Do not worry about the decisions of others at this time. Go home and be patient."

The horses and cats began to disperse. Many would stay for several days still, until all the wounded had been moved. Thracis and Aeos waited until they were alone with Phrenicos before inquiring what he wished of them.

"Thracis will return with me to continue his training. Aeos, you will go with Lady Alcina. She will take you to the delphae of Boudica. From there you will be sent to Sanctuary. We cannot put off your psychic training any longer, not if what Queen Hippolyta suspects is even partially true."

Aeos nodded. He had known he would be starting his own journey soon. "When do you wish to leave?" He kept his voice respectful even though he wished to stay and help in the medical tents for a little while longer.

"It is not safe for Thracis to remain here. He and I will return to Boudica today. You will stay with Alcina. Echo was severely injured and Alcina will not leave her. I am not sure if Echo will survive the day. Do not think to comfort Alcina in any case, just make yourself available whenever she decides to leave." Aeos nodded. He knew enough about Lady Alcina to know the mare would not take comfort from any stallion for any reason.

Phrenicos turned to Thracis. "Go and find your lady. Tell her you are leaving."

Thracis' throat felt dry. He knew he would have to return to training but he had hoped that he and Psyche would have a little more time.

Phrenicos inclined his head. "You have a little time. I don't want to leave until the sun rides low and the day begins to cool. Meet me at the eastern edge of the camp by the standard with the three horseshoes on a green field in the late afternoon."

"I thank you, Phrenicos."

"Don't look so downtrodden, Thracis. You will see your lady again someday soon. This is only a temporary separation. And you can always contact her mentally."

After a nod to Aeos, Phrenicos moved off on more errands. Thracis watched his white coat disappear among the tents. He cocked his head at Aeos. "I envy your position. If Echo holds on, you and Alcina might be in this camp for a week before Echo can be moved."

Aeos tossed his head. "That does not mean Psyche will be here. Eno should be able to move by tomorrow. I would assume that they will be returning to wherever they are from."

"And Psyche will return to ignoring me."

Aeos nipped Thracis neck. "She will be busy, as will you. Perhaps now that you know where your lady's heart lies you can concentrate better."

Thracis nipped back. "Perhaps. I will miss you. Psychic training can take years, can't it?"

Aeos nodded. "But I don't think I will have the luxury of becoming fully trained. I believe a war has just begun."

"I agree. I will contact Pyrios within the month and find out what the Registry thinks of this Baroquian invasion."

They were walking back to the medical tents. Aeos flicked his ears. "Psyche will not like to hear of your eminent departure."

"She is accustomed to the regimens of training. She will understand."

"Understanding will not make the pain any less. She is strong, but she is also young. I feel she has many worries that she does not share with anyone."

"She is not much younger than the two of us."

Aeos tossed his head. "No, but she holds different ideals."

"So, what am I supposed to do? Make a bunch of empty promises that will ease feminine feelings?"

"No promise you make will be empty. The problem you will have is making Psyche realize you are not like other stallions."

"That is a challenge. I think I would prefer to go back into battle."

They entered the tent in which they had left Eno and Psyche only to be told by a bedraggled Felisian that Lady Psyche and her friend had been summoned to the queen's pavilion.

Thracis twitched a shoulder. "I don't think I can just walk up to the Queen's pavilion or that Psyche would want me there for that matter."

"The pavilion is open to everyone, but I understand that Psyche would be uncomfortable if you met her dam unannounced. Let's walk up to the Queen's camp and you can wait on the edge. I'll go in and find Psyche and Eno."

"What am I going to do while you're away learning to use your head?" Thracis asked.

"Hopefully learn to use yours as well."

Thracis pinned his ears, but refused to comment. They were nearing the queen's tents. All the banners in this area represented herds that were part of the queen's council or other important members of her court. While Aeos walked with head high, inspecting the different tents and occupants, Thracis kept his eyes lowered, trying to not to draw attention to himself. Psyche would not be happy that he had taken it on himself to go in search of her. He should have contacted her mind and asked her to meet him somewhere else in the camp.

An armed guard met them at the perimeter of Queen Hippolyta's private tents. "State your business." The guard was a buckskin mare with hard eyes. She had a bandage around her upper neck.

"We are looking for Lady Psyche and her companion, Dias Eno." Aeos kept his voice smooth.

"They are busy with the queen at this time. I will tell them you were inquiring about them. Tell me your names."

"Quintus Aeos and Zephyros Thracis." No indication of recognition from the guard. "Time is of the essence as Thracis will be departing the camp within a few hours. We must speak with Lady Psyche before then."

The guard cocked her head. "If it is that important, I'm sure you can contact Lady Psyche mentally."

Certain he would get no further with this mare, Aeos bowed his head and turned to walk back through the camp. Thracis fell into step beside him after a glance back at the guard. "She is right. I should have just contacted Psyche's mind."

"I doubt Psyche would have answered. Not until she was away from her dam at any rate."

"Why should that make any difference?"

"Thracis, the dynamics of royal herds are somewhat different than those of the ruling herds. They tend to be more...formal."

"Psyche does not behave very formal with me," Thracis laughed.

"No, but you should understand that when dealing with her herd, you must be on your best behavior."

They had returned to the medical tents. Aeos caught the eye of a Felisian. The cat nodded at Aeos and pointed into the tent. "I must go," Aeos said. "If I were you, I would go graze for a bit, then take a long walk to loosen your muscles. If I see Psyche I will tell her to contact you."

Thracis nodded and headed out the surrounding fields. He grazed for a little while then took Aeos' advice and began walking around. He watched as Equines and Felisians alike broke down tents and packed gear. They either loaded their items on hovering movers or secured them in wagons that they would pull home. Some Equines wore packing cradles on their backs in which they or their Felisian companions stored food and equipment. By evening, a quarter of Queen Hippolyta's forces would be on their homeward journeys.

Thracis heard a harsh cawing and turned to see a congress of ravens winging across the sky in the direction of the battlefield. Queen Hippolyta had ordered a group of horses to see to the burial of the dead. It would be a hard job, but with their mental capabilities the Equines would make short work of it. With the amount of carcasses, the ravens would have their fill of meat before every body could be buried.

The sky over the battlefield was dark with heavy smoke as the Felisians fed their funeral pyres. Unlike the Equines, who buried their dead, the Felisians believed the only way for a cat to find peace was to have their remains burned and given to Bast. The wind was blowing away from the camp, but the acrid smell of smoke and the sweetish smell of flesh was hinted every time the wind died for a moment or two. The thought of cleaning up the battlefield turned Thracis' stomach and he headed farther away from the smoke and death.

In the quiet of a field, Thracis' mind turned back to the battle itself. He felt he had proven himself against his many opponents, adapting to multiple enemies and changing tactics in the heat of battle. He had come a long way since the ambush in Levadia. He now understood Phrenicos' careful attention to detail and why the white stallion had stressed the need for balance and stamina. The scholars claimed the battles of old could last for days, but Thracis had never believed that statement. Now he thought the scholars may have had a point.

Looking around to make sure he was alone, Thracis began to trot in the cadence defined by Phrenicos. Letting his mind flow where it would, he moved his feet along the patterns he had learned over the past weeks. His muscles, flourishing in the remembered movements, began to loosen at once. Thracis moved effortlessly through his laterals, his half-passes flawless. He collected himself, creating more impulsion. He cantered a large figure eight, shifting leads in the center without a hitch. After a large canter circle, Thracis shortened his stride to a fast trot and then shortened it even more until he was performing a perfect piaffe in the green open field with the dark smoke of the pyres rising behind him in the distance.

He finished the movement, then stood for a moment with head bowed. The wind shifted, bring the scent of another horse. Embarrassed of being observed without his knowledge made Thracis' face heat as he turned to see who was watching.

"I had thought you were having difficulty learning the High Dances." Psyche ducked her head. "That is what Aeos is telling Eno, anyway."

"Aeos and Eno seem to be discussing a great many things." Thracis felt his flush of embarrassment turn to one of pleasure. He was thrilled to have performed so well for Psyche's eyes.

"They have a lot in common. Both ask too many questions. They will keep each other occupied for hours with their boundless curiosity." She joined him as Thracis began to walked around the perimeter of the field to cool himself.

"Did Aeos tell you I would be leaving soon?"

"Yes. My dam has told me I am to return to my teacher, the Lady Moirae, for further psychic training."

Thracis nuzzled her shoulder. "When must you leave?"

"At first light. I've already procured a mover for Eno. I'm sure she'll complain during the entire trip that I am treating her like an invalid."

Remembering how stubborn Psyche could be, Thracis kept his mouth shut.

Psyche tossed her head at the smoke in the distance. "I offered to help with the burials, but my dam forbade it. She doesn't want a member of her herd out among the dead."

"Given how frustrated you sound, maybe it is a good thing that you will be leaving in the morning."

Psyche flattened her ears. "Do you think I could not do it?"

<u>Do what?</u> Thracis thought. Then he noticed she was still preoccupied with the battlefield. "Are you asking whether or not I think you could bury bodies or whether I think you should have been in the battle to begin with?"

"Both."

"I did not see you fight, but given your lack of injury I would surmise that you handled yourself better than most." He saw her relax. "As far as digging holes...I'm sure you could, but I think your heart would break long before your legs tired."

Psyche twitched a shoulder. "You don't think I am strong enough for battle?"

Thracis thought about the question. He knew the truth would hurt her because she would not understand his reasoning. He didn't think she was physically incapable of defending herself or of holding her own in a fight. It was her mental state that was not strong enough, not yet. Of course, he couldn't say that. "I think it is a decision you have to make for yourself."

That seemed to satisfy as Psyche dropped the subject. "The sun is getting low. I will walk with you to Phrenicos."

"Will you think of me? Once you return to training?"

Psyche flicked her ears, feigning to consider. "I guess I might. If I have enough time."

"I will think of you."

She was silent for a few steps. "Don't think of me too much. I do not want Phrenicos to blame me because you can't concentrate." She stopped walking.

Thracis stopped next to her. Psyche pressed her forehead against his shoulder. He brought his head around to nuzzle her neck.

"If I even breathe this to another Diomedean mare I would be laughed out of camp, but I wish we could stay together." Psyche's voice was muffled against Thracis' shoulder.

"We can contact each other in the evenings."

"Yes, but we must be careful. Too many others are trying to harm you."

Thracis lipped her neck. "I would know if it were not you. I did before."

Psyche rubbed her head against him. "They will try harder next time."

"Don't worry. I like to think I have learned a few things." He felt some of the tension drain out of her.

Psyche stepped back. She lipped the corner of his mouth. "Maybe a few things."

Thracis nuzzled the underside of her jaw. "Do you think Phrenicos will wait a little longer?"

She nipped his cheek, hard. "I think we better get moving before he comes looking."

Phrenicos was watching for them as they reached the banner he had specified. Aeos was with him, as was Eno. Psyche pricked her ears at the sight of her friend. She had thought Eno would have gone back to the medical tents and given her ribs a rest. Eno must have thought Psyche would need moral support. Given the turmoil inside herself, Psyche had to agree.

"I was ready to send Aeos in search of you," Phrenicos commented when Thracis and Psyche arrived.

"It has been a long day." Thracis kept his regret at leaving early out of his voice.

"It's not over yet. Say your farewells so that we can leave. You will all see each other again soon so don't be overly dramatic." Phrenicos walked a few paces away. Experience had taught the older stallion that goodbyes should be quick, else the parting was all the more difficult.

Thracis spoke to Aoes first. "I wish you luck in your training."

"And you in yours."

The two stallions nipped at each other's shoulders in brotherly affection. They would keep in touch whenever time allowed. Thracis had no doubt that Aeos would not ignore him as Pyrios did.

Thracis and Psyche walked a few feet away. In front of an audience, Pysche turned shy and unsure. She wanted to reach out to Thracis, but didn't want to appear weak in front of Eno.

Thracis had no reservations about showing affection. He lipped Psyche's cheek and rubbed his head against her neck. "I will miss you, Psyche."

"We must have hope that we will see each other soon, though I wonder what Phrenicos considers 'soon'." She nuzzled his shoulder. "Keep focused and remember that meditation is not a waste of time, foolish colt." She stepped back and looked at him. "Good journey, stallion of Thetis."

"And the same to you, Lady of Augean."

Thracis said a farewell to Eno then left to join Phrenicos. As he walked, Thracis could hear Psyche's retreating footsteps as she went to Aeos and Eno. Phrenicos began to move as soon as Thracis fell into step beside him. They walked in silence until they reached a small rise. The camp would disappear from sight as soon as they went down the other side. At the top of the rise, Thracis turned back to look at the camp. Psyche and the others were still watching, standing in a loose group.

"Come along, young Thracis. We've miles to tread."

"I only wanted to look back once."

Phrenicos chuckled. "Turn and face forward, stallion of Thetis Stable. Your journey lies before you and it has only just begun."

Stables, Locations, and Characters of Note

Thetis Stable

A. Bailus Zephyros

    1. Ruling stallion of Calabria

    2. Chestnut with white stripe

    3. Sire to Pyrios, Thracis, Aquina

    4. Mate to Calypsa

B. Maestoso Calypsa

    1. Mate to Zephyros

    2. Dam to Pyrios, Thracis, and Aquina

    3. Gray shading to white

C. Zephyros Pyrios

    1. Oldest son of Zephyros and Calypsa

    2. Gray

    3. Heir to Thetis Stable

D. Zephyros Thracis

    1. Youngest son of Zephyros and Calypsa

    2. Chestnut with white stripe

E. Zephyros Aquina

    1. Youngest foal of Zephyros and Calypsa

    2. Born dark but will lighten to blue roan

Augean Stable

A. Athene Hippolyta
   1. Queen of Diomedea
   2. Dam to Psyche, Alastrina, Lachesis, Zeva
   3. Pewter with dark mane and tail

B. Hippolyta Alastrina
   1. Oldest daughter of Hippolyta
   2. Heir to Diomedea
   3. Dapple gray

C. Hippolyta Lachesis
   1. Second oldest daughter to Hippolyta
   2. High Delphae of the Temple of Consciousness
   3. Black as onyx

D. Hippolyta Zeva
1. Second youngest daughter to Hippolyta
2. Exiled for attempted assassination of Psyche
3. Black

E. Hippolyta Psyche
1. Youngest daughter of Hippolyta Psyche
2. Black and white pinto
3. Seer and *ammoni*

Acadia Stable

A. Lord Quintus
   1. Ruler of Acarnia
   2. Sire of Aeos
   3. Buckskin
   4. Present at King Pedasos' council

B. Quintus Aeos

1. Only foal of Quintus
2. Dam died shortly after his birth
3. Silver dun

Calpernia Stable

A. Lady Ithia
   1. Dam to Aethon and Phlegon
   2. Ruling mare of a small but significant stable in Pendaria
B. Ithia Phlegon
   1. Oldest son of Ithia
   2. Gray
   3. Has political ambitions and becomes an aide to Lord Kantaka
C. Ithia Aethon
   1. Youngest son of Ithia
   2. Gray

Mykenia Stable

A. Memnon Pedasos
   1. King of Myrmidonia
   2. Mate to Helena
   3. Sire to Salia
   4. Bay
B. Zeus Helena
   1. Queen of Myrmidonia
   2. Mate to Pedasos
   3. Dam to Salia

4. Palimino
C. Pedasos Salia
1. Only foal to Pedasos and Helena
2. Buckskin
D. Desiree
1. Lady in waiting to Queen Helena
2. Originally from Emor in Acarnia

Hapsburg Stable

A. Favory Demas
1. Gray
2. Oldest son of Hapsburg Stable of Levadia
a) Hapsburg Stable is ruling stable of Lipizzania

Arion Stable

A. Dimitri Alexi
1. Ruling stallion of Kigeria
2. Buckskin
3. Mate to Nerissa
B. Stephanos Nerissa
1. Mate to Alexi
2. Red dun

The Romanium

A. Commander Talos Dias
1. Current Asapatish of the Hippikon
2. Bay with white stripe

3. Sire to Eno
        4. Connections with Lord Kantaka
   B. Othello Iago
      1. Andalusian
      2. Head student at the Romanium
      3. Bay
   C. Ilarches Platon
      1. Instructor to Thracis

University of Piber and Registry of Breeds

A. Lampos Nonios
   1. Head Sentinel
   2. Gray
   3. Comes from Trakania
B. Xanthos Kantaka
   1. Representative of Mongolea
   2. Sorrel
C. Claudius Adonis
   1. Palimino
   2. Representative of Calabria
D. Lady Adelpha
   1. Representative of Courbettania
   2. Gray
E. Lord Nicodemus
   1. Welsh representative
   2. Brown

Boudica

A. Alois Phrenicos
    1. Legendary trainer of the Romanium
    2. White stallion
    3. Mentor to Thracis
B. Kebi
    1. Felisian who meets Aeos and Thracis first
    2. Black cat
C. Alcina
    1. Black
    2. Diomedean mare in charge of Boudica
    3. Nickname The Raven
    4. Small main herd
        A) Dysis -- Palimino
        B) Echo -- Gray
        C) Haidee -- Sorrel
D. Titania
    1. Barkeep
    2. Clydesdale
E. Neema
    1. Calico
    2. Helps in bar

Hippolyta's Forces

A. Horus -- Felisian
    1. Falcon Master
B. Lady Liana
    1. Lead mare of Argos Stable
    2. Dam to Belen
    3. Bay

C. Lady Melantha -- Felisian
  1. Black
  2. Close advisor to Queen Hippolyta
D. Lady Dendera -- Felisian
  1. Lead cat of assassin cats
  2. Lisimba -- male follower

Felisians of Note:

A. Adjo
  1. Helped Zephyros find Calypsa's circlet
B. Kamuzu
  1. Sent by Psyche to save Thracis
  2. Companion to Alcander
  3. Orange cat
C. Nefertiti
  1. Queen who spoke with Bast about Canan invasion

Other Characters of Note:

A. Dias Eno
  1. Daughter of Talos Dias
  2. Bay with white stripe and four white socks
  3. Longtime friend of Psyche
  4. Brilliant in strategy and weaponry
B. Alcander
  1. White miniature gelding who helps Thracis
  2. Companion to Kamuzu

Pantheon

Chimera

1. Ruler of the gods
2. Mate to Hippocampia
3. Creator of the Universe
4. Lives in Land of Tranquility
5. Underworld is Pandemonium

Pegasus

1. Planet Equus
2. Escort is Selene, Lady of the Moons
   a) Selene's brother is Helios of the sun

Bast

1. Planet Felisian
2. Twin of Lupios

Lupios

1. Planet Canan
2. Twin of Bast

Volga

1. Planet Mustel

Countries and Provinces:

Myrmidonia

1. Calabria, Pendaria, Acarnia

Lipizzania

1. Levadia, Courbettania, Capriola
2. Borders Myrmidonia

Diomedea

1. Athenia, Artemia, Amazonia

2. Southern continent

Baroquia
1. Andalusia, Friesia, Lusitania
2. Located in an area known as the Baroquian Peninsula

Rebecca McCullough has lived with horses, primarily Lipizzans, and cats her whole life. Their intelligence and interactions, not to mention the author's own love for the interweaving of history and legend, were the foundations that created the realms and civilizations contained in these pages. She lives on her family farm in Florida where she and her daughter continue to promote the Lipizzan breed through public performances.

Visit her website at www.herrmannsroyallipizzans.com for more information.